MA

+

NO LIMITS

Martin Walker

This paperback first edition published 2023 in Great Britain
by Amazon.

ISBN 9798857441978

1 - LIMITS

Without too much hesitation, I am always happy to kick the crap out of someone if I believe they deserve it. That does make me sound like some sort of psycho, but my training has left its mark on me, more than I want. Since being housed at MI6, I have been teamed up with a very select bunch of teens, testing my patience and my training.

Alex, is one I could happily floor as he tripped me up (on purpose), causing me to smash my face on a bollard. My nose already has had too many dislocations which makes it far too bendy.

Jules, the OCD, is another testing individual who has tried to rearrange all my personal stuff so many times it drives me crazy. Who wants a bloke to interfere with your designer chaos where every item of clothing and stuff is stored according to your own order?

Then, I am plagued by a bizarre girl called Jazmin, who spends all her time sweating profusely and appears to be away with the fairies. Her incessant use of joss sticks makes me choke, impregnating all my clothes with an 'eastern promise' of sandalwood.

I have my limits.

Ayanna, my sister in arms and mentor at MI6, has teamed me up with these teenage recruits who, she thinks, will bring out the best in me. Well, I'm proving her wrong, as this crew should be sent to the scrap heap as far as I'm concerned. Their insane nature shows mine to be quite normal and average. I thought being trained in an organisation with such kudos would be of benefit to me, but from what I've experienced so far it has dragged me down into despair. I'm seriously considering whether I should stay.

"Ayanna; you know this joss stick use. Is it a fire hazard? The room is filled with smoke every day and besides, it's like living in London from the 1800's!"

She stares at me as if I've insulted her grandmother.

"I know you are finding teamwork difficult Maisie, but tolerance is a prerequisite to success. If we are to send you on missions, you must learn to rely on the backup of your team. The training we have designed will ensure that you depend on each other." She cocks her head to one side, giving me a knowing look.

"Your experience in solitary espionage has to be retrained and moulded, I'm afraid. You will benefit from it, I'm sure. I was a wild cat when I was first recruited, and now look at me." I do look at her and purse my lips, trying not to laugh.

Ayanna has the complexion of a model, dark and glossy plaited hair, bright purple lipstick and dangly earrings. She would not look out of place on a catwalk or Chanel fragrance promotion.

Since joining this British security institution, she has been my mentor and confidant, as well as being the sister I never had. We have shopped, ate pizza, visited the sights of London, and generally bummed around for the past few months and I *have* changed my ways - slightly. It has shown me a different side to life, which I never had with my adopted mother, the all-controlling Olga. So, I am grateful for her company and the freedom it has brought. However, this team business is grating and being thrown into a mix of people who I would never touch with a soggy joss stick, is pushing me beyond my limits.

I am sitting on my bed staring at Jaz who is lighting the fifth stick of the day. The smoke rises gently towards the air con unit, thankfully sucking out the stifling cloud before it drifts my way.

Studying her face has become a pastime of mine. Her auburn hair, constrained by her clips and scrunchy bands made from lace or some defunct 19th century design, forms an unruly heap on her head, that would rival any hurricane torn neighbourhood. Her green eyes are droopy and dozy, giving the impression she is high on some drug-induced trip. Her clothes are diaphanous and reminiscent of an impressionist painter, floating around oozing creative nonsense. So, as you can see, she is not my choice of roommate and patience is not one of my best talents.

"Jaz; has it occurred to you that these smelly sticks are doing you more harm than good? It is creating havoc with my breathing, and I would appreciate it if you didn't burn so many." She looks up in that drippy way, with a wistful smile, as if I have confirmed unicorns are real.

"Oh Maisie, you really need to chill; I think you take life too seriously. And besides, this heavenly scent will transport you to a peaceful place where your soul can rest."

I hesitate to reply, as I am on the brink of using her stick as a flue brush to send her to a peaceful place - *for good.*

"Well... this isn't a hippy convention; we are supposed to be well trained, precise tools of MI6. To fight injustice and corruption, not welcome every screwed-up individual and let them drift on the evening breeze to blissful Manyana!" My frustration is growing, and I bite my lip. She again smiles and wafts the smoke towards me. Is she goading me or just stupid? I am really very close to 'wafting' her away.

"Yes...I know. Ayanna is training us for whatever, but we need rest and realignment so we can function well in stressful times." My brow is beginning to furrow like an expertly ploughed field. This is not helping me do either.

"Hmm... I think I am going to ask for another room if you carry on like this. Can't you just cut it down to one a day, then my lungs can recover?" She looks devastated by the suggestion; *I haven't killed your dog.*

"That would be hard; adjusting my alignment and inner peace would take time." Oh, my goodness. Jaz, *you are extreme.*

"If you could at least try. Then I won't have to consider leaving." Again, she looks shocked at the prospect of me going.

"Oh, please don't do that; I wouldn't know who to talk to. The lads are far too detached from reality." I uncontrollably laugh and cough, as Jaz has *no* grasp of reality at all. "And I really enjoy being with you." At this, I'm not quite sure what she means. I hope she doesn't have a girl crush, as I am not well versed in dealing with that.

"Yeah, ok then. Let's have a go, and then I'll reassess. I'm going out for a walk - to clear my lungs." She appears less hurt and returns to her weird, crooked smile.

Since settling down in MI6, I have found my *own* peace of mind by consoling myself with reconstructed memories of my parents working here. No end of people have commented to me about how they miss them and have either worked or trained with them. It is like a strange reunion, with me in the middle with amnesia. One thing it has given me is the feeling of a wider family as anyone who did know them seems to be quite friendly and often sympathetic to my upbringing.

I get to tell them that I have no actual memories of my mum and dad and that their collective stories are very welcome, helping me piece together some of my past. Many try to encourage me to explain about my life with Olga and the work with the organisation we operated under. I am still wary of sharing as I don't know where

Olga is or what she is doing at present. Being whisked away from the hospital gave her the anonymity she needed, and I still have some allegiance to her, even after the revelation that she killed my parents.

Ayanna is the most insistent, as I am assuming she has been given the task of deconstructing my past so it can give MI6 a better handle on the dealings of the agency I and Olga worked for and stop it in its tracks. After all, it was them that put out the hit on my parents and other agents. So, they have been, and still are, a threat.

"Since you are our only contact with this organisation, any information would be extremely valuable Maisie," Ayanna would say, like some sort of mantra.

It usually comes up in conversation over a pizza at the local Pizza Express. Her manner can be quite disarming, and I am often finding myself divulging more than I should. A pain in my arm seems to be a welcome distraction, probably the scar that twinges in vengeance from the Versailles horror. Ayanna senses every time I divert her attention away from her questioning, shown by her bottom lip skewing to the side. Then she has the presence of mind to carry on talking about the latest trend in lipstick or clothes. It is a cat and mouse sort of questioning. Only time will tell who wins.

2 - WIN OR LOSE?

As previously mentioned, kicking the crap out of someone is one bit of my programming under Olga, which is imprinted within me, even expressed in my dreams. Jaz has commented how I can end up fighting the duvet and strangling the life out of it before relaxing again into a peaceful slumber. This doesn't bode well if I ever want to share a bed with someone; they may well end up phoning the police or shooting me. This morning, the bed has survived yet another one of my night-time attacks and we are sleepily dragging our butts to a training session.

Today it consists of Jiu Jitsu along with fitness exercises to test the strongest physique. The team, as I mentioned, is a motley crew from all around the UK. Their British heritage has been scrutinised down to their toothbrush usage. There are two guys, Alex and Jules, and Jaz, which seems to me to be a little light, seeing that our seniors are training us to work as undercover operatives for various projects.

Now, just a point of reference; when I was working with Olga, my mother, who wasn't my mother, we called the completion of our jobs 'despatches'. Here in the world of MI6, they are called 'projects'. Yet, I'm unclear as to whether this means when the job is complete it will be called a 'projection'; a bit like an 'execution'. Anyway, a small detail, no doubt I will understand one day.

Alex is the arrogant one, who is determined to make a fool out of me. Every training session, he finds some reason to make me look small (even though I am small, it's not the point). Today is no exception.

"Hey Maiz," he utters, without my permission to call me that. "Are you up for the long rope? I'll give you a head start." I look at him and can't quite ignore his bulging biceps. They stand proud, forcing their way through his tight fitting, sweat stained shirt. At six feet two and probably 200lbs, I am no match for his brawn. He unfortunately knows that and will demonstrate it in every strength contest.

I twist my nose and blow it out on the floor mat. I take great joy from his reaction, as he winces a little. I think his high school and elite college background has left him with some weakness when it comes to etiquette. Since Harmony Chase smashed my nose, it has a bendy nature which I can use to dislodge any unwanted bogie quite easily.

So, with a quick wipe on my arm, I nod and saunter over to the parallel ropes hanging from the roof timbers. He looks me up and down, with that annoying expression which I assume he is either checking me out or, he can't wait to prove his masculinity.

Gripping the rough jute, I twist my fingers around it and pull. Why I do this, I am not sure. I know it's secure. He looks at me with a disdain I could trample on. The other two have finished on the rowing machines and walk over towelling themselves. Jaz shouts "*come on Maisie - whip his butt*", which I appreciate. Except, his butt is not my main concern. I am a competitor who does not enter unless I win. Too many times has this asshole beaten me and it stings. I feel my face grimace and unfortunately Alex takes this as a forced acceptance that I will lose again.

"Ready or not - three, two, one…" he shouts.

I feel the adrenaline kick in and immediately my hands are racing upwards, my left foot quickly wrapping around and locking, finding the rope jammed against the top of my ankle. My right foot pushes hard down on it. I let out a squeal because I didn't position it quite right and the pressure forced a pain to shoot through my leg. I have to forget that and repeat the process again.

In the corner of my eye, I see Alex now shifting up a gear, as he reaches above my position, his long arms reaching far further than mine. A sense of injustice bites at my throat, as this contest is no way even. But still, I want to win, so ignoring the pain, I increase my rate. The next time I position well, and this thrust up gets me going quicker. The roof panels look to be higher than normal. I know this is rubbish, but when you are behind, *everything* seems further away.

I can hear his effort wheeze through his breathing. He is a no compromise winner too. Looking across, I hope he slips or misjudges his foot wrap, anything to give me a chance. I judge now he has a couple more reaches and he'll win - *again.* I push hard and feel the strength in my arms failing but my legs are stronger. Sweat is not helping with my grip either. I concentrate and focus. *Bend with the wind; be one with the rope.* These sayings are racing through my head like a waterfall. There's clapping from the floor, as Jaz and Jules are willing us on. I hear a swear word, Alex's grip slips. It gives me hope. I force the last couple of reaches and rush my foot wrap. The misjudgement is my undoing. I slip and my hands flail in thin air. My head outweighs the rest of my body and spirals towards the crash mats.

Jaz screams and I blackout.

***

I wake with the team gazing at me as if I'm some fish out of water. Ayanna has knelt beside me and is wafting a vile smelling substance under my nose. I jerk to one side and throw up.

"Oh dear," I hear Jaz say. The other sound is Alex chortling. Ayanna is rubbing my back.

"Take it easy. The fall has knocked the wind out of you and that crack on the head won't help," she says, with her usual unruffled calmness. I slowly get to a sitting position and put my head between my shivering legs. Jules is scurrying around wiping up where my breakfast lay, his hands securely encased in surgical gloves.

"You pushed rather too hard on this one, Maisie. You will have to pace yourself." Ayanna gives me this parental advice every time I apparently overstep some predetermined line in my endeavours to win a challenge. I give her a side look, my brows heavy with sweat.

"Yeah, maybe so. I'm sure one day I'll learn, *too*," I say with more sarcasm than I expected. This releases another laugh from Alex.

"I doubt that. One day you might beat me, *too*," he says with more laughter.

From the reflection off her lanyard, I can see my face glows a shade of ruby red. Ayanna's hand is heavy on my shoulder. She must have known what my response was going to be. I give her an annoyed stare. All I see are those deep brown eyes creasing to slits, enough to tell me to cool it.

"Ok, Alex; you win today; we *all* win one day," she says, "Now, team; we need to get to a briefing meeting. Get showered and look less dishevelled and meet up at 11 in room C 12." She gives me a warm squeeze on the shoulder and rises from her crossed legged position, as if on a bungee rope. Jaz offers a hand and I grab it.

"I was sure you were going to win today, Maisie. What distracted you?" she asks. I shrug.

"Maybe his stink. You know how much he smells." Jaz hides a smile and then nearly chokes.

"Ha ha-ha…Maisie. You are so funny." I smile at her. She is the one who is funny.

"Come on…let's get cleaned up. Hey…I wonder what this meeting is all about? Do you think we could be getting our first assignment?" Jaz asks wide eyed. I shrug again.

"Maybe. Maybe it's just a pep talk on how not to fall off ropes," I say.

"Don't be daft. We all know how to do *that.*" I give her a push in the back.

"Ha ha… *Maisie G, the one who falls from grace, to only wind up in heaven,*" she says with a wistful tone. I frown, not really understanding her meaning.

"What the hell are you on about?"

"I know you don't speak much about your past, but we hear whispers of how you were involved in, shall we say, underhand dealings? Crooked organisations and the like…" I wave my finger around.

"Hmm …yes and no. It's not something I'm proud of to be honest, and MI6 are trying to get more info out of me than I am wanting." This conversation sends a tingle of uncertainty down my spine. "I do hope they haven't asked *you* to wheedle more out of me, have they?" I study those droopy eyes. Surely Jaz couldn't be underhand, even if she tried. Her gaze drifts to one side and she wipes her brow with the workout towel.

"No. I'm just curious as to what you were into. My upbringing was less exciting than yours. I was an angel at school and was chosen for this work by my head of department." I give her an incredulous look.

"Head of department? What sort of school did you go to? Prep school for spies?" I snigger. She gives me a stern look for her.

"An all-girls school for high achievers, *actually!* I excelled in Math and problem solving, so much so, they contacted the intelligence services asking if any of them would take me on." I give a wry smile. Jaz is more than a fairy on speed then. "GCHQ were after me originally, but a friend of my mother's suggested MI6 as he had worked for them in his youth as well. He said it would suit my character." I nod. It does, I think.

"So, being selected from this all-girl school and paired off with me must be pretty disappointing for you," I say, expecting her to agree.

"Oh no, far from it. To be honest, the girls at school were boring and traditional. All they were interested in was which car they wanted, along with the designer house and boyfriend. It never really appealed to me. I was more into the spiritual side of things."

We wander the corridors as she continues to tell me of her dreams to set up a yoga retreat in Bali, whilst applying her knowledge of code breaking and computer programming.

"Fascinating Jaz," I conclude, "I didn't think you had so much depth. Maybe when you get your yoga club, I will come and visit. Always wanted to go to Bali. Sounds idyllic." She nods and her face flushes.

We turn into the shower rooms, and I see Alex wandering around with nothing but a skimpy towel around his waist. Jules has already showered and is combing his dark hair into a precise wave. He nods as we walk in. Jules is a guy of few words, and I have yet to extract a decent conversation out of him. Another challenge yet to win.

Alex hogs the other large mirror. It appears that he can't get enough of his own reflection. I feel his eyes follow us as we walk past towards the changing area. He stands there preening himself, like a Greek god; not that I have really seen any so self-absorbed as he. Without hesitation, he slides across to block our way. I look up at his cheesy grin.

"Yes…what do you want, Alex?" I ask. I know what I *want* to give him.

"Silly that you should slip today. I even thought you might have beaten me," he hisses through his exquisite teeth. I give a false smile. "Maybe we can try out some of your Jeet Kune Do and see if you can beat me at that? There must be something."

My lips tingle, as I run a dry tongue across them. I can't really account for what happened next. All I can say is that I slipped again, and the result was *very* satisfying.

3 - A BRIEF MEETING

We file into the briefing room smartly dressed, the smell of freshly showered bodies shadowing our walk. Ayanna and two others are sitting at a round table, just about large enough to accommodate all of us, without touching arms. I raise an eyebrow as Alex sits down. He visibly winces and an audible groan emits from his face. Jaz looks away and stops herself from giggling. Alex stands up again to rearrange his trousers. They seem to be giving him some discomfort around the groin. I give him a long deliberate smile.

"Good morning recruits. My name is Agent Delaware, and this is Chief Analyst, Catherine Short. We are wanting to brief you over some intel we have recently been made aware of. Agent Bolt has been presented with it and she considers you are the best team we can prepare for the task."

Agent Delaware appears to have a mid-Atlantic twang to his accent, so I am assuming he is either a CIA operative or has been seconded by MI6. Either way, he doesn't say. My mind just makes the necessary notes. He is an older guy, dark hair, losing it at the temples with sharp piercing blue eyes.

"I will ask Catherine to explain." He motions to her, and she stands taller than I expected. Her long legs elevate her to a dizzying height of at least six feet. Clothed in an apricot suit, she reminds me of a giant ice lolly.

"Yes, good morning. It has come to the MI6's attention that a serious breach has occurred in a section of the security forces. They are tackling the likelihood of classified information leaking to foreign governments who will benefit from this and will use it to hamper our operations in the far east."

She has the tone of a headmistress and I notice that Jaz has sat bolt upright as if she is attending one of her all-girl school meetings. Alex and Jules seem to be attentive, with Jules taking copious notes. How is he writing so much down? She hasn't said anything yet. I can feel my back sweating and I shuffle in this squeaky chair. Catherine Lollipop Lady stares at me.

"It is important that you pay attention to what I am about to tell you. As a matter of national security, you four are to infiltrate and apprehend the people who have masterminded this. It will take a disciplined team effort to accomplish this mission…,"

"Should we wish to accept it…" I whisper to Jaz.

"... *and* with the support of each other, you must succeed. Any failure will result in a catastrophic imbalance of power in the West." Catherine continues to give me her harshest stare. Not that I know what other she has, but it looks likely to be her worst. I give a sarcastic shudder and roll my shoulders.

"Excuse me young lady, I have been reassured that your involvement on the team is necessary, so I am hoping you understand the importance of this. You seem a little disrespectful." I nod in agreement. Ayanna moves forward in her chair.

"I must apologise for any unseemly attitudes that the team may give off. It is their first assignment and especially Maisie; she is a recent recruit and still has to learn about our protocols." She gives me that slit eyed look which is as good as a rebuke.

"Very well, I can make allowances." She clears her throat. "Here are the pictures of the people of interest." She switches a video on and the opposite wall flickers into life.

"The first person is Erin Bogslava; a Slovakian national who has been dealing in national secrets with the Russians and Chinese. Don't be fooled by her youthful looks; her kill rate is quite extraordinary. She has been on our radar for the last year and has managed to evade our attempts at reeling her in." I act out throwing a mock fishing line. Ms Short frowns. Ayanna gives me another stare.

"The next person is Henri Fontaine; a French national who was until recently under the protection of the DGSE, the French security services. He has since been aligning himself with this band of conspirators." The mention of that organisation sends a ripple up my back. My thoughts wander off, thinking of my boyfriend who I have had no contact with for over six months. His father apparently worked for these people. I must have wandered too far as Ms Short gets *'short'* with me.

"*Maisie Greene*; you are here to be an asset to this team, not a pain in the backside," she hisses.

To my surprise, she continues this rant, probably in the hope I will capitulate and behave myself. When is that going to happen? I smile at her, which only seems to send her hair into a spiked frenzy.

"Ayanna; this girl has to be reined in, or our arrangement will be terminated." I don't like the sound of that. What arrangement? Ayanna nods and waves a magic hand as if to make me fall asleep.

"Maisie, you must learn to respect your seniors here. It is in your best interest and ultimately, ours too."

Alex hides a smirk and Jules lifts a timely hand before coughing. Jaz has maintained her upright stance, as if a pole has been rammed down her back, just staring ahead. This does make me feel like a misplaced puzzle piece, with nowhere to fit. The squeaky chair continues to complain as my bum is sweaty as I relieve my discomfort.

"I think it is *you* that wanted me to be here, not the other way around, Ayanna," I say with annoyance. "I have always considered that my presence in MI6 is for your benefit rather than mine. So, I think we both must walk a fine line… *if* you want me to stay."

Ayanna purses her lips. I know she knows what I say is true. One of the few reasons for me to stay is find out more about my parents and try to piece together the long-lost memories I so want. But, if this becomes too untenable, I'm walking.

"Sorry, I will *try* to behave," I eventually say. Ayanna nods in appreciation. Ms Short pulls her apricot jacket down and continues with her preach.

"The other main person of interest is Moiran Cafferty, an Irish national. Her involvement seems to be triggered by the failing peace process in Northern Ireland and has wanted to bring down any government that doesn't agree with her misaligned beliefs." She sneers when saying this. I sense she has a nasty taste in her mouth. Clearing her throat, she gulps some water and flicks onto the next picture which has documents strewn across a table.

"These files were discovered in a flat in Paris recently and indicate that this team of conspirators want to acquire information as to making a 'dirty bomb'." My ears are on fire now. I sit forward quickly noting that Ayanna has spotted my change in enthusiasm.

"They were tracked down by the DGSE and MI6 in a joint effort." I flinch. This sounds too close to what I was involved in prior to joining MI6. How did they get hold of them? Has this anything to do with my mother's sapphire?

"They have been verified as having the potential for the completion of the said 'dirty bomb'," butts in Agent Delaware. "All they require are the right ingredients and the opportunity. That is where you come in, team."

I stare at Ms Short and Delaware. Is this what Ayanna wanted me for? So far, she has gleaned from me that my mother held some vital information, but as to where and on what, I have never said. The blinding flash from my mother's sapphire fills my mind's eye. For a second, its intense brightness causes me to blink. Ayanna clears her throat.

"Maisie; I know this may be difficult for you to grasp, but the department had doubts as to what your mother was up to, prior to her death." I exit my dream world and frown at her.

"We have to find out what she knew so we can neutralise this threat." She gives me that concerned look; one I have encountered several times when she has tried to tease information out of me. I find myself biting my lip.

"Have you not found that man who nearly killed me to get that information?" I ask.

"No; we are still unsure as to who he is. The description you gave us came up short." I glance at the apricot lady and grin.

"We have planned a series of training expeditions to make sure you can cope with the rigours of life in the field," Ayanna says. "They will start with you going to the Outer Hebrides, islands off the Scottish coast." Jaz glances at me, with a look of rising horror.

"There, you will be put through your paces with combat and survival training. It will push you beyond any comfort zones you have, but I have utmost confidence in you all." Ayanna smiles and nods at Agent Delaware. Ms Short sits and shuffles her paperwork.

"Ayanna, I smell something..." she looks at me puzzled. "Bullsh**t...". Ayanna shakes her head. Ms Short uncontrollably bangs her fist on the table, making us all jump.

"You better get that attitude sorted, *Miss Greene.* If you think that we are going to be easy on you because of some sentimental attachment to your parents working for us years ago, then you are very much mistaken!"

I'm sure her tongue spit in two and whipped out of her mouth. I shake my head and push back the chair harder than I expected, rattling into the wall. Everyone stares at me.

"Well, thanks for the welcome...I'm *off.*" I march towards the door and as a last statement, I turn and give Ms Short the finger.

End of meeting.

4- PILLOW FIGHTS

"Maisie, I can't believe you did that." Jaz is gawping at me as if I killed the head of MI6 with a cheese grater. "She was seething when you left. Quite funny actually…her face looked like a cherry on top of that apricot suit." Jaz giggles and I return a self-satisfied smile.

"Well, she had better watch her step as I'm in no mood for bowing and scraping to these people. They are a bunch of assholes, as far I'm concerned. How could they think that my mother would be a part of this conspiracy? That gets me so mad." Jaz looks at the floor and then shuffles across the bed.

"Maybe, they are clutching at straws. You know, trying to join the dots without any guide. From what I've heard, your parents were hugely respected here." She is obviously trying to be empathetic. I appreciate it. It's nice to have someone who is *for* me.

"Yeah, that's the impression I get. So, what is with Lollipop lady? Is she trying to smear crap over their memory?" I lean back on my cushion against the corner of the bedroom wall. *Safe place...* I can see all angles. My training even kicks in when I'm in the bedroom.

"I think they are concerned that this information is too sensitive to be floating around people who don't give a crap who it hurts or destabilised," Jaz says. "We are here to make a difference to the world. That's why I joined. Working a typical 9 till 5 has never appealed to me. It's more like an obsession to make the world safer and brighter." I look at her and smile. She really is Florence Nightingale trying to put a plaster over the world's ills.

"You are a treasure Jaz. I have never met anyone quite like you." She colours up and looks away. "Most people put themselves first, sod everyone else." I punched her shoulder. She looks shocked.

"Hey! That hurt." Yeah, as if.

"I think maybe before we start sorting the evil megalomaniacs of this world, we need to toughen you up a little." She nods.

"I'm terrified to be honest when she said we were going for survival training. What will that be like? I've only ever camped in the summer and that was a trial. The bugs and cows were constantly attacking the tent *and* me."

"Don't fret, I'll look after you. Have you never been in a fight?" I ask.

"No, I mean at school I used to get bullied when I was more interested in sitting at my computer than playing netball or football. I retreated into my meditation and cut myself off." I shake my head.

"If we are out in the field and someone is pointing a gun at you, it wouldn't work if you became a tortoise and disappeared into your shell, would it?" Her eyes widened and shivered.

"I suppose not. Have you been in those situations?"

"Too many to remember. Each one is different. You have to react *and* adapt. That's why my Jeet Kune Do comes in so useful. I can still be aware and react quickly to any threat. Let me show you." We stand and face each other.

"Ok, throw a punch at me." She looks sceptical.

"Are you sure? I don't want to hurt you." I shake my head.

"You won't, honestly." She prepares by facing me head on. As quick as a flash, she flings a right uppercut at my face. To be fair, I didn't expect her to be so enthusiastic. I glance her arm to the side, as my fist lands millimetres from her nose. She looks shocked and nearly stumbles backwards.

"Shit! That was frightening. Shall we try again?" she asks.

"Ok then," I reply, not expecting her to be up for it so quickly.

Her stance changes and now jumps around to her right, bouncing on her feet. Who is she trying to copy, Neo from the Matrix?

Her foot comes up towards my knee and I twist and brush it to one side. Her follow up comes from a spin and her other leg comes crashing down towards my head. I nearly allow it to contact, as I stumble into the side of the bed, but manage to roll and kick her in the stomach. The force pushes her back into a cabinet, all her joss sticks clattering on the floor. She sits there, coughing.

I reach out a hand to help her up. Then, Jaz, the unpredictable, slaps me on the ear, sending my balance all over the place. She pulls on my arm, and I tumble like a drunken fool across her bed. Has she become possessed? Why has Jaz, the dozy, now become Conan the Conqueror? It takes me a few seconds to adjust and bring my senses into fight mode. I jump onto the bed and stare at this raging bull. Her eyes have become alive with anger.

"Are you ok, Jaz? I didn't think you had it in you, all this aggression." She stares at me, dribble running down her chin. Without any warning, she charges me, shouting like a crazed zombie. Her shoulder barges me into the wall knocking the wind out of me. I instantly react by sinking my elbow into her back, bringing my knee upwards into her face. She finally collapses, the fire in her belly hopefully extinguished.

"What the hell has got into you girl?" I ask, trying to get my breathing steady. She mumbles something. I lean a little closer, but not that close. She isn't going to catch me unawares again.

"I'm sorry. I didn't mean to get so aggressive. I sometimes lose it and I can't control myself." She rolls over and drags her limbs into a lotus position, forcing her breathing to be calm and deliberate. I stare at her wondering why this side of Jaz has been hidden. She raises her shoulders and shakes her head. "It comes over me when I feel threatened. I can get so angry."

"I get it - I've had to learn to channel that anger into a positive response. But losing it like that is going to get you an early hole in the ground," I say and sit again studying this quirky girl.

"Yes, so impetuous, not good," she breathes out heavily.

"I'm glad it's happened now though. We can work on that. This training session we are going on will test our limits. We will make a lethal weapon out of you yet, Jaz." She opens one eye and allows a smile to stretch her face. I pick up a pillow and throw it at her. She catches it like a ninja and throws it back with interest.

What happened next would only be appropriate for a seventh-grade school kids' party. Feathers and sheets went everywhere, the air in the room heavy with swear words from Jaz, who again bemused me as to the extent of her vocabulary. But it was great fun and such a relief from the all-important Ms Shorty. I did wonder if the cleaners would report us, as I wasn't in the mood for clearing up *this* mess.

5 - COFFEE AND CROISSANTS

It was one sunny afternoon that Ayanna and I went for a ramble, downtown London. We sauntered around Covent Garden's shops, although the floaty clothing here would suit Jaz more than myself. We visited every clothes shop on Oxford Street I could find; I was in buying mode.

It was still within my capacity to shop until I dropped and with my newfound wealth left by my parents, it was tempting to buy anything I wanted, however trivial. My obsession with crop tops and designer trainers was not going to go on the back burner. So, in my new wardrobe, hung every colour and shade, Converse trainers stacking up. Ayanna wasn't impressed. I think she was a little jealous of my carefree attitude.

"You are like a kid in a candy shop, aren't you?" she said. Her dark features would crease up as I came out with yet another set to slay the unwary. I would try to encourage her to be more adventurous, but she was always resistant to it, saying she had enough clothes to last a lifetime.

"Did Olga treat you this way?" she asked. "I mean, let you loose on the high street to gobble up everything?" Her expression was searching for more than an answer to that question.

"We would travel to a country, and she would allow me to get most things I wanted; I guess a thank you for helping her out. She *was* acting as my *mother*." I look into Ayanna's eyes and wonder how long she will patiently tease information out of me.

"Hmm…not a good one really," she replies. I shrug.

"I can't go back in time and tell her to do it differently, can I?"

"Indeed. You are a mix of the spoilt and impetuous," she states.

"Well, better than being a boring old fart!" She frowns and then laughs.

"Less of the old, and, how do you know I fart?"

"Unless you are an alien and have no butt hole… then you fart." She laughs again.

"Ok, you got me there."

"Shall we get something to eat, as these bags are weighing me down."

"Ok, come on. I'll treat you. I know an old coffee shop where they make the most exquisite croissants and serve heavenly arabica coffee," she says.

I know I tend to distrust people, but when that word slipped into the conversation, my back bristled. Olga was obsessed with taking her own coffee blend everywhere we went, saying that the local beverage was never up to her standards. So, I now find myself averse to anything that Ayanna is going to say which attempts to extract further knowledge about my background.

We wander down a side street, with nothing special going on, a few warehouses and a gantry overhanging the road. Then the smell grabbed my senses. The coffee scent drifted like an invisible velvet cloud, dragging drool from my mouth. As we got closer, the croissant's aroma was making me so hungry, I'm almost chewing my tongue!

Sitting at a table situated in a small courtyard at the rear of the coffee house, I rest my multiple bags on an adjacent chair. The old London feel of this place sends a shiver down my back. It reminds me of the sort of place dirty deals are done in pleasant surroundings, making the agreements more palatable and justified.

I scan the other residents sipping their drinks and crunching on pastries. They're mostly millennials, probably wealthy beyond any reason, other than they work in London and huge inheritances are waiting for them, so, what the hell; live the rich, fast life; tomorrow we may die. Coming to think of it, that was my style, until recently. Ayanna distracts me from philosophising by rattling the tray onto the table.

"There you go - a feast for the senses," she says, pleased with herself.

"Thanks. I could get this for *you*, you know? I do have money." She looks at me and shakes her head.

"I know, little rich girl. I have wondered where your money comes from. Do you want to enlighten me?"

Her head shifts to one side as the coffee cup drifts up to her ruby red lips. I twitch my nose and grab a croissant. It crumbles in my hand and hot cinnamon and almond syrup streams through my fingers. *Soo nice.* It finds its target and my teeth rip into it like a gorging lion.

"That coffee does smell gorgeous," I say, crumbs spraying over my own drink. She has instinctively bought me a coke along with an iced coffee, which she is trying to wean me onto.

"Forever the politician; never answer the question, do you Maisie?" She wipes the froth from her top lip and sucks it off her finger. I shrug, sipping my iced version and look away.

A small man with white shoes and a fawn and white suit wanders in looking like he owns the street. His eyes search the courtyard. I try not to catch his gaze, as it has caused too many problems in the past. These guys can think I'm interested in them if they think I'm checking them out. He walks slowly around as if he's temporarily lost and decides to go into the shop.

"Maisie. I know you still regard me as an interrogator, but I am seriously trying to understand your background and try to be friends with you." I nod.

"Yes…I know. But it's hard to trust anyone after what I've been through." She looks kindly at me and has another sip. Her pastry is steaming with expectation. The man comes out of the shop, again scanning around. I can't resist and kick Ayanna under the table. She nearly chokes.

"What?"

"That guy. Don't you think he looks suspicious?" I whisper.

Ayanna's eyes drift into surveillance mode. Creasing to half their normal size, her eyes seem to be calculating the threat this guy might be. He continues to wander aimlessly, his jacket swinging open and shut. I see a dark concealed object tucked under his armpit.

I place my croissant carefully on its plate. Tension is building in my chest. I have not felt this for months, being closeted in MI6. Ayanna has reached for her hidden weapon; a Walther PPK. This one was not the popular air pistol anyone can buy online. This one is for real. Talk about James Bond.

Her preparation sends more anxiety through my body, as I feel vulnerable. If I was with Olga, I would be continually ready to tackle thugs, but I feel like I have become soft and non-reactive. I have no weapons on me and with this potential threat, I am unusually nervous.

The guy is still whirling around as if he is waiting for someone to tell him to sit down. Ayanna keeps her eyes fixed on him. I consider what I could use for an attack or self-defence. The pottery on the table would come in useful, although an iced coffee would do little to stop an attacker. The chairs could be a distraction and if the tabletop were loose, then I can use it like a giant frisbee and slice him in half.

Finally, he sits down and crosses his legs. From his inner pocket he pulls out a dark folder. It wasn't a gun then. Ayanna relaxes and covers up her weapon. She glances at me and nods. We are ok - no threat.

"Sorry. That was me overreacting. I must be rusty when judging people. This would never be the case when I was…" I shut up. Ayanna cocks her head and raises her eyebrows.

"Yes?"

"When I was working for the agency. It would need me to be on point with any threats, that's all," I say. She scans my face, for any trace of admission, an arrow to more revelations. I shrug.

"What? I'm not telling you anything… anything that might make me look like an evil swine," I say in self-defence. She nods again.

"It was hard to hear that about your real mother, wasn't it?"

"Yeah, of course. I'm still trying to piece together who they were and what they did. To think they were doing something bad, hurts - especially after finding out that Olga killed them." She again does her sigh and gives a sympathetic look.

"Maisie - in this world of espionage, anyone can be turned. We all need to be accountable and before your parents were terminated, there were rumours that something was being hidden from MI6. It allows a mistrust to grow." I see her trying to reel me in.

"So, they are guilty before they can be judged. A bit unfair, don't you think?" I twitch my nose and attack the remnants of my croissant.

"Listen - when you showed up on our radar, it meant we could try and piece together if there *was* any wrongdoing and contain any threats. If you know anything, it would be extremely helpful. This operation we are preparing you for is dangerous and so much hangs on its success. I believe you are wanting to break free of this life that Olga led you into, correct?" She resumes sipping her coffee.

"Yes - but I want to know why my parents became targets and were duped into lowering their guard. From what I have seen, they would not be so easily hung out to dry."

"Well…this bomb we are talking about was being investigated at the time they were killed. The hiatus in the meantime has kept us on our toes wondering if it would reappear and catch us unprepared. That's why your appearance and this threat emerging seems coincidental. You get my drift?" I look across my coke and nod.

My gaze wanders across to the well-dressed man, who is still reading his paperwork, small round reading glasses perched on the end of his thin nose. A waiter comes across to him and places down a drink and a pastry. He thanks him and continues to study the document in his hand.

This is when I notice something. The back of the folder had some inscription on it that sparked a memory. It was a motif with a horse and thistle. Why does that stir up something? Ayanna is continuing her reasoning for my inclusion in the operation, but I'm distracted now and inwardly kick my brain groping for an answer. *A horse rearing up and a thistle…*I glance down at the cobbled ground, squinting as solitary pools of rainwater reflect the sunlight. A voice drifts through the fog of my memories.

"*Maisie…Maisie.* Oi, are you listening to me?" I nod, and then shake my head.

"Sorry…something is coming back from the past…I think." She meets my eyes with a spark of expectation.

"Really? What do you think it is?"

"A horse and thistle." Ayanna frowns.

"Ok…sounds random. Is it something you might have seen as a kid, something your mum might have talked about?" I hold up my hand.

"Just a minute," I say, shaking my head. I stare at the man again and my heart jumps. He's staring straight back at me.

6 - HORSE AND THISTLE

I know my mind can sink into dark recesses which amaze me and probably appal most people. But this motif has sent my head in a whirl. What is freaking me out is that my eye contact with this eccentric man is opening the floodgates to a world which until now has been locked away. I feel a shudder down my back and glance at Ayanna. She appears to be on high alert, as she has noted my look of anxiety. The man seems to have frozen and through the steaming haze of his drink, his eyes barely move.

"Maisie…are you ok? You seem to be in shock," she says. I agree. The chill racing through my body is freezing me.

"That motif…*that motif*…is something to do with… my mum had a broach," I say and break eye contact.

"Are you sure? Can you remember what it represented?" I blink a few times; this brain freeze is excruciating. More memories start to emerge.

"I can see a pub, with mum and dad drinking in a courtyard…I was playing on the swings. They were laughing and chatting with another couple." The haze slowly lifts revealing more. "Yeah…they were handing each other packages. It was like a birthday party, I think."

Emerging through the mist I see a cake with four candles. I start to well up; *it must be mine*. I watch myself as I run over in slow motion and blow them out, one by one. Mum claps her hands and dad cuddles me. I feel the warmth of his arms wrap around me, and I can't help but cover my chest with my hands. Ayanna reaches over and adds a reassuring squeeze to my arm.

In my dream, I gaze around the table where my parents are now becoming clearer, and a smile cracks my face. The elation of my birthday floods me with joy, along with sadness, in a toxic mix. For some reason I look upwards and the pub sign above my mum's head clearly presents itself.

"A horse and thistle - the pub was called '*The Horse and Thistle*' - that's it."

"Ok. Great that you are getting some memories back…but I am not sure that is so important, is it?" Ayanna is now subsiding into disappointment. I think she was expecting some great revelation to help her crusade.

"Yes, but it is!"

"Oh, why?"

"The other two people there … were *Harmony Chase's* mum and dad!" Ayanna frowns.

"Ok…who are they?"

"Sorry…the woman that tried to kill me in Versailles was Harmony Chase. She said to me that my parents had caused *her* parents death. The mystery man also said something about my parents being reckless with the lives of others. I just thought he was winding me up, telling me a load of crap."

"How do you know it was them at the party?"

"The waiter came over and asked who Mr and Mrs Chase were, so to give them their food."

This memory is increasingly shocking as the implications of what Harmony said to me hits my gut like a boulder. My parents and hers *did* know each other. They did work on operations, maybe. I shake my head and stare at Ayanna.

"I can't quite see what the packages were…I thought they were presents. Maybe they were something more sinister." I blink at Ayanna who is patiently waiting for the big fish to be caught.

"Ok, I know you are traumatised by this flood of memories, so just breathe and chill. I think you may be reading too much into them."

She smiles and relaxes again. I glance across to the man. He's back to reading and drinking his latte, seemingly not interested in me at all. *Did I imagine all this?* I'm starting to doubt my own sanity. Or did the fall in the gym do more damage than I thought? I continue to force the rest of the memory out.

I see that my mum has a broach, more like a pendant you wear when you belong to a club. My back bristles with an electric shock as I see something more surprising.

"What's wrong now?" Ayanna asks.

"Not just the pub sign, but they all had a pendant or a badge."

"Oh, ok. Can you describe it?"

"A horse's head with a thistle wrapped around it. The thistle flower is a bright blue gem." I shudder. Maybe this was like the sapphire on my mum's necklace.

"Great. Now *that* is interesting. I seem to remember some dossier on a group called the *'Horsemen of the Apocalypse'*. It all seemed a bit fantastical to my thinking, but what you said now brings it into sharp focus. Thank you, Maisie. This is the breakthrough I've been looking for."

I stare bleary eyed at her. I feel like I've been sent through a very tight space and squeezed until all my blood has squirted out.

"Oh wow. Are you going to abandon me now that I've given you something?" I have a feeling of dread rising.

"Of course not. You are under my care. I am just pleased the gaps in your past are coming out. I'm sorry that it might be more traumatic than you wanted. Come on. Let's get back to the office. We can chill and I'll do some digging."

I get up from my chair, feeling my legs buckle. Steadying myself, I collect my bags and glance at the man. He rustles his papers and places them neatly on the table. He drinks slow and long from his latte as we glide past him. I'm sure I feel his eyes burning into the back of my head.

7 - INTELLIGENCE. WHAT INTELLIGENCE?

Our trip back to the 'office' was painful. These memories were harsh. I still can't accept there was some collusion between the Chases and my parents. I also wonder why I have no memory of Harmony in this collage of mental pictures. Maybe she wasn't at my party. She was older than me after all. Anyway, that isn't relevant. I hate the woman. She got what she deserved.

Why, though, were my parent's friends with them? Were they in some sort of secret society? I muse over these pendants on each of their lapels, inviting me to doubt their integrity. This sends me down the old street of retribution and I wonder if Olga was told to kill them because of this association. I notice Ayanna close to me, probably aware that I'm distracted from walking safely along the sidewalk.

"Take it easy, Maisie. This is going to take time to process. When we get back, I'll check the archives to see what we have on this splinter group."

I nod and shuffle my bags from one hand to the other. The cords are cutting into my skin. Everything is hurting me. Olga's words of '*preventing a worse situation'* as the reason for my parent's deaths, stings my gut. Added to that, I'm replaying Harmony's dying moments in my mind, making me wretch so I must stop, propping myself against a lamp post.

"Hey. Just take a moment. The shock of all this is messing with your mind, Maisie. Let me take your bags. We need to get back so you can rest," Ayanna says. Her welfare towards me is what I need at a time like this; someone to lean on, trust in.

"Thanks. It all seems… so overwhelming. It's not what I expected, all these memories." In a moment of weakness, I feel compelled to tell her something. "Have you ever heard of *'Trojan'*?" My heart escapes with my breath. She stops and turns, her eyes closing to slits.

"Where have you heard of that, Maisie?" she asks.

"It's complicated. A 'friend' was helping me find Olga in Paris and came up with this code name. I read a report on it. It appeared that my parents were involved." She continues to stare.

"Hmm…this memory shake up is loosening your tongue. I think we need a good sit down and unravel what you know. You have suddenly come up with two major code names which MI6 officials have been scratching their heads over for years." She continues to study my face, making me squirm.

"Yeah…ok. I'll tell you as much as I can. Now this stuff is rising to the surface, I need some answers myself. If nothing else, I want to clear my parents' name. All this crap is unjustified as far as I'm concerned." Ayanna nods.

We catch the underground train on the Victoria line to Pimlico station, and I ponder over what I've divulged. Glancing across to Ayanna, I do wonder if what she implies is going to bring me down along with all the other conspiracies. Can it be true that my parents were rogue agents?

As we walk from Pimlico underground station, we walk past the Lithuanian embassy. It sends a chill down my back. What if Olga suddenly appeared (being from that country) and invited us in for coffee? I shudder.

A passing black cab reflects a flicker of sunlight, making me squint. As I look up, I notice a woman who is loitering across the road and keeps glancing my way. I feel an increasing readiness to escape, and I catch up with Ayanna. I touch her deftly on the arm. She turns and raises an eyebrow.

"Yeah. What is it?"

"I have a feeling that someone over the road is watching me. This time, I'm not hallucinating, honestly."

She screws up her face, probably expecting me to be still paranoid. She glances across and fixes on the woman straight away. Ayanna quickens her pace and I follow. We keep checking whether this person is keeping up with us. Being not that far from the SIS building, I'm guessing that Ayanna will make sure we take a diversion.

As we head for Vauxhall Bridge, we pick up the pace, whilst keeping a fixed eye on our tracker. Ayanna points to a section of the bridge and nods. I am confused. What does she want me to do? Jump off?

"Head for the Riverside Walk Gardens; we will assess what her intentions are." We skip across Millbank and end up standing around some weird sculptures. I stand gazing across the river to my new employer's building and wonder why I am entertaining this at all. It's like being at sea without an engine, tossed from one allegiance to another.

Ayanna prepares to grasp her concealed weapon, as she hands my bags over without much care and one spills my carefully chosen clothes across where the pigeons have their communal toilet. Great! I quickly rescue them from any further grubbing and stand with my back to the river wall. We watch this person trace our steps and doesn't appear to be worried that she has been spotted. As she approaches, Ayanna shouts out.

"Hey! What are you doing? Are you following us?" A daft question as far I'm concerned.

"I need to talk. That's all," the woman says, glancing around.

"Ok. Talk then." Ayanna wasn't in the mood for entertaining any pleasantries.

"You are in danger, Maisie Greene." My back bristles.

"How do you know my name?"

"That isn't relevant. I'm just a messenger." I can't stop a frown screwing up my face.

"What is that supposed to mean?" I ask.

"An associate asked me to advise you to watch your back - especially those who you believe to be trustworthy." I continue to frown and glance at Ayanna who is poised with her Walther PPK to conclude the conversation.

"Who is this 'associate'?"

"All I can say is that they will contact you directly at some stage. In the meantime, be careful. Trust no one." She turns away about to leave, but Ayanna was having none of it.

"Hey. You can't just wander off after giving that warning. You need to justify yourself." The woman half turns and delivers another warning.

"Ayanna, you are in danger too. That isn't my concern, but you can have this intelligence free of charge." She continues to walk towards Millbank. Ayanna follows, determined to get more out of her. Quickening her pace, the woman sidesteps a car racing towards her and screeches to a halt. Ayanna instinctively draws her pistol. I instinctively dive for cover. This has the makings of an abduction. Except, it wasn't.

Masked people emerge and confront the woman, revealing a silenced weapon. She halts but then tries to run in another direction. She slides across a car bonnet and races for cover. Ayanna is now vulnerable, with no cover and faced with a shoot-out. One of the masked gunmen fires at the escaping woman, a spray of red escaping her shoulder. She collapses on the sidewalk, rolling into railings. People who were innocently enjoying an evening's drink at the local pub are sent yelling inside. I can't quite get myself into gear. I know I should, but again, I feel soft and unprepared.

Ayanna screams out *'police'* and aims at these assailants. I hear a shot ring out and one of them staggers into the open car door. The other retreated from the woman sprawled across the ground and ran back to the car, muffled shouts telling the other person to get going. They sounded foreign. The car screeches off, blue smoke wafting around creating a grey haze. Ayanna hesitates and re-holsters her gun. I emerge from behind one of these sculptures and race across to hear the moans of a dying woman.

We approach her together with both of us kneeling beside her. Ayanna tries to stem the blood flow. The woman whispers something to me. I leaned closer as her last breath was hacking and horrific. I picked out something that meant so much to me. A name whom I will always treasure.

"*Maria Giogorgi sent me...*" Her last sound gurgled as she slipped into unconsciousness. Ayanna felt her pulse and shook her head.

"What did she say?" Ayanna asks.

"A name… my real mother's stage name."

"That's odd, don't you think?" I nod. She turns to the lifeless body covered in blood, and grimaces.

"We had better get this cleaned up. I'll ring SIS and they will dispose of the body. We will need to identify her. Get back to MI6, Maisie. You need to get safe." She grabs my hand and shakes it.

As I scuttle across Vauxhall Bridge, I feel a sensation rising in my throat, making me choke. I stop for a second and spit some bile out into the river. The stream of pedestrians makes my hands greasy with sweat. Could any of these be a threat? Who are the people this woman was trying to warn me of? My mind goes through the list of people I am with day to day, including the team. Did she mean *any* of them?

8 - POOL PARTY

I stagger through the main entrance of MI6 feeling like a car wreck. The burden of the woman's death, given the simple job of telling me to trust no one, weighs heavily on my mind. To be honest, I didn't need her to tell me that. I don't trust anyone. Olga drilled that in me from an early age.

For instance, I have vague recollections of playing with a girl at a park once. She was taunting me to walk across a rope bridge. I was not impressed when she started to jump up and down, sending a shock wave along the bridge which sent me flying. What made it worse, she had reassured me that she would steady it and I could cross safely. Lesson learnt.

The gate guard glares at me and asks for my pass. I didn't take one with me. I shrug. He thinks I'm trying to get in illegally and asks who I am.

"Maisie Greene; trainee assass-*een*." He attempts to stare me down.

"Don't be clever with me, young lady. Where's your mentor?"

"Tor-mentor," I reply, pouting.

"I'm sorry. I can't let you in if you have no pass. Is there anyone who can vouch for you?" I give my withering look and sigh.

"Try Agent Tupperware or Ms Shorty." He continues to stare at me, adjusting his weapon. I'm not helping him, I realise that. Ayanna hurries in behind me and nods to the impatient guard.

"She is with me, Steven. I'm sorry, we skipped out and we got separated." He nods in reply and grins to himself.

"Got a crush on her, *Steven?*" I ask. He glares at me and colours up. I laugh and follow Ayanna through the scanner.

"You can't be serious. Has he got a thing for me?" she whispers. I can see the motors whirring in her head.

"I would say - probably. But one of those things where he knows you are out of reach, so it's a bit of a fantasy. You know, all alone, at home, watching romantic movies, that kind of thing." She frowns at me.

"I hope you are not implying he's stalking me."

"Neh…just wishful wanting. I've seen it so often with Olga. Some men could only get so close then she would shut them down like pulling the plug on a generator. You could hear the disappointment ooze out of them, like a dropped melon." Not one of my best analogies.

We arrive at our floor and Ayanna waves me off to my room. My head is not made any easier as the smells drifting along the corridor would draw me in blindfolded. I suspect Jaz is having a yoga session.

"Oh my god! What are you doing?" I stare at Jaz who is leaning against the wall doing a handstand.

"Just realigning myself," she replies in a muffled voice. I throw my bags on the bed and kick off my shoes.

"With the upside-down world, Eleven?" I ask. She mutters something and then collapses.

"Sorry?"

"You know, the Netflix series of a few years ago." She still looks clueless. "Oh, never mind. So, what have you been up to, other than draining all your blood into that dozy head of yours?"

"I have been reading about the assault course we are destined for. Scares me to death!" She has that look of revulsion which would sour cat's cream.

"It will be fine. All you need to do is stick with me, I'll take care of you." She now has a vacant expression.

"Hmmm…"

Moving to her bed, she proceeds to wrap a leg around her neck. Why would anyone want to do that, unless under threat of death?

"What is worrying you?"

"Just the boys - you know how idiotic they can be."

"Yeah, I know; remember I've been through worse times than sitting on a windswept mountain side, waiting for my butt to be bitten by a bug." She shivers.

"You can't keep them away as well, can you?" I nod.

"I have a hellish yell; easily scare the ass off any beast." She laughs.

"Ok. You have reassured me of that, at least." The bedroom door silently opens, freaking us both out.

"Who the hell is that?" My nerves are more on edge than I thought. Jules pokes his head around.

"Want to come for a game of pool? Alex and I are heading for the games room." I'm shocked. Not because the lads have invited us, but that Jules has spoken at all.

"Yeah, ok. Could do with a distraction from Jaz bending things that should not be bent." He grins as he glances at her, still with her leg in an unearthly position.

We wander into the games room as Alex is chalking his cue. Not a surprise, that. He chucks the chalk cube at me with force. I catch it just before it embeds in my forehead. Jules shakes his head.

"Alex, really? You are a poor loser," he says. Again, I frown at Jules, who is issuing more words from his mouth than I've heard for months. Alex shrugs and places the balls in a precise order in the triangle. Jaz and I select our cues and circle the table.

"So, is this going to be another one of your challenges, Alex?" I ask.

"We will see. I *was* the college champion." Of course, you were. "But I'm prepared to be beaten by a better player." Of course, you are.

"Well, Jaz. You better give him a chance, then. You know how childish he gets if he loses." She glances across to me and grins. Jules wins the toss, and we start to play, girls against boys.

The game goes as predicted, Alex and Jules leading with some lucky shots, I think. Jaz is getting redder with each shot. I am wondering if another explosive session is about to kick off. The last balls on the table are ours, except for one of theirs, precariously kissing the black ball next to a pocket. I whisper to Jaz to take it easy, as a nudge will give the game away. I have noticed her approach to potting balls seems somewhat erratic.

Taking her time, she focuses on a long shot to down two balls in one. I bite my lip, thinking this is going to go wrong. Her deft nudge has an astonishing effect. The first ricochets off the next, potting them both and positions kindly for another. I nod, impressed. She sinks it beautifully, leaving only one more and we could be onto the black. She eyes up the isolated ball, fighting with an unruly wisp of hair dangling across her vision. I am compelled to reach across to tuck it behind her ear. *Wrong move.* She scuttles the shot, and it goes careering into theirs and pots the black.

"*Bastard!*" she shouts.

"Sorry. I should have told you what I was doing," I say apologetically. She glares at me, as if her drippy eyes could. Alex does his silly chortling laugh and gets the rack ready for the next game. Jules has an emotionless face as usual and tilts his head.

"Shame, that. You were close to beating us. Next time." He repositions the rack and balls even though Alex has just done it. Alex gives him a stare.

"Jules. What was wrong with that? It was ok, you know." Jules' face flashes with the briefest of grins.

These games go on for another two hours. Our tally is close to 15 games each as Jaz and I get our act together and the lads appear to falter.

"Next game wins all," Alex commands. I shrug and watch Jaz nod.

Preparing for the last game seems to be the final challenge for a great Olympic competitor, as far as Alex is concerned. He is flexing his muscles and stretching. Jules watches with patient breathing and I can't help but giggle.

"What's wrong? I have to get rid of all this tension," Alex says looking offended. Winning at all costs obviously winds him up.

It's our turn to break and Jaz gives it some welly. The balls explode across the table and miraculously she pots two. A great start. Alex looks perplexed, his face colouring up. She gets another positioned nicely. Jules pots one and fails on the next. I come to the table and have to reach high, my leg perching on the edge. Not my best look.

"Be careful. With that position you might turn me on," says Alex.

I lower my leg and turn to face him. Before I realise what I'm doing, the cue is folding itself around his smug head. He reels backwards, I think more with shock than my power. Jaz shrieks and Jules moves on a cushion of air away from harm. Alex recovers and stares at me, rage firing up his eyes.

"Bloody hell, Maisie. You don't take compliments well, do you?" He faces me with his cue now raised to a fighting position. I am shocked by my own response - but *no one* takes advantage of me.

He takes a swipe at my legs and instinct kicks in. I jump and use the broken cue like nun chucks, swinging at his arms and torso. We are now in full attack and defence mode, with each of us trying to score a headshot, our arms flailing. He pushes me back with a forceful kick to the stomach. It winds me and I take too long to recover. He bears down on me, his breath and stink making me wince.

"No one has a go at me and wins. Remember that, Maisie. I'm not here to collect friends. You are certainly not one I want to win - except as a trophy." He smirks. That comment was not wise.

"I am not a trophy to be won or lost!"

I slap his ears with force and bring my knee up quickly to his groin. He reels to the side, and I roll the other way. Grasping my sticks, I swipe his face, the splintered end cutting his cheek. Blood flows freely.

A hand halts my other intended blow. I spin round and frown at Jaz who is holding me back.

"I think you have made your point, Maisie," she says.

My breathing is racing. The rage in my chest took me further than I wanted. Seeing the woman dying on the pavement in my mind, creates a desire for vengeance. An unnecessary death, for what? I must weed out who she is warning me against before it's too late.

9 - SECRETS

Ayanna reprimands my behaviour in the pool room by telling me that her arrangement with Ms Short is hanging by a thread. She doesn't want me to get hung by it. *What is this arrangement?*

"I agreed to keep you here as I convinced her that you have a special connection with this operation, being so close to the last persons of interest," she states. I assume they are my parents.

"What happens if I pull out and walk?"

"Then, you would be on your own, vulnerable to anyone who wants to get what we want." I think for a moment.

"Surely, the mystery man seems to be the one who holds the key." I picture my mother's sapphire releasing its hidden information into his futuristic computer.

"So, what has he got?" I wince. I am leaking information like a melting iceberg.

"Just something that could give the 'dirty bomb party' the means."

"What? The making of it?"

"Hmm…maybe…" She stares at me.

"If this information is correct, you do realise that we are closer to an attack than we thought?" Is she trying to make *me* feel responsible?

"Look. I was at the point of losing my boyfriend at the gun of Harmony Chase; I was compromised." I bite my lip and consider if this secret is ready to be released.

"Look, if this 'thing' the man holds is the key, we need to know. Surely you can see how important that is?" I sheepishly nod.

"To get a better handle on this threat, I have been digging into the archives. Let's see if it shakes any more information out of you," she says impatiently.

We wander to a room decked out with cupboards and a large computer screen. The archives room. I know that because it said so on the door. Ayanna sits at the computer, and she punches in her password.

"That's not a good one you know," I casually say.

"Hey! You are not supposed to see that. How did you know?"

"Observation has been one of my primary skills as Olga was either half drunk or sleepy, so I had to be on point." She frowns.

"Well, I'm changing that, asap."

"Good idea."

She brings up a file named:

'Horsemen of The Apocalypse'.

She reads out the summary of who and what these people may be. It states that four people held such dangerous information, that if it got into a rebel nation's hands, it would create a potential escalation to a regional war, even a world war.

It was believed that they were from different nations, colluding to use this information to threaten or manipulate governments to extort money and resources. Searching through this document I notice a reference to the other great secret that Olga and Anton both referred to:

'TROJAN'.

"So, as you can see, these two projects were closely associated. That's why mentioning both made me pay attention immediately. If you are holding information on two confidential projects that MI6 have put on hold for years, then I am justified including you in on this team. Come on Maisie, you must give us what you know. If we put you out into the field all your lives could be in jeopardy, along with whatever these individuals are planning."

She gives that puppy dog look. I glance back at the screen, wishing Anton, my AI friend, would whisper in my ear the correct response.

"Ok". I sigh and prepare myself for the big reveal.

"I came across a necklace my mother had. It was beautiful. The first time I wore it, a holographic message projected on a mirror." Ayanna stares at me, transfixed.

"Yeah, I know, crazy. Apparently, it held information, which the Parisian man, who was British, wanted. He said something about making lots of money and retiring with Harmony." She continues to stare, her mouth still gaping.

"It was unlocked by my voice." At this, her mouth could have easily swallowed a bus. "At first, I wasn't aware that I had that power, but faced with the death of Freddie, my boyfriend, I was forced to find it. Olga sparked a memory of something my mother often said to me, apparently."

Closing her mouth, she taps away on the keyboard, flicking through the onscreen pages. She stops abruptly and points. I squint.

"*Talisman*...that's what I said! *I am your Talisman*. Why is that in there?"

"It was a code name that your mother and father were known by in the field. It was only known to the senior staff and obviously on this secured file."

"Well, that's more reassuring than you know. I had to say it, because no one else knew about it, not even Anton..." Damn! A name I should *not* have mentioned.

"Who?"

"An associate, someone who helped me."

"This associate seems to know too much, as far as I can see," she said, her eyes searching me like a CT scanner.

"Hmm...yes, he has an investigative mind."

"I would like to meet this, Anton."

"Yeah? That would be difficult. He's like - *toast*." She frowns.

"Dead?"

"Sort of." Her eyes narrow.

"Either he is or not. Stop being so cagey. If what you say is true, then we have a serious security breach." I give her a side glance.

"Maybe more than you know…"

"Oh, for God's sake, Maisie, this is not a game. We are on a knife edge with world security, and you are messing around with a cat and mouse approach with me."

"Look. I was freaked out when I found out about him. Anton knew things that not even senior security people knew. It was like he had access to every security service's secrets."

Ayanna is lapping up my admissions I have held onto for months. I think her brain is going to explode with all this intel. She shakes her head.

"I *knew* you were key in all this. Thank you, Maisie; you have justified my faith in you. Catherine will have no reason now to eject you."

"You mean she was going to kick me out?"

"She was very sceptical about your involvement at all. You see, she had close connections with your parents, before all these accusations came up. I think she became suspicious of their activities. When their deaths were reported, she even doubted they were dead. She thought it was a set up." I wince and want to kick an invisible apricot effigy.

"She can go to hell. I refuse to accept my parents were into espionage. I was told that 'Trojan' was to prevent rogue nations turning into dangerous enemies of the UK. Weren't my parents' negotiating deals with governments to bring them under NATO's cloak?" She gave me another glare.

"You are revealing stuff that my seniors would kill for," she says with a wry smile.

"Well, there has been enough death for today, thanks. That woman: did you get a fix on her identity?" She shakes her head.

"Not yet. It would appear that these people who you come across don't have any ID; not on any of our data, at least. Maybe, if this Anton can be contacted, he could enlighten us." She raises her eyebrows looking hopeful.

"I'm not sure how to contact him anymore, to be honest. His last words to me were that he had to disappear…" If rebooting himself, was like disappearing.

"Arr…gone into hiding. I see." I'm glad you do.

"Hopefully, he will contact you before it's too late to stop any catastrophe." I nod. I am missing his incessant chatter these days.

"Ok. Now we have some intel which will enable us to be more prepared. To be on the safe side, we must keep this information from the rest of the team. If what the woman said is true, we must be extra vigilant." I agree.

At least I feel I can trust Ayanna. She is showing a similar approach to myself; not trusting anyone. Secrets are powerful tools, giving you the advantage over your enemies, even if it rips at the very heart of you, making you feel alone and isolated. At least, I feel I have an ally in Ayanna.

I hope.

10 - WARM MEMORIES, COLD CLOTHES

The day for our excursion to colder climates has arrived and Jaz is looking paler than normal. Her rucksack is packed with most of her joss sticks and other items that she insists will ground her in testing times.

"This trip is freaking me out, Maisie. I do hope it doesn't involve dangling over precipices and being submerged in freezing cold water." She shivers and pulls her floaty dress ever tighter.

"Probably," I say, with mischief. "I am sure that whatever is thrown at us, we will conquer it." Unfortunately, my mind runs wild at the mention of water, as I am averse to being *under* water and heights are not a favourite either.

"You promised to watch out for me." Her dreamy eyes demand my affirmation.

"Yes, of course. These trials are designed to pull us together as a team, not that Alex is a team player. He's out for himself and that is concerning. Jules, I don't have a clue about. Maybe he is the one that will lock us together; you know, bring Alex into line." She nods, without any enthusiasm.

Alex pokes his head around the door, followed by Jules. He flings his rucksack with no regard to what else is carefully placed there. It has little finesse, clothes stuffed in at all angles. Jules, however, has packed immaculately, with no wasted space. He carefully places it down next to mine. I smile at my own packing and like to think I am ordered too, ensuring I can find anything in a hurry, especially underwear in case of an accident. Alex wouldn't find a bath in his, even if it had a signpost.

"So, are we ready? It's going to be fun sleeping out in the wilds and testing our strength," says Alex smiling with that same arrogance that indicates that he wants to find any weakness in us to exploit.

"Yeah, I think it will be a test for all of us. How much wild living have *you* done?" I ask.

"Enough. College took us out into the forests, where we learnt bushcraft and survival techniques," he replies, a smug expression resting on his face.

"Hmm…I think it will be different from that. This is professional stuff. None of your elite snobbish crap." He gives me a glare. Jules releases a cough, a prelude to him stating something of value.

"We must assume that this will push us beyond our comfort zones. So, in the best interests of all, we need to pull together, if we are to survive." We are drawn to his face and wisdom. "Ayanna is relying on us to succeed with this mission; I believe we can't mess it up," he continued.

You have such a sensible head, Jules. I do feel a kindred spirit. I feel compelled to add my morsel of insight.

"Remember; to come through this, we need to be ready to face anything thrown at us. What I've learned over the years is that you must adapt to every situation; or you're *dead*."

"Yeah, of course you have Maiz. *'The all-overcoming assassin'*. Tell me; how many people have you killed then?" Alex is fishing and I'm not biting.

"Enough. It's not the number that counts - it's the way you do it." Jaz frowns.

"Are you really that calculating about it?" she asks.

"Yep." I give Alex a stare, trying to gauge how much I can freak him out. No sign of it today.

"Hilarious! I bet she hasn't done anyone in. All a mirage to impress or misdirect us," Alex chortles.

"Just be careful you don't find out," I reply.

Jules interjects. "We are about to leave, so let's pick up our packs and get to the coach." He strides away and takes the lead.

We wander off to the pick-up point, behind the MI6 building. Ayanna is standing ready to tick us off the list like we are going on a school trip.

"Hi team. I hope you are prepared for this. Don't be concerned over the tests. Work together for success. I will be coming with you to assess your progress and intervene if anything is pushing you too far. As much as I want you to complete, I would rather you be alive than dead." I nod, pleased that she is being considerate, at least to Jaz.

The journey takes, what feels like, a day and a half. I have slept for most of it, taking time out to eat and go to the loo. I am pleased that they supplied coke, (the drink), as I would be gasping for a sugar rush. Jaz has been sitting in a semi trance like state, humming to herself. I can't help but prod her occasionally, to stop this noise which is boring into my brain. I see from her frowning that she doesn't appreciate this interruption of her meditation.

"Stop disturbing me, Maisie. This is the only way I can get through this. To blend mind and body and soul in a state of calm. You know how out of control I can get." Yeah, the pillow fight still got me spitting feathers.

Staring through the window, I transport myself to a different place like Jaz, remembering the trips Olga and I did, to escape the rigours of the assassin lifestyle. We would often go to Santorini or other less well-known destinations, especially in Africa. Malawi was a favourite as no one would know us there and it is such a gentle country to travel around. We would find a lodge beside the lake in remote areas where there were few tourists and lots of sun. The shore of Lake Malawi or Nyasa is stunning. Often, I would wake up listening to the subtle lapping of freshwater on gritty sand, followed by local doves cooing. The lake would shimmer with a turquoise blue, gentle waves titling catamarans and the dugout canoes locals used for fishing. The villagers were always friendly, some offering their hand made bracelets and carved animals, in the hope we would buy.

Olga would lie in the sun, with her oversized shades and all-in-one swimsuit, ensuring that all who passed would give her a second look. If any of the touters became too insistent, she would shoo them away, along with the ever-present flies. I learned a few words to say thank you and hello, but beyond that, I smiled and feigned sleep so no one would bother me.

The heat of the day was overpowering. It was well over 30C in the summer months, so we had no reason to come away without a decent tan. I preferred the lodges with their own swimming pools as I could chill gazing out at the tranquil lake. Floating, with a freezing coke in one hand and my current playlist plugged into my head, it was always the best distraction from our somewhat chaotic life.

A trip out on the lake was fun. I once endeavoured to snorkel and swim amongst the host of multi coloured fish which the lake is renowned for. Averse to being underwater for long, I couldn't resist diving in and then regretting it, surfacing, and spluttering. Olga would be acting like a solar panel on the deck and gave little concern to my choking. I occasionally thought she had a sadistic side to her beyond work, even with her own adopted daughter.

This memory is a delightful way to ignore Jaz and her repetitive acoustic assault on my senses. However, Alex's snoring has now joined the chorus, so I'm forced to sink further into my memories.

I recall when we sailed on a catamaran to one of the uninhabited islands that scatter the lake. It was a breezy day, the captain ensuring we skimmed over the waves with the ease of an ice skater. The sun was baking us into a crisp pastry, so I smothered myself with suncream. I do tan beautifully, but the process can be a painful one if unprepared.

I was sprawled out on the net that overhung the bow gazing down at the fish scattering around the hull. Swallows dived around us, like ariel dolphins, with such accuracy, missing the sail wires and rigging. Some perched on a suitable taut rope and chirped away as if chatting to me about the latest trend in fishing. I find myself smiling, as these times were amongst my favourites. Olga may have killed my parents, but I now appreciate that she was, in some twisted way, trying to repay her debt to me.

Anchored off the shore of the island, the captain insisted we watch as he summoned a fish eagle from the dense treeline. He waved a fish in a tantalising manner and whistled. Along with a few chosen words and sounds, it encouraged the raptor to dive towards us. I expected it to grasp the man by his arm and drag him away to its secret lair to be torn apart and fed to its furry young. Instead, he threw the smelly carcass into the lake and the eagle scooped it up with ease.

He insisted that I take a swim around the boat and checked out the 'live' fish surrounding the hull. So, carefully I slipped into the lukewarm water, and lowered my head beneath the surface, taking a large breath to ensure I didn't drown.

A multi coloured aquatic world flashed before my eyes, bulging in the goggles I misplaced on my head. For a second or two, I watched a dazzling display of fish called cichlids swimming with ease, almost mocking my ridiculous efforts at floating. And because of my goggles-mishap, the water flooded my view and then sent me into a desperate thrashing. Once again, panic, instead of controlled behaviour, overtook my logic.

The next reaction I had, could also be described as illogical. My mental 'National Geographic' video was abruptly interrupted by water splashing my face and subsequently, down my jacket and trousers. The shock of water hitting me made the memory almost real, but it was not from a warm lake, but from a stone-cold water bottle.

A man, who had joined us on the trip, with no introduction, stood over me with a smirk. I looked at Jaz who had suffered the same interruption, her face flush with annoyance. I suspected she was ready to take him down if she transitioned into her evil zombie mode.

"What the f…?" I couldn't respond any less appreciative. I hear Alex and Jules using foul language too.

"What is *that* all about?" I ask again, staring at this idiot.

His grin didn't diminish, but as an answer, he again emptied the said water all over my head. The sugar rush or lack of anger management propelled me to throw a punch into his face. It would have floored him, except he moved enough to allow my fist to overshoot and open me up to a counter block with his open hand, contacting my shoulder with the opposite force I had used. *Damn, that hurt.*

The bus screeched to a halt and Ayanna, who seemingly wasn't interested in our predicament, told us to get off. We dragged our dripping bodies down the bus and out into a windy, cold night. My clothes had soaked in so much water, every movement was awkward and uncomfortable. Lining up alongside the coach, we looked like a line of badly rinsed washing, dripping, and seething.

"Welcome to your survival training," the water dispenser spouted. "We will be getting on a ferry taking us to our home for the next few days. Be prepared for the unexpected. It will hone your skills and teamwork."

Yeah, looking forward to honing your arse, pal.

11 - CROSSING INTO HELL

The said ferry appeared to be a small fishing boat that forced our cold bodies to unwillingly squeeze together, making for many weird noises, as water squelched between wet jackets and shoes. The night was black and foreboding with a biting wind only adding to my frazzled nerves. The waves were swaying the hull with random movements, making it difficult to predict where the next hit would strike. Our head torches shone on ghostly faces or into spray, brightly shining like jewels chaotically cascading over freezing bodies.

The man, who was to be our trainer, stood like a Viking captain at the front and appeared to roll effortlessly with every wave. Man, I wish I could push him overboard and my mind would find peace.

Jaz was huddled next to me, her teeth rattling to the point of escaping her mouth. The lads were in a near embrace, which distracted me for a moment, seeing how comical it looked. Ayanna was suitably ensconced in a wet and dry suit. She looked ready for an expedition to the Arctic. Nice, when you know what to expect.

"Wwwhhaaat dooo yoooo thhnik weee arrrr doing herrrreee?" Jaz said through locked jaws.

"Perhaps ssssuffering some retribution for past ssssins?" I replied as best I could. I wasn't sure Jaz smiled or not, the head torch glare forcing her eyes shut.

I couldn't judge how long this journey took, but as we neared the island, a wave hit us with venom and tossed us across the boat. Our bags flew up into the black air in unison, saved only by the strap that Ayanna had sensibly tied to them. Rescuing my stomach, I dragged back my rucksack along with Jaz's and we stood to our feet, only to be toppled again. A rope thrown to an invisible hand on shore, reassured me that we had arrived and not lost at sea; a statistic adding to the drowned mariners of old.

As the rope pulled tight and then slackened, the 'waterboy' leapt across the enraged void and disappeared into the abyss. I was hoping he might have misjudged and slipped into the inky black, but his smug face shone in my head torch light, beckoning us to make the same death-defying leap. I summoned all my energy and jumped, with my foot slipping off the rim of the boat. It forced my heart rate to accelerate as if I was being shot at. My feet landed on slimy rocks, creating a fear of falling backwards. The guy, who I wished ill health, shot out a hand and grabbed mine and yanked me back.

"Thanks," I said.

"Last time," he said with a gruff voice. I wasn't sure if that meant for the whole trip or for anyone else. "Stay there and help the others." Ok, I can do that.

"Mmmaisie." Jaz extended her arm with a limp hand. I grabbed it as the boat lurched to shore.

"Jump!" I shouted. She did, but with the strength of a lettuce leaf. It was only my upper body strength that

held both her and me from falling. She crumpled into my arms reminiscent of two lovers desperate to be with each other after a long separation.

"Thhhhanks," she spluttered.

"No worries. Get over there with Ayanna and that bloke. I've got to help the others."

Jules was positioning himself to do a standing leap, only Olympians would be capable of. His preparation was immaculate as usual and needed little assistance from me. Alex was the last one being tossed from side to side by the unrelenting waves. His head torch light flicked all over like a frenzied search light. His bulk didn't really help his attempt and the force he used to push across heaved the boat further away from the shore. His arms flailed and as best I could, I reached out to catch his faltering arm.

"Maisie!! Grab my hand, you idiot," he shouted.

A little unappreciative I thought, seeing I was nearly sucked into a wave urging me to be devoured. My fingers managed to grip the material of his waterproof. The resulting ripping noise barely registered above the noise of the raging sea as I yanked with all my might. Alex crumpled onto a rock at my feet, shouting some expletives.

"Well done, Alex; you nearly pulled me in. Good job I'm stronger than you think."

If his head torch illuminated my face, he would have seen a smug grin, but I'm glad he didn't as his lack of appreciation was apparent with his angry push against my hip.

"I could have been swept away then!"

"Yes; it would have been a shame, but there you go; not everything works out as I would like," I reply.

"You are a little f…!"

"Thanks! You deserve to have something push you to the edge." Ayanna grabs my arm. For what reason I'm not sure, but it makes me swing round, as I see a dark shadow fly above my head.

"*Alex! Cool it. You are lucky that Maisie grabbed you,*" she yells. "Come on, we need to get to our shelters." She waves to us, as the rain penetrates every crevice along my body.

The trudge up the cliff side was as treacherous as the leap of death from the boat. The rough path is slippery and crumbling, as we stagger in single file, the flickering torch light guiding our footsteps. Jaz is faltering as her feet keep sliding. I think she is picking the worst route possible. It was a good job I was following, forever putting out my hand to steadier her.

"Oh god, oh god," she keeps whispering.

"Jaz; you are ok, just concentrate and breathe."

"Okkkkay," her shivering voice echoes back.

"A little further and we will be over the ridge," Ayanna yells back to us from the darkness.

"See," I say. "Not long and we can rest."

"Oh god...Oh god," Jaz continues. Jules and Alex are now racing up alongside us, as if this climb was an easy pathway.

"Come on girls; no need for farting about," Alex spits. Jules climbs with the skill of a mountain goat, and I see his face briefly enough to catch his look of disdain at Alex's comment.

Scrambling a few more metres, we collapse with our bags twice the weight they were. In the distance a dim light gives me some hope of a warm dry place, where I can disrobe and get into some dry clothes. Ayanna gives us a few moments to catch our breath, and then motions to get moving again. At least now the ground is horizontal and not perilously vertical. Even so, Jaz seems to stumble over every miniscule stone.

"Pick your feet up Jaz; no one else will do it for you," I say with as much force as I dare. I don't want her to give up before we have started. At least she responds and now looks like her legs are overstepping reminiscent of a cat on its tiptoes.

The hope that the light gave me, is now replaced with increasing despair, as it doesn't bring the expectation of a warm, dry shelter. It is a lamp swinging freely on a pole, with no Premier Inn room attached.

"Where is our shelter, Ayanna?" I ask.

"Over there," she points.

I gaze into the darkness and make out the shadows of some ghoul flapping around. My heart sinks into wet sodden boots, as I realise that camping is the vehicle for our rest and not a warm cosy bed, with duvet and fluffy socks. *Stop it, Maisie! You're going delirious.*

My attention is drawn to Jaz who, despite my own disappointment, is displaying signs of greater desperation. Her face is ashen, even without the head torch lights, and appears to be heaving. Alex brushes past her and marches quickly to find which is the best tent, I guess. Jules follows, stimulating me into action.

I stride to the nearest tent and assess its viability to stop the weather from hitting us hard for the rest of the night. I catch hold of the door and kneel checking to see if the interior is dry. Yes! It seems to be ok. I beckon Jaz over. She stumbles across, leaving her rucksack at the mercy of the incessant rain. Without any hesitation, she dives into the inner and lies flat, leaking water across the once dry floor.

"Jaz, you *waz!* It was dry until you crashed the place."

"Sorry, I needed to get out of that awful weather," she gasps.

"Yeah sure. Come on, we need to get out of these wet clothes and get something warm on, or we will both be corpses in the morning." She responds quicker than I expect, shelling her wet stuff at the speed of Supergirl.

I drag her rucksack into the doorway and find the whizz of the zip very satisfying, finally pushing the dark and wet away from us.

I whisk my outer layers off down to my knickers, quickly replacing every item with its warm dry counterpart. Jaz and I sit and stare at each other. Then we start to giggle and laugh. It's strange how you get this hysterical when your mind is numb, and the circumstances are dire. It must be a release mechanism. I admit that when I was working with Olga, I occasionally burst into fits of giggling when I should have been on point, ready to help with a dispatch.

"This is extreme," I finally say. "I didn't expect our trip to be so crazy. Are you feeling better?" Jaz gives me a coy look.

"Yeah. I never dreamed of doing anything like this, though. I thought I would be in an office, sitting at a warm computer table, sipping Oolong tea." I grin. That option seems almost desirable. I hear a voice telling us that we need to sleep and be prepared for an early morning start.

"Well… we better get some kip," I say to a calmer-faced Jaz. She wiggles into her sleeping bag, her nose the only evidence of her in there.

"How are we supposed to sleep in this hurricane?" she asks, quite rightly. I shiver as I sink into mine, scrunching up the pull tie. I feel like an Egyptian mummy ready to be entombed.

"I've got a playlist which distracts me, so I would suggest you find something too." I didn't think about the implications of what I said, as Jaz now starts with a low ruttling throaty sound. Her Buddhist inclinations are what carries her through times like this, I guess. Good job I can turn up my own music and soon her vibrations are as distant as the rain whipping against the outer tent. Then, my mind wanders to what the woman said to me:

"An associate has told me to advise you to watch out for those around you - those who have led you to believe to be trustworthy - trust no one!"

I roll over to where I see the faint outline of Jaz and her nose pointing to the North Star. Can I trust her? She has the perfect opportunity to despatch me in my sleep. This would be the place. But she is so dependent on me, I can't see that it could be her.

The other two. Alex seems to be the main one who doesn't give a shit about me. The times we have confronted have given me more reason to mistrust his motives. Yet, he hasn't made any compelling moves towards me other than motivated by his arrogance. Then there's Jules. I know so little about him. He keeps all the cards close to his chest like a poker player.

Oh, I don't know. This is not helping me sleep. The wind has seemingly dropped from the howling gale to the occasional blast. I feel my shoulders relax, as I think about warmer climates and happier times. I think of Freddie in Paris and wonder what he is doing now. Our last time together could not be more extreme, and he is probably content without me being around, causing him anxiety and pain. Funny thing is, as I recall his face (before it was messed up by Harmony Chase), I feel a strong desire to hold him again. Like in a virtual game, I feel his hands around my hips, drawing me closer. If I allow myself, the desire for his body next to mine sends a tingle down my belly.

Unfortunately, this exquisite moment is shattered by Jaz. She rolled towards me, her arms breaking out from her sleeping bag like a bug exploding free from a chrysalis, reaching out to hug me.

What the hell are you doing?

I hear her murmuring something. I doubt she is awake. The need for comfort must have propelled her onto me. I allow this to continue, as my own need to be close to someone, at least for warmth, compels me to snuggle up to her as well. Oh well, let's see where we end up tomorrow. Maybe the trials will separate the weasels from the rats, and hopefully I will come out holding a scalp.

12 - CLOSE TO THE EDGE

It *was* an early start to the day. I know this as I awake with Jaz wrapped around me like a baby monkey and the tent enveloped in an orange glow. The sun is barely rising, the rain and wind having ceased. The night cold has caused condensation to hang like stalactites dangling from the roof. They are dislodged by the slightest shimmer of the tent lining, somehow finding the sliver of facial skin I've allowed to be in the open. The dripping feels like torture, whilst washing away my night-time haze.

I dare to extract my arms and push Jaz over to her side. I snigger at her disgruntled noises. Sitting up I shake my hair and tie it in a loose ponytail. My rucksack is still damp, it's cold clamminess clawing at me. I'm hoping that I can find some warmer, dryer clothes in the dry bag hidden inside. Jaz prises open an eye and peers at me. I don't think she has registered where she is.

"Are you ok? Sleep?" I ask.

"I don't know. Why is it so cold? I didn't leave a window open, did I?"

"We are in a tent, Jaz, not in our room, you idiot." A look of horror stretches across her face. She brings her fingers up to the brim and looks around wildly.

"Oh no…I thought it was all a dream." Yeah, I know what you mean.

"Welcome to MI6 training. It will probably be more of a nightmare than a dream; don't worry, it'll all be over soon." I can't help but grin at her. Her response is predictable. She clamps her wild eyes shut and the humming resumes.

"I think we need to get into our day gear and find a wash place and a loo." She nods reluctantly, as I grope around for the clothes I need for surviving the day's training.

Finally encouraging her out of her cocoon, Jaz and I unzip the tent and get our first view of our temporary home. Stretching out before us, is a landscape of green bracken and grey rocks. Our tent is surrounded by the other ones in a semicircle, backed by a small wooden cabin. I guess this is where Ayanna has spent the night. Counting the tents, it looks like the man who is our trainer has slept in a tent too. Give him his due, he seems to be as hard ass as anyone. Perhaps, he is making sure he doesn't get soft in his old age.

"Morning," a voice softly calls. It's Jules. I bet he's been up since the crack of dawn and ran a marathon.

"Hey," I reply. "Where is Alex?" As if I care.

"He's still asleep. I don't think his college bushcraft prepared him enough for a wet, cold night's camping," he says with a grin. I laugh and then cough. My throat is so coarse this morning. Spitting out the phlegm strangling my airways, I drag Jaz's butt out into the morning light.

“Come on. Let’s get exploring, before the adults wake up.” Jaz gives me a look of disbelief.

“Really? I’m hardly awake and you want me to wander around like we are at Disney world?” She gives a huge yawn and shivers. I nod enthusiastically. It’s not every day I’m on a Scottish island.

Jules, Jaz, and I walk up to a high point and gaze at the beauty of isolation. The cliffs are filled with squawking seabirds, some dive bombing us. This would have really freaked out Olga, as her dislike of any bird sent her into a meltdown. Why my thoughts descend to her, I don’t know. Perhaps my life with her is so intrinsically linked, I can’t break free even if I wanted to.

I peer over the edge of a cliff and feel my head swim. I have never really got on with heights; same as with going under water. My curiosity always gets the better of me though, and the clown-like puffins are a delight to watch. The crashing waves below compliment the bird chatter, the white froth foaming against the unforgiving rocks. Jaz tries to peer over the edge too. By the way she creeps, I know she is even *more* unhappy about this drop than I am.

“Careful Jaz; I don't want to scrape your body off those rocks,” I say, my hands tingling.

She falls to her knees and crawls the remaining couple of metres. Jules stands perched on a rock outcrop as if he was born to be a watchman of old, seeking enemy ships arriving from distant shores.

"Wow! Those birds know how to fly," Jaz states. I wonder where she has lived all these years.

"Yes… amazing, isn't it?" I grin at Jules, who rolls his eyes.

Distracted by Jaz's surprising obsession with all things avian, I hear movement behind me. Swiftly turning, I instinctively crouch. A figure is lurching towards me, and I roll to one side. This would have been fine if I was on a level floor with walls or some sort of boundary. Except, we are in the open on a precarious rock cliff edge. You can imagine my dread when I stumble and my face is peering at a grey and white drop of several hundred feet, the waves beckoning me to join them.

My hands scramble at loose slippery rocks, my feet and legs feeling useless, except for adding weight to my potential fall. My clothing rips and wraps around a sharp protruding rock and shudders me to a halt. I shake my head and try to refocus. I'm lying on my side, my hands gripping onto rocks hoping this stops me from falling. Looking around quickly to work out how bad this position is, I hear shouting above me.

"Hang on Maisie! We will get someone to haul you up." *What do you think I'm doing?*

"Reach up with your right hand…I can grab you," Jules shouts. I turn my head to look up at him. He has perched himself on an outcrop above me, his hand dangling down. In the background I hear Jaz screeching.

"It's ok…I can reach you here," Jules continues. I move my hand to let go and my heart flutters as the clothing rips again as the weight shifts. My fingers reach his and he edges closer. We interlock and I feel sweet relief.

"Now, move slowly and push up with your other hand." I do it as obediently as I can, for me. As he pulls, my body shifts into an upright position. At last, my feet are useful again and wedging them into a solid cleft, chases away the fear that was strangling my thinking. Now I can push more, and Jules grabs my arm, propelling me up. I blow my cheeks out as the last effort launches me onto stable ground and I roll onto my back breathing heavily. I look up Jules' nose and thank him.

"Mate…I thought that was me over and out. Thanks for being there." He smiles and nods. Jaz runs over and crashes down on me.

"Oh, I thought you were dead meat then." Thanks Jaz; nice analogy. Now if you could get off me. We are not lovers.

"What happened then?" I hear Ayanna's concerned voice carrying across the rocks. I get up and see the reason why I reacted so crazily. The man, who is still nameless, stands with hands on hips staring at me. I regain my composure and stare back at him, a ripple of a sneer creeping across my face.

"This idiot crept up on me and nearly made me fall off the cliff; that's what happened," I say with annoyance.

He adds a snarl to his stare. Ayanna turns to the man. Her stare can be disabling at times, and this was a perfect example. She motions to him to follow, and he breaks eye contact. The other two surround me and we fall into a spontaneous bearhug. Passing the two retreating trainers, Alex wanders over, looking bleary eyed, still wrapped up in his sleeping bag.

"Did I miss something?" We all laugh at his ridiculous question and dishevelled look.

"Yeah, something that would have pleased you, actually," I say.

We filled him in on my near-death fall. Alex shook his head, confirming that he would have been quite happy for me to crash my head against the cliff. His smirk makes me tense, wanting to smash *his* head with a suitable rock.

Ayanna walks with purpose towards our gathering. She nods to me to follow. We wander out of earshot of the camp. She turns to me, her face pensive.

"I'm really sorry you got into that situation, Maisie. There was no need to get you on edge like that." I thought that was a pun worth grinning at. "I have reprimanded him for it. We are here to train you, not kill you!" *I'm glad you confirmed that, Ayanna.*

"So, what *was* he trying to do?"

"He was out for a morning jog, apparently, and saw you guys standing too close to the cliff edge. He said he wanted to drag you away. It's loose shale there and people have fallen before." I skew my lips.

"That's an improbable reason seeing we were nowhere near the edge, as Jaz and I are unhappy about sheer drops. Jules was the courageous one. But I guess we will have to put it down to experience." She looks at me with those dark searching eyes.

"I know… we have to be aware of what the woman told us." I nod, kicking some loose stones around.

"In your opinion; do you think this is worth it? All this outdoor crap. Anything could happen out here, and no one would know or care. Not exactly a safe environment, is it?"

"Yes, but if it is one of the team, we would expose them clearly out here…"

"... and die in the process," I conclude. She purses her lips, still as shiny red as usual.

"Yes, point taken. Come on, let's get breakfast and then some training." She wanders off to her 'Holiday Inn' and we get on with making our own food off a gas stove and outdoor kitchen area. Disappointing; I was looking forward to being Bear Grylls; eating raw fish and bird eggs.

13 - TRIAL BY WIRE

Full of porridge and renewed pride, we make our way to a disused quarry. The man, who I have very little faith in, directs us to someone who is donned in climbing gear, leaving little to the imagination as to what the next task involves. Jaz pulls a crazed face and stands rigid while the man kits her out with harness, ropes, safety hat, carabiners and all the equipment we apparently need. We eventually stand in a line waiting for our task details, resembling a school outing to the local climbing club.

"OK. Now you are to traverse the quarry edge over here," the man instructs and points. "You will have a range of ways to cross over to the other side, but as you work together, it will be safer and easier. The ropes and carabiners are to be used in unison with each other; passing them to one another as you edge along the wire foot way."

I can't stop my mind tripping down the usual avenue of anxiety, as again, heights are being used against me. And what is more worrying, we have to trust each other to get through this task. *Stop it, Maisie! Steady, breath and bring calm.* Jules and Alex are going along first. Jaz has to be extracted from the ground where she is frozen.

"Come on Jaz. We can do this," I say. Her eyes give away only fear. "Now let's watch the guy and copy what he's doing."

We shuffle along to the quarry edge and gaze at the man and his careful walk out onto a wire attached to the edge of the cliff. At shoulder height another wire follows the route, one which we have to attach to, making our harnesses and our lives secure. He shuffles along on this taut wire and passes his carabiner over the fixings into the rock. Showing us how to pass ours on to the next person safely, he carries on encouraging us to follow. The lads start their journey, Alex acting as if he needs no tuition and strides ahead, with Jules noting the man's every move and reacting like a clone. They are making good progress, which encourages me to get going.

I step out first as I think Jaz will dither and never complete it. That first step out is the worst bit. Steadying the bouncing wire and my heart rate is a trial in itself. Jaz has a skittish approach, threatening to send us both off.

"Come on Jaz. Just imagine we are on a rope about a metre off the ground and concentrate…*please*." She nervously reaches out and grabs the rock as if she's making love to it.

Slowly we get our footing and confidence. The first passing of the carabiner makes me shudder as for a breath-taking moment nothing is attaching us to the rock face. But as we gather pace, we make good strides. Jaz now starts her chatter, evidence of her internal chaos.

"That dream of mine to be in Bali - you would come and visit, wouldn't you? I have so many things I want to do. Just the money, as always. Could find a quick way, I suppose. If this job doesn't do it..." I give her a quizzical look.

"Are you expecting to get a good return from working for MI6? I don't think it's that well paid." Thinking about it, I haven't received *any* income from it yet.

"Ayanna said you had resources that are from your parents or something. Is that true? They were wealthy, weren't they?" I frown again, wondering why she is talking like this.

"Hmm...yes they were, but a lot of my inheritance is tied up, except for expenses and stuff." We stagger around an outcrop, forcing us wider and making us more wary of unclipping and reattaching than earlier. She grabs my hand, which startles me. Her face has that mental look she had in the bedroom before she went crazy.

"Yeah...so it seems. What about letting us in on it? You know, giving us a handout?" I grimace. Why is she asking like that?

"I don't get where you are going with this Jaz. Of course, I would be happy to help, but not just yet. I'm not old enough." I quiz her eyes. I then look at her hand; she holds the unclipped carabiner. My heart skips a beat. The next thing that happens is just as startling.

I hear a crack and small stones rain down on our heads, followed by larger boulders, bouncing off the outcrop. We get showered by this gravel downpour and we instinctively hug the rock face. I grab her hand and force the carabiner onto the wire, securing us both. The hard hats get a pounding, as do our shoulders. Jaz shouts out, screaming like a banshee warrior. I am swearing and praying together. *What the hell is going on?*

Another crash louder than the first signals more rock fall. I stare at Jaz and scream out that we need to move quickly. That slow motion thing kicks in as usual. As if we are wading through thick blancmange, we force our legs along the wires as more of the avalanche cascades. I hear shouting from above, Jules and Alex, anxiety in their voices.

Getting further along, I think we are out of the danger zone. We both sigh in relief. I find myself staring at Jaz distracted over what she asked. Then before I can make any sense of it, a greater threat hits us. The rock outcrop that shielded us groans and collapses falling directly onto the wire bridge we are attached to. A pang of fear hits my stomach. All I can see is us being dragged down to the quarry floor with this wire violently ripping out from the rock face. *What do we do?*

Jules shouts out, telling us to get moving. My feet are frozen on this taut wire. Jaz's face is ashen and seems to have gone into a meditation haze. *Come on Maisie! Shift!*

Forcing a response from deep within, I pull the rope we are attached to and drag Jaz by her harness and almost skip along the wire now tense enough to support a herd of elephants. We have one more switch of carabiners and then up a wire ladder and then to safety.

As we get to the wire ladder, I shove Jaz's ass ahead of me, shouting to her to get moving. The lads are waving their arms around as if they can magically control the situation. I watch her get to the top rung and I start my ascent, my legs shaking.

The wire bridge only has two more secure fixings and then it'll be the wire ladder. I must increase my pace. *Get moving Maisie!* I look upwards and focus on the top. The other three are waving at me frantically. I can feel the quake of the other fixtures screeching out of their moorings making my feet quiver with the shock wave. The ladder below me is now being dragged into the beast below, my anxiety confirming that I will be too.

Jules slings down a rope, swinging beside me. *Do I carry on or grab this?* I don't think, I just do. Reminding me of the rope chase in the gym, I wrap it around my leg and push down on my ankle. The wire ladder whips past my head, nearly slashing my face as it writhes like a serpent down and away from me. I'm still thirty feet from the top and a pang of fear again freezes my brain. No crash mats here to stop me. Alex has now grabbed the rope along with Jules and they are pulling me upwards.

"Hang on, we are pulling you up," they shout in unison. I hear Ayanna joining them along with the trainer man acting as anchor. My grip is sweaty, slipping as I adjust.

"Oh God, please help!" I can't help but pray.

My leg has a biting pain as the rope burns my exposed skin, but it stops my brain-freeze, keeping me focused. Finally, they drag me over the lip and onto sound ground and I collapse, breathing heavily, my eyes shut tight. Ayanna comes down to me and says something reassuring. I open my eyes again and prop myself up. Gathering my thoughts, I look around for the one who I think is responsible. Is he the one that started the avalanche?

"Where is that bastard? I want an explanation. Then I'll beat the shit out of him." I can't help my anger pouring out like a torrent. Ayanna looks sympathetic but shakes her head.

"He wasn't anywhere near what happened Maisie. He was back at the camp. And the other guy who was leading you, was up here waiting with me." I give her a hard stare.

"Well…that wasn't an accident. I heard a crack, like a shot." I stare at each one, trying to force an admission. The adrenaline kicks in and I leap to my feet, and storm off towards the camp, Jaz trailing me. I walked up to where I thought the avalanche started, being wary of any shifting rocks. I stare in horror at the amount of stone that has disappeared. A gaping wound sits on the quarry edge.

"This is where it started. Make use of yourself, Jaz. Look for anything that shouldn't be here." She nods and searches around, making sure she isn't too close to the edge.

The thing is, I'm doubting if there would be any evidence as it's all down there in the mouth of the quarry beast. We search for ages as the others wander up to us. I finally give in as it's futile trying to find anything in this mess.

Jaz links her arm through mine. She smiles in her coy way and apologises for her inappropriate money talk. Trouble is, I'm still wary of her.

"It's ok Jaz; I know you were frightened, and we do stupid things when we are scared. But … I am wondering why Ayanna was talking to you about my parents' wealth, though? How did that come about?" She again looks all coy.

"Actually…it wasn't her…I overheard you talking once about how you could spend at will. I was a touch jealous I suppose. It's never been easy for our family. Always struggling from one crisis to another. I have an alcoholic father and he regularly loses too much gambling. My mother found it increasingly difficult to make ends meet. I suppose that's why I went into my meditation to get away from it all." I look at her and feel some empathy especially with the way Olga was with her drinking.

"I understand that…it destroys so many people. I'm sorry Jaz. That's tough." She smiles and pulls herself closer, as if for comfort, but I can't help myself shun her, as this whole episode has made my mistrust rise to the surface with vengeance. *Who can I trust?*

We wander slowly back to camp, and I watch the shifty eyed man give me a furtive glance. He makes my skin crawl, as he tops the most-likely candidate for this so-called accident. I sit by the campfire as it burns with a welcome ferocity, mirroring my internal anger. Life is so complicated. Once, I was in a job with my adopted mother, Olga, where we knew what was expected of us and we dispatched with some sense of satisfaction. That is, until I discovered that it was a front for the agency, placing their own pawns in position. I still can't believe that I was involved in it all. Ayanna distracts me.

"Hey, everyone. I think we have enough drama for today. I suggest we head down to the beach and have some chill time." We grunt our approval and return to our tents to get our swimming kits. Jaz again tries to get friendly.

"Maisie - I'm sorry about what I said. And... thanks for saving my life. God, that was so close. We could have been mush on the quarry floor. You were amazing." I give a half smile.

"All about what I've been telling you - adapt and respond. In the field, we must - or we die." She grins back, as if it's her birthday.

"Yeah, that's what I'm learning about you - adapt and live!"

Damn right girl!

14 - WATERY EYES

I scramble down to a small cove, white and pristine. The waves are crashing on the beach dragging the sand back into the sea. The sound of gulls fills the air, as noisy as the London morning traffic, but more soothing. Placing my towel near a large half buried rock, I sit staring out to the horizon.

That rock fall was bloody scary. I have felt death close in on me before, but that was somehow malicious; a desperate attempt to get rid of me. Someone was trying to make it look like a freakin' accident. Laughter and joking echoes behind me as I hear the rest of the team clambering down.

Jules walks upright and stealth-like, which compliments all he does. His dark skin is smooth and muscular, without the appearance of being gym obsessed. His dark hair is smoothed back by his right hand, revealing something I've not noticed before. Along his side there is a tattoo, scrawled in a foreign language. He glances back and quickly moves his arm down. He smiles and throws the ball he brought. I catch it.

"What's that you've got there, Jules? A lovers note?" He grins and shakes his head.

"No…just a warning and reminder." That sounds intriguing.

"Oh, ok. Who to? You or others?"

"Anyone who gets too close." I grimace.

"That's unfriendly. I thought you were a decent sort of bloke. A bit restrained, but at least not an asshole like someone I could mention." Alex jumps onto the beach as if on cue.

"What? Are you guys talking about me again?" How could he be vainer, even though we were?

"Nothing asshole…not for your ears anyway." He kicks sand my way and misses.

"You are a little shit; are we going for a swim? I would love to see you drown." My eyes shrink to slits, my heart pumping loudly in my ears. Jules waves his magic hand.

"Cool it, Alex. No one wants anyone to drown. Have you not understood the meaning behind team yet?" Alex's bottom lip curls. Was he thinking of having a go at Jules? That would be interesting. Instead, he makes for the surf and dives in.

Jaz has finally arrived. Her hair is chaotically tied with bands of patterned material and a matching delicate wrap-around. I think she would look good on the French Riviera, alongside Lily Collins, drinking cocktails and smoking long thin cigarettes. Her towel is unfurled beside me, flapping in the unruly breeze, which kicks up from nowhere. I throw a rock on it.

"Thanks Maisie. This is more like it," she says, smiling for the first time since we have been here. "The sound of breaking waves and sea air…so invigorating. I feel my sense of harmony returning." I can't help but bite my lip at the sound of that name, even if it is out of context.

"Not the word I would have used, but I know what you mean." She breathes in deeply, descending into a cross-legged position, placing her pale fingers on her knees. I give a chuckle and return to looking out to the horizon.

A small boat is bobbing around in the waves about two hundred metres away. Alex is about halfway out towards it, arms thrashing around as if he's punching the white crescents out of the way. He is obviously an accomplished swimmer, more than I can say about myself. If I could only overcome my fear, I would actually enjoy being in the water. However, amongst this crew, I'm not about to achieve that today. Time to relax and shake off the threat of someone trying to kill me. Jaz reaches into her bag and pulls out a book.

"Do you read much Maisie?" she asks.

"Sometimes; depends on my mood. I like sci-fi, gadget manuals, some history stuff; whatever takes my fancy at the time. You?"

"Oh yes…I love horror, anything that sends a shiver down my back." I shake my head.

"You're an enigma, Jaz. I wouldn't have expected you to like that genre. Maybe Jane Austin or something like that." She shakes her head vigorously.

"No, no. Too feminine. I like a bit of blood and gore." I can't help but chuckle again.

"'Nightmare on Elm Street' or 'Scream' would be my film choice. Have you seen them? Couldn't sleep for days after bingeing on those."

"I'm not surprised. To be honest I've seen far worse than that over the years, so I suppose that seems daft to me." Jaz frowns.

"What? You have seen more gore than wild axe men chopping legs and heads off?"

"Yep…possibly watched my mum do worse things." Jaz appears to shudder.

"Oh, that is scary. Perhaps you could share some time."

"Maybe, maybe not. You need your sleep." She returns to her book, 'Death by Snu Snu'. I thought that was a sex thing on a cartoon show I once watched.

The sun has drifted around to the cove, its full intensity bearing down on us. I rub on sunscreen and lie on my back. Placing shades on my head, it sparks off old memories from where I had bought them on my last trip to Florence, Italy.

***

Olga and I had finished dispatching an Italian banker who had swindled thousands of retirees out of their pension funds, so some downtime was needed. He was Lorenzo Bianchi, not to be confused with a bishop of the same name.

His role in embezzling millions of euros was unbelievable. For years he had syphoned money invested into clandestine accounts all over the world. He was discovered by a clever investigative journalist, Henri Soldare, who was about to expose him, when he was killed in another 'freak' accident.

Our job was to dispatch Lorenzo but redirect the money back into accounts which were destined for those that had lost out. However, that heroic plan probably never existed, now I understand more about the agency's motives. They probably put another one of their own in place to salvage the laundered finance and spend it themselves.

The dispatch went well, for Olga. She had charmed him into her arms at a dinner function in the centre of Florence, around the Duomo Cathedral and lured him up to Giotto's Bell Tower. She was sharing the delights of the fading sunset from the top. Then the truth was violently revealed. She had a well concealed knife on her leg covered by a chic silk number and delivered the blow swiftly to his neck. Of course, I had to be on hand as the blood splatter was everywhere; all over Olga and the flooring.

Being so high up, I was reeling when we had our unorthodox escape via a zip wire across to the Baptistry opposite. My head swam with vertigo as I stepped out on the ledge, Olga smiling at me as if it were a fun ride at an amusement park. The partying crowds did well not to see us whipping across the sky above their heads; I did well, not to puke up over them.

On reaching the top of the building a small explosive released the wire, allowing us to re-wind it, disposing of our escape route. We had to climb down with some new tech which allowed us to grab onto the marble exterior and descend like those sticky blob things kids get at parties.

We joined the crowds again and continued enjoying the evening until we heard the screams from the tower as some guests had stumbled across his cold, blood splattered body. Time to exit. We decided to spend a pleasant week in the nearby city of Lucca, eating pasta and pizza, and cycling along the tops of the city walls.

***

I must have dozed off as I felt the shadow of someone hovering over me. Lifting my arm, I see that it's Alex, dripping salty water.

"Are you coming for a swim or what? It's cold but I'm sure it'll freeze when it meets your icy personality."

"I'm impressed Alex; you know how to use an analogy. Yeah, in a minute." I look across to where I thought Jaz was. "Where's she gone?"

"No idea. Jules and I have been here all the time; didn't even notice she wasn't."

"Gone for piss probably. Ok I'll come now."

I get up and dust myself down from sand-filled cracks and chase the lads out into the water.

We threw the ball backwards and forwards, me using it like a floatation device, as I kept drifting out further than I meant to. It's great fun though, and I feel like we are at last bonding. The ball skids along the water's surface and I try to outwit Alex in particular, aiming for his head. His arms seem to stretch everywhere, and it becomes a matter of distraction and timing. Jules dives and resurfaces as if he's imitating a dolphin, avoiding all my assaults. I get bashed too many times and regularly curse them. I then notice Jaz wandering on the sand, looking a bit dazed.

"You ok, Jaz?" I shout and swallow salty water. She waves a dismissive hand and sits. Hmm… a bit weird for her. I swim back to shore whilst getting a head strike finally on Alex, much to his disgust.

"Shit, that was cold. Are you ok Jaz? You look a bit pale," I ask as I wrap my warm towel around. How she could look any paler, I don't really know.

"Yeah… I'm fine." Tears start to stream down her face.

"Hey what's wrong?" I press alongside and give her a hug. She snivels.

"My mum…she's died…and I wasn't there to protect her." Her shoulders begin to bounce as her tears stream.

"Oh my god; I am so sorry. Had she been ill?"

"No…she was in a car accident…killed outright…I can't believe it. Why, why now?" Snot drips from her nose and she continues to blubber.

"That's really tough, Jaz. Are you going to leave to get back to your family?" She nods.

"Ayanna is organising a trip back to the mainland. Oh, how could this happen? Who would do something like this?"

"Usually, these things just have an insane way of happening. Nothing we can control. Do you have anyone to be at home with; any brothers, or sisters?" She shakes her head, splashing more tears on her legs.

"They are all older than me and live in different countries. Only my dad and I and… mum." She breaks into a torrent of howling.

I hug her tightly and wish I could do more. This is a shock to me as well. I sense the loss of my own parents rising from deep within. Shaking my head, I try to stem any emotion. This is not about me, but I can't seem to control it. Watery tears blur my vision and I quietly weep with her.

Ayanna arrives and kneels next to us. Her warm hand rests on my shoulder and she speaks softly to Jaz. It amazes me the empathy that Ayanna radiates. I have found myself melting in her presence, often whilst trying to divulge less about my past. Except, this moment brings up anger and I want to crush anyone who is out to get me. I think the attempts to shut me down permanently are grating in my mind. This whole journey here seems an unnecessary waste of time. Jaz now is distraught, and I have had two escapes from death.

"What are we doing here?" I say with annoyance.

"We are reassessing the training; I understand your frustration and there has been a development which forces us to change the timetable." I look up into her dark eyes, trying to decode that statement.

"What changes? Are we all leaving?" I hope we are.

"Yes. I have arranged transport to get us back to the office. Jaz will be sent home for a few weeks to be with family. This is very sad news, and she will need time to recover." I nod and hug Jaz again.

"Thank God we are getting away from this island. I shan't be missing it one little bit," I say. Jaz nods.

"Yeah…I need a warm bath and warm bed…if only I could hug my mum again…" she splutters. I help her up and we gather our kit. The lads are still in the water, so Ayanna calls them and obediently they swim back. She unexpectedly pulls me away from Jaz.

"You need to be aware that the death of Jaz's mum was suspicious. We haven't told her that," Ayanna whispers to me. I frown.

"Why are you telling *me* this?"

"It has the characteristics of an agency hit."

I shudder.

15 – LAST CHANCE

The crossing over to the mainland is thankfully less traumatic this time, with the sea behaving itself. Everyone was gloomy. The news of Jaz's mum's death has silenced us all. The trainer who I had doubts about stands on the stern, hands-on hips, *looking* stern. I stare at his face, trying to determine any predatory intent. Still, I have that feeling in my gut *he* is the one that tried to kill me. But so far, he has hidden it too well.

What if the *agency* were trying to kill me? Would they go to this extreme? And for what end? The jewel is not mine anymore and the man, who no one knows, seemed happy to have escaped with it. So what threat am I anyway? It's a puzzle, one I am determined to crack. Jaz nuzzles up to me. I feel her breath on my arms, sweaty humid breath.

"I feel crap, Maisie. What am I to do now? My mum was the one who wanted me to succeed; my dad was too entangled in his own mess with his gambling addiction to be bothered."

"Life delivers some nasty blows at times – we must learn to adapt. Sorry, I sound like a bloody robot. It's what I've had to do most of my life though. When I found out about my real parents, it was like a knife dug into my gut." She looks up into my face, the dozy eyes watery and red.

"I have to learn so much, Maisie. I can see you have had to – the hard way. I'm so glad you are here. It makes me feel secure." I laugh.

"I wouldn't bank on it. My life has had all the trappings of destruction, dodging bullets, and perverts. Not a life I would wish on anyone." She nuzzles closer.

"Yeah…the all-conquering *Maisie G.*"

"Don't start that again. I'm just a teenager like you. I've learnt how to survive with what has been thrown at me. As I've said before – you adapt, you live."

"Wish I knew what happened to your parents. It sounds horrendous. Was it an accident too?" I squirm as this conversation is passing an invisible no-go line.

"Why are you interested in that, Jaz? I think you have enough to deal with at the moment."

"I have always been intrigued by your past, that's all." She pulls herself upright and stares vacantly at the emerging coastline. "This mission we are doing…will we complete it? I mean, how are we going to stop a dirty bomb being made? You can see what a mess I am, most of the time."

I hesitate to reply, as I don't want to squash any ambitions Jaz might have. I do agree with her though. I think we are a motley crew, with no chance of succeeding on the strength of what I have seen. I would rather be sent on my own.

"Well…Ayanna seems to have faith in us. I think you need to get back home though and find peace of mind and grieve before thinking any more about missions."

She nods and wipes a snotty nose on her sleeve.

"Yeah…I am not wanting to face what's at home to be honest. It scares me." I sense a deep hurt in Jaz, maybe more than the death of her mother.

Staring at the waves lapping against the white sand of the approaching shoreline, I mull over the time we've had on this island and the woman's warnings. It seems that I must watch my back at every step. A pang of fear writhes through my chest. I have never been so alone. With Olga, I had a certain routine; although deadly for our marks, it was a sense of purpose.

Now, I am like a piece of driftwood, at the mercy of whoever is trying to kill me. Under the so-called protection of MI6, I should start to feel some sort of grounding, but as yet, it is sending me deeper into despair. Has the death of Jaz's mum had anything to do with me? Are they trying to apply pressure on those around me to catch me unawares?

We are within spitting distance of the landing bay, as the man walks down the boat followed by Ayanna. I glance at his face. The stubble is thicker, showing the greying of an older man, along with flecks of black and ginger. His muscular torso pushes against a hoodie top as it shifts upwards with his movement. I cannot resist the urge to have a go at him. This would be my last chance.

Without thinking of the outcome, I lurch towards his back, pushing Ayanna out of the way. I contact his shoulder with mine. The force catches him off balance and he spiralled away to the starboard side, bouncing off an upright stay supporting the roof. Ayanna gives me a yell, but I'm focused now.

He unfortunately manages to stop his fall into the water by grabbing a rope. He swings around, a fire in his eyes. Also, a knife has fixed itself in his right hand. I flinch as I know this could be dangerous for all of us, not just me. A fight at close quarters is strewn with unintended consequences.

His bulk now is moving forward, his hand in a jabbing position. I grab hold of a roof beam and pull up swiftly and kick out at his hand. The knife spins away and embeds itself in Alex's bag. Still dangling like a monkey, I kick out with my other leg, catching the side of his head. He stumbles, but not enough for me to follow through. With the rage of a bull, he charges me, my legs now wrapped around his head and neck.

The force wrenches me away from my hold and we both crash into the sea. For a moment, I'm submerged. Panic overrides my logic, but I have little time to allow it. We both thrash around in the waves, trying to get a fix on each other. His hand grabs my coat, and he pulls me under. I gulp a breath just in time.

My only response is to bring my knees up to my chest and then push out against his stomach. It has the dual effect of pushing me away and winding him enough to slow him down. I thrash around again searching for air. In an agonising moment, I glance at rocks which are bobbing up and down, threatening to bash me as the waves are getting livelier. A decision has to be made. Do I stay and fight, or flee?

I'm in water which I hate, and rocks are harder than my body. I have an assailant trying to kill me too. Not good. An opportunity offers itself. The rope which he had held is dangling in the water. I reach across and grab it. Through the splashing, I see Jaz has the other end. A tug encourages me to haul myself towards the boat.

"Hold on Maisie. I've got you," I hear Jaz shouting.

Within a second, I am dragged closer, the joyful expectation of freedom rising from this freezing water. I grope at the side of the wooden hull, scratching paint under my nails and reach up on the upward swell of a wave to meet a hand. At the very moment of joy, I see a face which sends a deeper chill into my bones.

16 – DEEPER

My eyes meet grey, slits staring with venom. At first, I couldn't process what I was seeing. How could this man who I had sent further away from the boat be now standing holding out a hand to me? The hesitation made me falter. I lean back pulling on the rope for reassurance. I can't see Jaz anywhere and I'm glancing across the boat for any sign of the rest of the team. *Where the hell are they?*

"Are you coming aboard or what?" his gruff voice bellows. I stare back at the man scowling at me. "I can leave you to freeze and then drown – no skin off my nose."

I glance around for another alternative. None seemed remotely sensible. I throw across my hand and hope this is not a trick. He drags my shivering body up and out. I roll away from him and bring my knees up to my chest in a sodden mush. I see that the boat has moored up and the rest of the team are sitting or standing on the quayside.

"Stupid, that was. You really must choose your fights wisely," he chugs on. I grimace. I'm not taking advice from this idiot.

Ayanna steps back onto the boat and comes over. She offers a hand and I pull myself up. I am so cold I can hardly walk. My clothes are like ice packs stuck to my skin. Ayanna wraps me up in a blanket and leads me off the boat. Through my matted hair, I glare at the man, the only thing I can do to show him that I am totally pissed off. He returns a smirk and nods his head.

"What were you thinking?" Ayanna whispers. "That was reckless to say the least. You realise that both of you could have drowned." I'm too cold to reply.

Jaz runs over to me and attempts to hug me, then realising that I'm drenched, is repelled by the wet.

"My God, that was crazy. Are you ok?" I nod.

"Thanks for the hole in my bag, *Maiz*," Alex says. I nod again.

"Glad you are ok," Jules says, rubbing my arm and then wiping his hand as if it's infected.

"Come on. I need to get you out of this wet gear. Let's go over to the lifeguard station," says Ayanna, leading me.

The warmth of the room and a welcome cup of tea, begins to revive me. I am now sitting in clean, warm clothes again and life is returning to my body. My teeth are no longer chattering and I'm staring at a halogen heater which is now my best friend. Ayanna and I are the only ones in the room.

"Maisie. I get it. You are super sensitive to things at present. This whole journey has been a trial, more than I had anticipated. But you must trust what I am saying at least." I look at the heater. *That* is what I trust at this moment. To keep me warm. She shifts in her seat.

"Hey, look at me. I am as concerned as you are about the threats that hang over us. The trainer was *not* trying to kill you, honestly. If he was, don't you think he would do a better job at it?" I shrug.

"Maybe he's an incompetent asshole." She laughs.

"You really are a case. If he hadn't pulled you out, it was only a matter of minutes before your body would shut down, followed by death…not the actions of someone trying to kill you!" I shrug again. I know when my intuition is on point.

"So…what happens now? Are we travelling back to MI6 HQ? When is this mission supposed to be happening anyway?" I ask. Ayanna looks down at the table piled with National Geographic journals and weekly papers.

"Soon after Jaz has grieved, we will be preparing. We must do a thorough reconnaissance of the site and ensure we have the right cover for you all. At present, we are sending you as servants for the mealtime during the event." I grimace.

"What?? We're dressing up as *waiters*? So old school. I suppose we will have stupid whirly earpieces that make us look like CIA agents…" I say shaking my head.

"No actually, we have an in-ear piece that sits snugly without it being obvious. We use it all the time when we have an operational situation." I raise my eyebrows.

"Well, that does give me confidence. Where is this project or mission - *what do you call them?"*

"Operation, mission, field ops, project – all mean the same, only at a different level of danger."

"So what level are we?"

"High level. The risk to national security, both here and abroad is potentially huge. As I have told you before, the risk of a dirty bomb being used is deeply worrying."

"I really think you have the wrong people for this then. The rest of the team are a bunch of buffoons. How can you trust them with this mission, or whatever?"

"To be honest, I am hoping from your experience and skill set that you could bring them round." I glower at her.

"I am not a trainer or mentor to them. I have never wanted to pass on what I've learned or experienced. It's vile, dangerous and I wouldn't want anyone to be trained like me. What the hell are you thinking?" I turn away from her and stare through the salt smeared window.

"I am really hoping that you can; I am relying on you." I turn back to see her black eyes give away a glimmer of anxiety.

"Well, I really don't understand why. Is it still this obsession with what my parents were into that drives you to believe I can help?"

"Your parents had more to give, and I believe that your survival from the assassination has to be key to the continuation of their work."

"You're sounding like Anton now," I say, shaking my head.

"Hmm…this Anton intrigues me. I hope that we can meet soon." I look at her squarely in the face.

"It's like this…he's, or it's, a computer." She pulls back as if I let off a fart.

"What? This surveillance person is a computer??"

"Yes. Something my father created. Something to help me in case they died. I don't get it really, but he has saved my life a few times." She still has that expression of vague emptiness. Shaking her head, she comes back into the room.

"Every revelation from you opens a deeper doorway. Amazing. So, when you told me he's no longer available, what did you mean?"

"It was like he had to reboot himself – get rid of a hack that went into his systems. He went a bit weird towards the end. So, I'm guessing, he's in some sort of self-clean mode. I have no idea when that will end."

"So, do you have any access to his data?" At this, I consider; do I tell her of my home in the UK or act dumb?

"I have no idea." Dumb it is.

"Ok. That will have to wait." She gives me a motherly look and waves to the door.

"Time, I think we moved. The others are waiting in the coach. Say nothing about this to anyone else. I don't want any further complications, especially with Catherine; she would be on you like an avalanche."

That analogy makes me flinch.

17 – PLANNING

Sitting on the coach gives me the time to reflect on the situation I face. I have been given the opportunity to lead this team on a potentially dangerous mission and stop a group from exploding a dirty bomb. *Wtf*! I have had better days with Olga.

Jaz is quietly sobbing next to me whilst Alex and Jules are playing on a gaming machine, shouting with excitement about killing zombies. *Oh! Give me strength.* Staring at the traffic whizzing past sends a numbness to my brain. Then, a plan begins to form.

If Ayanna wants this from me, I am going to have to give some ground rules. I can't have a chaotic approach. It doesn't suit my style. Jules, I think I can rely upon – he sticks to the rules like super glue. Jaz needs oceans of confidence pouring into her, but I think we could do something with that aggression of hers. Alex is the stumbling block.

He's only given me grief ever since we met. It's as if he has no respect or belief in my ability or past. Perhaps I need to divulge more? Or do I prove myself beyond doubt that I have what it takes and blow him away? I know. I turn to Jaz.

"Hey…how are you doing?" She snuffles and coughs.

"Crap." Expected.

"Yeah…life sucks. I'm thinking…when you come back how do you like the sound of weapons training?" She stirs from her scrunched-up foetus position.

"Maybe. What would that involve?"

"Shooting loads of rounds into dummies," I glance across to Alex, "and getting to grips with an array of weapons for hand-to-hand combat. Also, some martial arts training." She sits more upright.

"I think… that would be great. I would worry over my lack of control though." I nod.

"Yeah, that's workable. When the training kicks in, you don't have to think about it. It's going to be a crash course though; it doesn't make up for all the years I've had." She gazes at me in her weird way. *Stop it Jaz!* It feels like you are sucking the life out of me.

"What I need though, is your total commitment. I believe you have what it takes. What I'm not sure about, is MI6's ability to bring out the best in you. So, I'm going to make a pact with Ayanna that we train my way…or it's the highway." Jaz gives the briefest of grins.

"That's a line from a song," she says.

"Maybe, but it's what I have lived by all my life. I'm not having anyone dealing with my shit." I turn to Jules and Alex.

"Hey, zombie killers. Are you up for some serious training when we get back?" Their heads jerk upwards and stare at me. "Sorry, didn't get you killed, did I?" Jules smiles and nods towards Alex. His face is distraught.

"Yeah, Maiz. Was on the final level and now I'm back to the start. Pain in the arse…" I shrug.

"Well…I am putting a plan out here to save *your* arse in the real world. Would you both be up for training my way?" Jules and Alex glance at each other. I am surprised by their reaction.

"If it means we get hold of real weapons and beat the shit out of you, then yes," Alex replies. Jules sniggers.

"It would be quite cathartic, Alex, to watch you do that." Thanks Jules: I thought you were on my side.

"Excellent!" Jaz and I break into a spontaneous air guitar solo. "You can return to your zombie sesh."

I press back into my chair and allow a calmness to settle me. At last, I am getting things the way I want, not being dictated to by others who think they know best. Ayanna will have to be on board with this, as she has to convince 'Shorty' that I'm worth it.

As long as I know I am, that's all that matters. I have absolute confidence in my abilities, even if Alex doesn't. I reach across to where Ayanna is sitting. Her headphones are perched on her head, and she appears to be nodding to whatever beat is pulsing.

"Oi..." She turns, taking them off.

"Yes, Maisie."

"I have some planning to do with you if you want these cretins to do a good job." She smiles at me and nods.

"Ok then. It seems you are coming round to my way of thinking. We will chat when we get back."

Headphones back on again. I push my pods in and turn up the volume. Today is turning out to be a good day, after all.

18 – DUMMIES

"This looks like a job for me,
So, everybody, just follow me.
'Cause we need a little controversy.
'Cause it feels so empty without me."

My playlist has strayed into rap and bass but is now firing me up for training. I need to get this team to the right standard.

We waved Jaz goodbye and good luck with the funeral of her mum. It was heart-warming to see the lads give her a hug and show some sort of empathy. To be honest, I never expected it from Alex. But there he was saying sorry and that he was looking forward to her returning. Miracles do happen!

So, I am currently in the gym on the weights and resistance bands. I have felt rubbish since coming back from the Outer Hebrides and need to get focused. This session will do just that - if I am not interrupted by anyone. Ayanna unfortunately does.

"Well, Maisie, it would appear that Catherine is in favour of you training the others – something about you giving something back to the state and proving yourself." I pull hard on the weights and let them crash into their housing. Ayanna flinches.

"Yeah…all about seeking approval from upon high. *Bullshit.* I know what I can do more than anyone here. Have I free reign to do it as I see fit?" I give a sweaty glare.

"Yes, with me as the mediator. I don't want you going rogue on us. Come on Maisie, I'm on your side. To be honest, I'm excited about you doing this."

"Hmm…you don't get wine from grapes unless they are pressed." A little philosophical for me.

"*And* left to mature…maybe we don't have enough time to do that for everyone."

"That's a fact, especially with Alex. What a moron he is. Anyway, I'm up for the challenge." She nods with modest approval.

"When Jazmin returns, we can set about putting together your ideas. Enjoy your workout." She wanders off, leaving me to pump these weights.

I have found working out like this quite relaxing, my mind can focus on nothing else, and I come out with an adrenaline rush which can last for hours. Weights then a rowing machine, followed by a treadmill. Running, I usually prefer to go outside on a sharp frosty morning. Today is too hot outdoors, so the air conditioning is pushed to its limits while I train.

A good breeze is blasting my sweat-ridden body. A chill runs along the rivulets of moisture on my arms and legs, whilst the crop top and shorts give me the best comfort for this sort of routine. I'm hoping that no one else comes into the gym, as I'm always conscious, especially of men and lads giving me unnecessary attention.

I speed up the treadmill to a satisfying pace and focus on my breathing. The music carries my mind back to a rave I ended up going to in Berlin.

***

Olga and I had dispatched a diplomat called Herman Schultz, (not the enemy of Spiderman). He apparently ran a drugs ring from the city, selling infected goods to the addicted of Europe. He held sway over many of the drug barons of Germany and Italy, having mafia connections too. After doing the deed, I had some spare time and wandered into a rave called 'Funkhaus'.

The venue was in an old underground pipe which had a past life as a shaft to a mine. Quite amazing. The lights and lasers bounced around the curved roof directed by large reflectors, the sound billowing out from the weird acoustics of the place. Stage smoke swirled around giving the effect of a forest fire. It was awesome.

The techno beat was so loud that my hearing went into sleep mode, a dull thudding in my head for days afterwards. Along with the rest of the writhing teens, I danced for hours. I nearly got off with one of the lads who happened to be dancing next to me. Except when I got close to kissing him, his breath smelt like a sewer. Nearly made me throw up. A quick dive under bobbing bodies got me away from him. Another guy was too pushy, and I had to give a pleasant jab with my fist into his gut as a reminder not to force a girl into something she doesn't want.

***

The drum and bass I'm listening to now, has that stimulating effect of giving a steady rhythm to my running and I feel strength surging into my legs. My mind is peaceful and rested, no need to be worrying about anything. So cool that state of mind, where nothing invades, and you are almost floating on a delicate heavenly breeze.

Sadly, the timer goes off and drags me back into the room. The treadmill slows to walking pace and I eye up the Wing Chun training dummy alongside another padded one swinging from a chain. This is where I really get a buzz. All my aggression and anger pour out on these things. I stroll over and wrap my hands in cloth, thinking of the people I love to beat up in my dreams.

First the punch bag gets a beating, my flying leaps and kicks thrashing the poor dummy who unfortunately stands before me withering away. Such a buzz. One, two; one, two. Smack hard and low. Twist and turn flick up and down with my feet. I push faster and my legs are whipping out harder and harder. The idiot on the boat is my main focus, as I'm still convinced he was trying to kill me.

Then I turn to the Wing Chun wooden dummy. I use this for focusing my attacks and parries, starting slow and then speeding up. This is where I know I can beat any opponent as I have uncanny speed and accuracy, that's why Alex had better watch out if we spar. I stray into thinking about that, and it distracts me. I smack my arm too hard on a wooden stay and I yelp with pain. Time to finish and get showered.

The hot water runs down my back and the gel froths up around my abs. My arms and legs sting from the bruising but a warmth rises in my chest. This is so relaxing I could stay here all day. I catch a glimpse of my reflection on the glass screen and nod. My body is looking great. My toning is increasing, along with my strength. This is what I've constantly tried to achieve. Not for any bloke to admire, but for my own satisfaction. Although, my thinking strays to my French boyfriend and running my fingers along my belly and further down sends a rush of pleasure through my head.

A bang jolts me out of my fantasy and I suddenly get a feeling of vulnerability and panic. I glance around, reaching for my towel. *Who is that?* The steam has partially hidden and enveloped the room. I drop down. I see a pair of legs in fatigues walking towards me. *Shit! Who is walking into the shower room dressed like that?*

19 – UNEXPECTED

I have no other option but to slide over the floor and get to the cover of the changing room lockers. The feet stop moving and change course. I feel tension rippling along my back. I hate being left open like this. It's the worst scenario for any woman being in a shower, stalked by an unknown.

"Maisie Greene?" a voice asks, almost a whisper. I freeze. It's not a voice I recognise. Not a man's either. "It's ok. I'm here to give you some information."

"Who are you?" I ask.

"Sergeant Jane McAlister, SAS. I was sent by a colleague to inform you that the mission that MI6 is sending you on has a greater threat than anyone here understands." I am wary of this, as I don't understand why she is coming to tell me and not Ayanna, or Shorty and Tupperware man.

"Ok…so what's the urgency and secretive wandering around showers. A bit creepy don't you think?" The fog is starting to clear, and I see before me the woman in complete army fatigues with the SAS logo on her shoulder. She stands at about 5' 10'' with blonde hair swept back into a neat ponytail. Her blue eyes are piercing. I feel them scan my soaking towel.

"Yes, sorry. I was here on a secondment under the premise of a cooperative interchange of security forces.

We occasionally have MI6 officers come over to our HQ for training." She smiles apologetically.

"Ok, but why have you come to see me? Surely others in authority are the ones to be told. I'm just a cog in the works." She knowingly smiles.

"You may think you are. However, your role in this mission is more crucial than you or anyone else understands. I am obliged to warn you that there are forces at work here within MI6 that are out to undermine the success of your mission."

"Really? I got the impression that *we* were the ones to be roasted if it went south."

"Not exactly. I would prefer to talk more about this away from the building. Could we meet somewhere outside?" She nods at my dripping state.

"Yeah, sure. Give me 15 and I'll meet you at a coffee shop near Vauxhall Bridge. I'm not sure how they will receive army personnel dressed like that in there though." She grins and says she will quickly get changed.

Fourteen minutes later I am sitting sipping a coke looking across the Thames with Sergeant Jane, with her hair tightly bound and her eyes still piercing my head.

"So, what is this information? Why is it so important that I know about it?" She glances around.

"We have to be careful, Maisie, especially whilst we are in the public domain. Threats are everywhere these days." I nod.

"Yeah, I get that."

Unexpectedly, she pushes her seat back and orders the barista to politely ask the remaining two other customers to leave. He gives her a shocked frown. She opens her coat to one side. This persuades him to comply. I'm not sure what she showed him, but I can guess.

"Now, that's better. OK, less of the smoke and mirrors. I represent a task force from the SAS with the strategic operation to counter this terrorist threat."

"What, the dirty bomb?"

"Exactly. I am aware that you have been briefed on the 'Trojan' operation." I nod. I wasn't aware that other people knew about it though.

"How come you know about that? I thought it was locked away in the files of MI6?"

"It *was* classified information. Trouble is, it's been leaked onto the dark web. It was picked up by some GCHQ geek. MI6 was notified but so were we. Being a possible terrorist threat, the SAS were alerted."

I study her face. There are signs of ageing around her steely eyes. Lines radiate outwards to her cheeks. A small scar sits under her left eye, raised and slightly red compared to the rest of her pale skin.

"So, if MI6 are aware, why are you approaching me? My seniors would be in the know already." This argument gives me the creeps. Is this Sergeant Jane all she claims to be?

"Yes, in theory. It came to our attention that whoever received the notification sat on it and hasn't reported it. I was informed that you were the daughter of the agents that used to be overseeing this operation. Correct?" I skew my mouth and wonder if I should engage anymore. I am feeling too vulnerable.

"What if I am? How does that have any bearing on this Trojan operation?"

"You are an integral part in its completion. Sources unknown have been banding about that you are a threat to any opponents of it. I am guessing you have had a few near scrapes with death?"

I feel my eyes shrink to slits and my bum is sweaty in the seat. My hands tense up. I stare at her and then quickly look around. Is there any other way out of this place? She moves slightly to the right pulling her coat open. As I thought, a concealed weapon. I shoot her a hard glare.

"What are you saying, Sergeant?"

"I am saying that I'm here to *help* you."

"Really? Cos' you better not be shitting me." She grins and settles back in her chair.

"I have been assigned to essentially guard you."

"Oh, that's nice," I say. "But I don't need guarding. I am very capable of looking after myself. It's all those around me that are holding me back."

"That may be the case, but I am compelled to advise you that no one is to be trusted on this team. We are not sure who is complicating the operation. It's like a phantom hovering over it." I roll my shoulders in mock fear.

"Well, you are not the first person telling me not to trust anyone. Why should I trust you?"

20 – SPIES WITHIN SPIES

She continues to explain that she and a small group of SAS soldiers have been given the covert task of covering the operation, mission, or whatever, my team and I are being prepared for. To date, no one from MI6 has been informed.

"That's the way it must be, or this mission will be compromised. I hope you understand that." She looks intently at me as I slurp my coke.

"Yeah…I get it. So, not even my mentor knows about it?"

"No one…except for you."

"Ok. So, what do you want me to do?"

"Nothing. Except be on your guard. The event will be at a stately home in the UK. The destination is only being released ten days before it happens. It will involve a banquet and auction. I am not sure what your team's undercover status will be, but I will be there with three others as guests."

"Sounds fun," I say. A slight frown appears above her scarred side.

"Not what I would call it, Maisie. I would appreciate any feedback if you discover anything relevant. It could save all our skins." I nod.

"I don't mind digging the dirt on MI6. Any covert organisation seems to have its nasty secrets. I've come across too many over the years." She tilts her head like a dog trying to work out a weird noise.

"Yeah," I say. "…that's another story. So, will I see you again? Do we have any passwords or codes to exchange info?" She nods and brings out a small case. From the lid she hands me what looks like a pen.

"What? An exploding pen? Or do I write a letter?"

"Ha, no. It has a receiver built inside which will relay a message from your phone and encrypt it to my workstation. It has no feed other than one way. So, if you do get anything of interest, you can send it to me directly. The message will not be seen on your phone – a bit like the old-style invisible ink we used as kids at school."

I look clueless, as I am. Invisible ink? What the hell is she on about?

"Don't worry. MI6 won't pick it up, or GCHQ. We have our own encryption software." Spies within spies, how quaint.

"Ok, I'll see what I can find out. One question though…how did you know about my parents?" She takes a long suck from her coffee cup and places it carefully on its saucer.

"Trojan involved task forces from many countries working together to form an alliance against foreign aggressors. NATO is a well-known one. However, unknown to all but a few, one of our tasks was to ensure that no one infiltrated the rank and file of the armed forces to undermine its effectiveness. Your parents were the courageous team that met with these undercover operatives. They were only known by code names to keep their anonymity. Of course, when they were murdered, we lost most of the intel they had accumulated. So, when you arrived on the scene, all our ears pricked up." I grimace at her.

"*All* our ears? Who have I been *alerting*?" I squirm in my seat again.

"As secure as MI6 thinks it is, we have eyes and ears everywhere. We have to. The defence of the country depends on us."

"Sounds like a friend of mine…" I say guardedly.

"Oh, who might that be?"

"Just a friend who's a bit of a geek with intelligence."

"Well, if your friend could help with obtaining any more information, it would be very welcome." I smile.

"When he reappears, I'll ask." She smiles and looks at her watch.

"Time for me to go. Maisie. I am relying on your cooperation. It is vital that this is a closed loop."

"Yes, I know. You can count on me," I say with as much sincerity as possible.

"See you at the auction. I'll have your back, don't worry." I give a thumbs up.

Sergeant Jane McAlister shuffles with her backpack and thanks the barista for his cooperation and slips through the door. I watch her march off towards the bridge and wonder what on earth I am involved with. Life with Olga, dispatching, has its attractions at this moment. My head is buzzing with all that could or might go belly up with this operation and I'm wondering if I should walk away.

I really don't appreciate all this attention. Jane's mentioning of escaping death certainly got me worried. I'm guessing she had a hunch that would be the case. Otherwise, I thought she might have something to do with it. It only confirms to me that my life is dangling by a shoelace.

I run back to the office as the evening is cooling and I need to relax my aching muscles from my workout. I show my pass at the gate and wink at Stephen who is on his shift.

"Good to know that Ayanna has a fan," I say in a girly voice. He gives a look of disgust and rolls his shoulders as if he isn't listening. "I guess you must have lots of fun at home…on your own." At this he tries to stare me down. I nod with satisfaction. How I love to wind people up.

The target of his love interest comes almost skipping down the corridor to me.

"Hey," she says. "Want to come for a swim? I'm about to get off."

"Yeah, sounds cool. Let me get my kit."

I ran to the lodging rooms. Pulling out my towel and swimwear, I gaze across to Jaz's bed and sigh. It reminds me of the hurt I felt when I found out about my parents. She must be suffering big time and I allow myself to pray for her. Strange that I do that. I'm not really sure who I am talking to, but that same one that has protected me all these years, I guess.

21 – DIGGING THE DIRT

The swim was great. We had a laugh, messing about, diving off the medium height board – the top one was far too high for me. It was bad enough on the lower one. My legs are still trembling.

The shower washes away that chlorine odour and I spray liberally to counter any after workout sweat. Ayanna dries her locks and twists it to contain its urge to frizz out.

"I love this hair, but it's a bitch to control at times."

"Ha, yeah," I say. "Mine just falls into place. Once I've tied it up in a ponytail, it behaves."

She packs her towel and kit into a holdall, and we wander through the sports hall. I can't shake the feeling that I'm in an alternative universe. Having been sworn to secrecy with Jane, I now have to navigate around Ayanna without giving anything away.

Looping her arm through mine, we head for a local bar, where Ayanna likes to hang out. She drinks with moderation, but her favourite is real ale. I'm unsure if that means that all other varieties are unreal. Even so, she downs a few tonight.

"You know…I'm really happy the way you have settled in. I did wonder about your tendency to irritate and provoke. But…you are turning into a decent sort of person." I look at her and wonder if she's getting pissed, as this doesn't sound like the normal Ayanna.

"Thanks…I suppose. What did you expect? I'm a kid from the darkest recesses of a clandestine world of assassins. I'm no fairy princess." I drink my coke with more force than necessary. It fizzes up my nose and I cough. She laughs at me.

"Ha ha…can't take your drink dear?" she asks.

"I'm not sure you can, to be honest."

We gaze around the pub taking in the locals and the buzz of conversation. A thought comes - I have never known where Ayanna lives.

"Where do you head off to after work? I don't know if you have a house, flat, or garage that you live in."

"I live overlooking Kennington Park, only a short walk away."

"I thought it might be nice to check out your living quarters – see if I can get an upgrade." She frowns and looks down at the floor. It's sticky with spilt drink and crushed crisps.

"Do you want to move in with me? That would *not* be appropriate. What would Catherine say?" She laughs.

"Sod Catherine. If Jaz continues with her obsessive joss stick burning, I am going to have to relocate," I say grinning.

"Well," she says, getting off her stool, "I think it's time for some shut eye. The days on that island have exhausted me. I suggest you get back too. And as far as moving you is concerned; we will only do that if it's *absolutely* necessary."

She waves at me to follow. I swig back the remaining coke and sling my swimming kit bag over my shoulder. I glance around the room again, making sure that no one is interested in following us. The only one with eyes on us is an elderly man emptying his glass before standing up and racing to the loo.

Outside that cool air hits my lungs with a refreshing thrill. I always feel a sense of warm cosy comfort after a swim. The evening twilight is mixed with the street lighting creating a waxy scene of an impressionist painting to the London skyline. Ayanna goes off to her flat, whilst I wander towards my temporary home.

I consider it temporary as I am not wanting to stay on after this mission. It feels all wrong and thwarted with danger. In fact, I have never been so uncomfortable with the people around me. Olga was at least dependable, stable, as much as she could be. This team, if it can be called that, gives me less belief in human trustworthiness. Now that Sergeant Jane has added her penny worth to the mix, I am even doubting Ayanna's integrity.

But should I make that judgement after a short meeting with a SAS officer? It could all be bullshit, to lead me astray. My mind was peaceful, but now these conflicting thoughts are invading. As I hurry along Vauxhall Bridge, a plan jumps to mind.

Nodding to the gate staff, wafting my lanyard around, I walk swiftly towards the archive room. I check around to see if anyone is already there. The door is slightly open. The lights are on. I sneak up to it and gently push it wider. I wonder who is in here at this time of night?

Catherine Short?

Late night working does seem to be some people's habit here to be honest. But I thought she was high up and would get a clerk to do this sort of work. I watch her, now fascinated with what she might be up to. I'm compelled to open the door wider and drift in behind a cabinet. It works, as I silently push back the door.

From here, I can just about see over her shoulder. I see the headline of the file. That name, which has hounded me for months, is at the top, alongside 'top secret'.

TROJAN – THREAT LEVEL 5

I wonder what level that is? The worst I guess after what I've been told. Also, I thought it was an MI6 operation, so why would it be a threat? I carefully lean around the cabinet, scared I'm going to be found out by making a squeaking noise, a fart, or a cough.

She is madly skimming through the file, looking for something. The screen freezes. She must have spotted what interests her.

I wish I had my skin suit which enhanced everything. After it disappeared when I was hospitalised, I was never told where all my stuff went. Then I was brought here. I am also wondering if Anton, my computer buddy, will ever return from his self-clean and be of help again.

Without any warning, my calf muscle starts to cramp up from all the exercise I've done, and I have to suppress a yell. *Arrggh.* It's excruciating. I try to stretch it out without making any noise. It doesn't help. I'm now losing my balance and I'm ready for my cover to be blown.

A phone buzzes. Shorty answers it. She asks for more time. She says "Ok, OK," about six times, and slams the phone down. Pushing the chair back, she gathers her bag and phone together and marches out of the room, switching the light off.

I stumble from behind the cabinet and prance about like a clown trying to get this muscle to relax. It's so tight it feels like rock. *Owww!!!!*

Gradually it releases giving me sweet relief. I hobble quickly over to the screen. If I can catch it before it goes into sleep mode, I will be able to see what she was researching. It jumps back into life. I scan the screen and try to make sense of it.

This page relates to a section on the importance of covert operations my parents were involved in. There is a list of people and places they visited. Running down the list, I spot a few I have come across before.

'Bucharest, Budapest, Sophia, Cluj Napoca,' all places I remember from Olga and I visiting. How can this be so similar to what my parents were into? Could it be

that MI6 were tracing the dealings of the agency we worked for? If so, was I under surveillance whilst this was happening? My mind is getting blurry. I read more.

The authorities in these countries were in league with armed factions becoming more unstable as Russia increased its pressure to claim back the countries it lost in the fall of the Soviet era. I recall this from various history lessons on National Geographic tv shows.

The intel implies that the code name *'Talisman'* was used by my parents to hide sensitive information and keep MI6 out of it. No wonder Shorty gets the feeling I'm here to be a pain in the butt. *So, the code that unlocked the sapphire, was the same one that withheld the information from the Secret Services in the UK*. I read on.

It implies that there was a fail-safe to this that no one knew about except my parents, and that MI6 had no time to find out who or what it was before they died. This forces a memory from what Olga said as she was bleeding all over the floor in Versailles:

"You are my talisman..."

The key was sealed away in my mind for over 12 years. Olga didn't really understand the significance of what that phrase meant, until she nearly died. Did she survive the fight at Versailles or not? I have no idea.

So, does what I have concealed away in my brain hold any more keys to this mystery? As I am digging deeper, I'm finding it uncomfortable that my parents were deemed unsafe, a liability. The claim that they caused the death of Chase's parents clangs like a raucous bell in my head. I am so desperate to clear my parents' name, but it feels like I am doing the opposite as each page of this nightmare narrative turns.

22 – HEART TO HEART

Returning to my dorm, I feel a prickly sensation ripple down my back. I keep pondering why Ayanna wants me on this mission so badly. Perhaps if these doubts are buzzing around in the back of MI6's mind, am I being set up as the conspirator like my parents? I crash onto my bed and kick off my Converse trainers. I stare at the ceiling trying to make any sense of these revelations.

My thoughts wander to Jaz and her mum's death. If what Ayanna says is true, perhaps the agency has an agenda to intimidate her and the rest of the team. What if something happens to any of the others? I would hate to think that it was down to me being here, working for the SIS. *Damn.* I would have been far better surviving on my own.

A knock on the door forces my eyes wider. It's Jules poking his head around.

"Any chance of a chat?" I'm in shock.

"Yeah, sure. What's on your mind," I say. He shuffles in and sits on Jaz's bed, rearranging her bedside table. Joss sticks and smelly bottles are now in neat rows.

"You see, since I started here, I've never been sure of what I was seconded to. I was training to be in the MET and being a student from inner London, I've had to fight my way through prejudice, intolerance, and misunderstanding. The UK is a pretty cool place to live but sometimes I feel, like, no one gets me." I nod, fascinated by this outpouring of Jules' inner thoughts.

"Yeah, I get that. I have had to live separate from most people all my life, so I understand how it feels to be different, distinct from others." I sit more upright and drag my knees to my chest.

"Where did you grow up?" I ask.

"Here and there. My mum had to find work wherever as a nurse. It has been tough, especially being Asian. At least London is multicultural. I sort of got an identity when I studied martial arts and progressed up to black belt in Taekwondo. Gave me confidence." I nod in agreement.

"Yeah, it gives you status, not dependent on anyone else. So, what brought you here, to MI6?"

"There was an advert circulating at New Scotland Yard for young, enthusiastic people to join the SIS to make a difference to the world. Sounded too good an opportunity to miss." I smile thinking of what Jaz once said.

"So, I applied, and I was dumbstruck when I got it. There must have been hundreds of applicants."

"Shows you have some special qualities, Jules," I say in a coy way, almost making myself blush. He glances at me and smiles.

"More than rearranging people's toiletries?" he says. I laugh.

"Yeah, that one is *very* special. So, what do you think of this mission we are going on?"

"I am nervous, to be honest. I know that Ayanna has confidence in us, but are we ready to engage in something so crucial to national security?" He shudders for the first time since I've known him. "And when you had that spate of attacks on the island, and now Jaz's mum dying, it made me really doubt that this was for me."

"I'm glad you thought they were attacking me. I was beginning to doubt my judgement. Also, we don't know how Jaz's mum died. Shit happens. Do you have any ideas about what happened on the island?" I stare at his eyes, dark and gentle eyes.

"I told you about the tattoo, yes?" I nod. "Well, when I was younger, a gang on our estate tried to intimidate me into working for them, you know, to be a drug mule. Told me to transport packages around for them on my bike." I am glued to his storytelling.

"I refused but they then threatened my mum. That was it. I broke. I was already a brown belt but didn't want to use it as a weapon. I found the gang leader and confronted him. He taunted me saying that I should go back to where I came from; used names and words that really annoyed me. Then he started pushing me and others of the gang hit me with a baseball bat."

"I can guess what you did," I say.

"Really? Well, I ran." Not what I expected.

"I felt so ashamed that I didn't stand up to them. I had the ability but didn't use it. After a few days I stoked myself up and found the leader and told him not to approach my mum again. He tried to bully me, but this time I was pumped up, ready for war. I unleashed all my training and left him broken and blubbering." My mouth drops in shock.

"So, you beat the crap out of him?" I ask.

"Yes, you could say that. It didn't end the intimidation though. These sorts of people never know when to stop. So, we had to move again and that's when we came to London. A new start."

"Cool. And what was the tattoo all about? You said it was a reminder, a warning?"

"Yes. To myself and anyone who tries to intimidate me again." He gives a look of defiance.

"Does that include *everyone?*" I ask, shifting my bum across the bed, closer to him. He gives me a sideways glance. I reach out and touch his hand. I squeeze gently. He smiles and places his other hand on mine. It's warm and comforting. Strong, yet reserved.

"Yes, I'm afraid so. The other thing about me is that …I'm gay. Sorry. I sense you are interested in me, but I'm not open for business, as you might say." I withdraw a little, taken back by this heart to heart. I then reach over and kiss him on the cheek.

"You won't be turned on by this then," I say suggestively. My hand wanders onto his leg and I squeeze.

I'm not really sure why I did that, maybe for my own pleasure more than his. He stands up and shakes his head.

"Heed the warning Maisie, heed the warning," he says mysteriously.

I'm now filled with regret. *Why did I do that?* He needs to be on my side if this mission is going to succeed. I shout out '*sorry*' to him, but I feel I may have crossed a line.

23 – HACKING

It was a week later, and Jaz returned looking crest-fallen and sad. She dropped her case by the bedside table and slumped onto her duvet. I can't help but stare at her. There must be a torrent of sadness raging in her head. I am trying to get eye contact, but her eyes are red and staring. I slowly shuffle across to her with the intention to hug her. She fights me off, shrugging her shoulders. I step away and find something else to occupy my failed attempt.

"Sorry. I get it. You want some space. I'm here if you need me," I say, climbing back across my bed.

I'm not normally this sympathetic, but we have grown close since I've been here. Shared quite a bit of life…and near death. She flings herself onto her back and sighs, snivelling. I copy and lie down fixing in my ear pods. If she's not in the mood, then I'm listening to music. No need for us both to be sinking into depression. I need to be on point when she is ready to communicate.

"Maisie," she suddenly says. I was halfway through a track and drifting. "I am really confused as to how my mum died. It was said that a car ran her down when she was coming home from shopping. She never shops on foot. Only to the corner shop and there is no need to cross the road."

"Maybe she needed something she had forgotten," I say.

"Not likely. She has a photographic memory…had…" She starts crying. I shuffle across to her, attempting to comfort.

"I know it's hard to accept, but these messed up things happen. Trying to analyse it can send us crazy. I know; I'm still trying to get my head around why my parents were killed and the reasons behind it." A loud blowing of her nose nearly deafens me.

"Yeah... I suppose. It's just that, along with the police's evidence, they said it happened with no witnesses. No one was around to see it. That is really odd. We live on a busy street, with people walking their dogs, chatting over garden fences. There's something weird about it." I put my arm around her and sigh.

"I really shouldn't tell you this, but Ayanna has suspicions about your mum's death." She pulls back abruptly and stares at me.

"What do you mean?"

"Well, while we were on the island, Ayanna told me that she thought that an outside agency had caused it." Jaz gazes puzzled at the floor.

"Who would do that to my mum? That would mean it was…*murder!*" She jumps up and begins to stomp around. I suspect this could be one of her moments of eruption.

"Look…as far as I can see, it's all speculation. No point getting worked up about it."

"Yeah," she says, pointing at me. "But if it was, does that mean it could be something like the agency *you* worked with?" She glares at me.

"No, not necessarily. There are a thousand and one rogue units out there, each with an agenda. Don't start joining the dots before we know." I am feeling the heat from her eyes.

"There must be a report, a file, that gives some detail of her misgivings, or she wouldn't have said anything."

"I know where the archives room is. Do you think we should investigate?" A tingle rises along my spine.

"Bloody well right, we should." She pulls on her jacket and we both attach our lanyards.

We march to the archives watching for anyone that might interfere with our mission. The door needs a pass. Damn, I forgot.

"Wait here, I know where I can get one," I say and leave Jaz pacing the floor.

The nearest person who would have access is a chap who works close to the office called John. I have occasionally talked to him, as he seems an ok sort of bloke. Not pushy, intelligent, but I sense a little interested in me.

"Hey John," I say. "Have you got a minute?" John looks up from his desk, and smiles.

"Yeah sure. What is it, Maisie?"

"I'm wanting to get a free pass into the archives room. I've been given a task to research the history of SIS and the files I need are in there. Any possibility I could get in?" I smile and look as coy as possible without making myself act stupid. His eyes flick back and forth between me and the computer screen. He knows it's out of bounds for a trainee like me.

"You know that's not allowed?" I smile again, my eyelids flickering unintentionally. I feel like my adopted mother, using her wily charms. He sighs.

"I'll give you 10 minutes. But don't tell anyone. I'm on a short string here." He hands over his own pass. I use a feather touch on the back of his hand as a reward and thank him. "Only 10 minutes…promise." I nod and race off.

"Here we go," I say and swipe the pass. Jaz is so eager to get in, she pushes past me and jumps onto the first screen she sees.

"Ok, how do I access the files?" she demands.

"I hope that Ayanna hasn't changed her password…" I say and start to type.

"*Yes*…that's got us in the system. Now to find the file." From here on, Jaz takes over and shows me why she was such a computer geek.

The system is barely keeping up with the speed she is searching. The files are tripping on the screen so fast I can't read them, yet she scans the screen with ease.

"It's got to be somewhere amongst the recent input," she burbles. I glance back to the door, feeling a sense of panic as I see shadows moving past the gap at the bottom.

"How long will this take? I've only got the pass for 10 minutes," I ask. Jaz nods and without any let up, types away.

"There!" Her surprise gives me hope. "It was logged the day before we left the island." She reads it to herself, mumbling.

"Yes…the accident was reported, and my mum was dead at the scene…" Jaz forces her mouth together to stop crying. I place my hand on her shoulder.

"Does it say anything about who might have done it?" I ask.

"*NO*," she almost screams. "But it doesn't say anything about mum shopping, but CCTV shows her talking to someone before it happened." I peer at the screen.

"Who is that?" she asks.

I recoil. I know. My heart is pounding so loud I fear that John will think I've got a thing for him. I back away and tell Jaz to shut down the computer and get out.

"I think we've had our time. Come on, we have seen enough. Shut the damn thing down." I almost have to drag her out.

I wander over to John and secretly hand over the pass. He glances around checking that no one has seen our little pact. I smile sweetly and tell him he was great, and that we must do it again sometime. He shakes his head.

Jaz and I walk with nowhere in mind and end up at the canteen. We decided to pass some time and get a drink.

"Coke for me please and..." I nod to Jaz, whose mind is elsewhere.

"...oh, a Camomile tea..." she manages to say.

We sit and stare at each other. I'm reluctant to reveal what I saw. It will complicate matters and probably send Jaz down the tubes. The canteen is filling with staff and the general hum of noise is rising along with my anxiety.

We sip our respective drinks. I think about how and what to say. Will it help her accept that her mum is dead, or just fire up the anger and frustration? She breaks the impasse.

"Who...who was she talking to? Why was I told that she went shopping? That's so much to cover up. This person must know something. I've got to ask Ayanna." She slurps her tea with determination.

"That might be a bad move, seeing that we have just hacked their system. We would be in deep shit, along with John, our collaborator." She shakes her head and asks the awkward question.

"So, who was it on CCTV? Do you have any clue?" Her dozy eyes are full of fire. I choose my words carefully.

"They looked familiar...but not from any agency I know of." Her eyes open wider expecting to receive a prize.

24 – BLACK AND WHITE

To my relief, revealing whom I thought the person was, gave me less grief than I expected. Jaz's eyes narrowed, indicating that some sort of plot was forming inside her head.

"So, you say that this person could be from the SAS? Do you think they had something to do with it?" I shrug.

"God knows. I am mystified by every new turn of the earth," I say, sipping coke, my own thoughts whirring in conflict.

Why was Sergeant Jane McAlister talking to her mum before she died? Was she warning her to be careful, like myself? Or was she part of a hit squad? I can't see that Jaz's mum would be that important to get killed by the SAS. Seems ridiculous. Also, why would Ayanna be peddling the story that she was killed in a hit and run accident? Perhaps she was softening the blow, covering up the real reason for confidentiality's sake. My concentration is broken, as the lads descend on us.

"Hey, Jaz you are back. Hope the funeral went ok. Sorry, again, about your mum. A real shock." Alex is showing a caring side again. I can't quite stomach this new aspect to his character. Is it genuine?

"Thanks…it was ok. Just so sad," Jaz replies.

Jules sits next to her and hugs her. He glances my way and I read the pain from our last encounter written across those soft brown eyes. He doesn't sit there for long and moves to his own seat, hand sanitiser being used.

"We are here for you Jazmin," he says with sincerity. She smiles for the first time.

"Apparently, we have a meeting in five minutes with our bosses," Alex declares. "They want to get on with some training for our role in this operation." Alex has a look of glee which means he has no idea that we are posing as waiters.

"I guess you don't know what we are going to do?" I ask. He shakes his head.

"Masked ninjas I hope." Jaz and I look at each other and she allows a snigger.

"You are so in for a surprise, Alex. Come on, let's go. I can't wait to see your face," I say. He glares at me in his usual dismissive way, and we saunter off, my arm looped around Jaz.

The room we enter has a large rectangular table, with an arrangement of glasses, cutlery, plates, and pottery. I scan the room looking for who is presenting this training. I doubt the Viking boatman would have the finesse to deal with this.

A slightly built lady stands to one side of the table dressed in black and white clothes, looking like a maid from a comedy sketch of the 1980's. I can't help but snigger. Sadly, Ms Short is standing at the head of the table, dressed in a fuchsia pink two-piece suit, with a cream blouse showing. This time the image of a strawberry split ice cream invades my mind. This is so hilarious, I must hide behind Jules, trying to contain myself.

"Team, this is Ms Isabelle Conforte. She will be your trainer for waiting at tables for this operation," Shorty announces.

The lady nods her head and smiles. I notice a look of worry flash across her face when her eyes scan us. Perhaps we are not the usual trainees she's used to. I glance at Alex who is looking puzzled. I grin and nudge him.

"No ninja suits for you today, big boy," I whisper. "Maybe a nice frilly pinny apron?" His mouth screws up, with eyes darting around the room.

"So, the dress code will be black trousers for the girls along with white blouses, black waistcoats and neckties. The lads will have black slacks, with white shirts and black waistcoats and bow ties. All will wear black shoes, clean and polished." Ms Conforte has a French or Belgian twang to her accent, making us all pay attention. "Your clothes will be made especially to your sizes and fit. Our tailor will take your measurements after this training." She waves her hand towards the table. "Let us begin."

Over the next hour, we are introduced to the world of serving. I am amazed at the intensity of this training. We must learn how to carry silver trays, observe guest's requests, and deliver drinks and hors d'oeuvres (plates with small packages of food). These consisted of Spinach Artichoke Dips, Baked Brie Bites, Guacamole Bites and Chicken Pot Pie Empanadas. I will not be able to remember these, except by scent.

We practised with each other generating a mixture of hilarity and accidents, parading around like some silly waiter's catwalk. I see that Jules is soaking up all this information like a dry sponge, whilst Alex is acting like an unreliable clown at a kid's function. Jaz and I make our best efforts at keeping a straight back and balancing these trays. We are instructed to always smile and be pleasant. I have a feeling that it may be more challenging than I thought.

"At all times, be polite and courteous as they are the guest and you are essentially a servant," Ms Conforte rambles. "Their needs are your priority. You may suggest alternatives if they are not interested in what you have to offer."

"A punch in the head, or knife to the throat?" I whisper to Jaz. She nearly drops her tray and coughs.

"You must appear competent and respectful. This is an essential front to your operation. Ms Short will now address the operational targets." She steps to one side as Ms Short strides across to the table.

"You must maintain your cover, as it will enable us to assess and neutralise the threat of this asset being passed on." I shuffle around and noisily clang my serving tray next to the silverware. She shoots a stare.

"The event we are attending is being held at a stately home in the Midlands, UK, "she continues. "It is a front for the sale and auction of unknown items which hold dangerous information. We will know more on the day. The people of interest we presented to you will be in attendance and we suspect they will be in the bidding process." She directs our gaze to a screen. A gallery of the suspects appears. "These are the latest pictures of our targets. Memorise, and when you can, approach them with care; if they suspect you are other than waiters, your cover will be blown. This opportunity will be lost, and years of work will be wasted." I see a sneer flicker across her thin sallow face.

"What exactly are we to do…other than serve drinks and expensive treats?" I ask.

"Observe, listen, and report. You will have cameras embedded in your ties and neckties. Small earpieces will keep you informed of what decisions are being made. Under no circumstances must you engage before you are ordered to." She moves her eyes in a shifty manner to me. "Especially you Miss Greene. I know you have been in the field before, but this is a team operation. *NO* heroics!" I glance away, resisting the urge to kick back at that comment.

"Do we have access to weapons?" asks Alex.

"Not directly; any encounters that are required will be by others in situ." Alex looks deflated.

"And who are the *others?*" I ask.

"Agent Bolt and I will be embedded in the event, one as your team leader and myself as a bidding guest."

I raise my eyebrows, trying not to look too sceptical.

"Seems a little light."

"Well, that is not your concern, Miss Greene. We have a fail-safe team on call if we need them," she replies.

"Now, please go to the person in the next room and he will obtain your measurements," she concludes and walks smartly out of the room.

"I hate black and white," Jaz says. "Makes me look like I'm from the Addams family." I snigger and push her towards the door.

"Yeah…a starring role in your own horror movie."

25 – SHOOTING RANGE

Thankfully the tailor wasn't too concerned where he put his tape measure when using it against the lads. Alex squirmed and Jules displayed a wry grin. It's times like this I chuckle and consider where my life meanders. It's comical to think a year ago I was out with my adopted mother killing scumbags around the world; today, I am being fitted for a waiter's costume. Can life be any more diverse?

Coming away with our measured statistics, we are directed by Ayanna to a shooting range. Alex has become animated again and his grin means he is aiming to, not only shoot effigies, but also try to impress us.

"This is more like it! Now, I can really shoot off some stuff." We all grimace at his word choice and shake heads. Really Alex? I am wondering how well he will perform, in all areas.

"Let's see if you have what it takes, Alex," I say.

"Are we using live rounds?" he asks gleefully.

"Yes," Ayanna replies. "The range has targets which can be positioned at 20, 50 and 100 metres. This will enable you to get your eye in and practise precision firing." I nod. This is where I perform well. "The rest of the day we will put you through your paces with a holographic virtual tour of the stately home we are operating in to give you some familiarity with the place."

We take up positions in the firing lanes, checking over our weapons. The choice for the day seems to be a Glock 17. I do my usual checks, making sure that the safety is on. The magazines lie to one side and look to be fully loaded. This is a potentially dangerous situation as I look back to the control booth. I want to ensure that Ayanna has my back. I don't want anyone surprising me with a bullet in my head.

She nods and gives me a thumbs up. I turn to the targets and load the Glock. The click confirms its ready. I put on the ear defenders and safety goggles. I eye up the target which is a silhouette figure with a rifle. Standard military pose. I aim, safety off. Ayanna talks through our comms and commands 'single fire'.

The gun discharges as expected, the kick-back a reassuring confirmation. I got a head shot. Glancing across to the other targets, I see a variety of hits. Jaz has shot the throat and Alex has gone for a heart shot. Jules is too far away for me to see. Another command hisses through my headphones.

"Take a few random shots, like head, arm, and legs to get the range and accuracy. When you are satisfied, then fire at will; empty this magazine and reload. Then, await instructions."

I position for a leg shot first. Ayanna shouts fire. We again discharge our weapons, the targets getting pummelled, shreds of material flying in all directions, the spent bullets clattering against the safety wall behind. I rotate around the target, first leg and then arms, followed by torso. I finish by blasting the head off completely.

The silence indicates that we have all succeeded in emptying our guns into the range. Ayanna congratulates us and asks us to reload. The targets are replaced and moved further away.

"What will happen now is that the lights will be dimmed and turned off randomly. The targets will be moved back and forth, so be prepared to fire aiming to disable, not kill. Take care where you shoot."

I'm liking the jeopardy introduced into this. I roll my shoulders and square up to the target. The lights go out. I'm surprised by the darkness. This is where my old suit with infrared via the face cover was so on point. I could see shapes and hot spots easily. I allow my eyes to adjust. The lights flicker on, and the target is further away. *Crack.* Leg shot. Lights out again. I blink. On again and now it's closer. Arm shot.

This happens five times and deciding where to shoot gets more complicated. Considering I haven't practised for so long, I think I've done pretty well. Ayanna tells us to put the safety on and return to the control booth. I spin round and find Jaz standing right behind me, staring.

"Shit Jaz! What are you doing?" The Glock is in her hand. I see the safety is still off. My instinct takes over and I flick out my foot, kicking her hand away and the loaded pistol. She winces at me, holding her bruised hand.

"Why did you do that? I was only coming to see how you had done." She gives me a pained expression.

"Well, that was a stupid way of doing it, facing me with a loaded weapon. You do realise that could have gone off?" I say, trying to keep my cool.

She turns and walks away, hiding a tear I suspect. I place the pistol on my lane table, safety back on, magazine released. I glance at the lads to make sure they are not wandering around with lethal weapons as toys. They, at least, are sensible.

"Well done everyone. You scored well on the placement and accuracy. Alex, you scored 59. Jules 63. Jazmin 56 and Maisie 71. Any score over 50 is commendable." I glance across to Alex who I guess will not be pleased that I whooped his ass. Ayanna scans our expressions and looks at Jaz, who has a face like thunder. "What's wrong Jazmin?"

"Maisie kicked my hand," she admits like a schoolgirl who's been in a scrap.

"Well, you did approach me with a loaded gun, you idiot." Sympathy has somewhat escaped me.

"Ayanna, it wasn't like that. I was only coming to see how she had done. Then she attacks me." I stare and shake my head.

"Safety is paramount Jazmin," Ayanna says. "The rules are in place so that no one gets hurt. Next time be more careful." She glances at me, pursing her lips. "Maisie - a word."

I saunter off behind Ayanna to an office adjacent to the control booth. She shuts the door.

"I know you are pent up regarding any threats but be mindful; these three are being placed in a dangerous operation where you must all trust each other. Treating Jaz like that will only cause tension."

"Yes…but, when someone is facing you with a gun, you don't have a lot of time to decide if it's a friendly chat or death, do you?" My patience is being stretched.

"Also, I am aware that you had a visitor." I quickly turn away, feeling a betrayal.

"What do you mean?"

"I have seen CCTV footage of you talking to a woman. I believe she was here on a training exercise. Also, what I find more worrying is that she appears on footage talking to Jazmin's mother. Would you like to enlighten me?" She gives that slit eyed stare.

"Hmm…yes. I know."

"What do you know?"

"I saw the footage as well…" She grimaces and then glares at me.

"How did you see that? It's a classified document!" The light dawns and she shakes her head. "You hacked into my login, didn't you? Maisie, you are going to be the death of me." I watch her face colour up.

"Well, I hope not. Look – Jaz wanted to know more about her mum's death and so we checked out the file. Why did you give a false story? You had to know she would find out eventually." She sighs heavily.

"We have intel which is unsettling. This woman, who I am informed is an SAS soldier, is meddling in MI6's affairs and we are not sure if she is for us or against us," she says with exasperation.

"She asked me to keep my conversation with her confidential – said it was crucial to keeping the operation safe."

"So, what did she want?"

"For me to be silent."

26 – VR

Ayanna gave up the interrogation after twenty minutes of grilling me. I wasn't going to say any more as I had the gut instinct that Sergeant Jane deserved anonymity. After all, I was curious how this whole operation was going to develop. Frustrated with the revelations that SAS combatants were likely to be involved in the operation, Ayanna told me to be guarded about any more contact with them.

After trying to convince her that I would, she took the team and me to a virtual reality session to be transported into a digital world around the operational location.

"Ok team, put on your headsets and we will take you for a tour of the site. It is a stately home, set in the countryside in the East Midlands." My heart jumps. That's where my safe house is, my dead parent's home, along with my AI computer, Anton.

"We will direct you through the servant's entrance, into the kitchens and then out into the main hall where the guests will be meandering and congregating."

We put on our VR headsets and stand expectantly. Alex and Jules seem the happiest about this, as most of their games are set in unreality anyway. Jaz is tottering around, seemingly feeling dizzy with the experience.

"This is making me feel sick," she gasps.

"Just let it settle. You'll get used to it," I say.

“Maybe like getting kicked,” she replies with venom.

“Well, don’t creep around with lethal weapons, you moron.”

“Girls! Be quiet, and put on your headphones and handsets,” Ayanna shouts. We obey and wait for the display.

The visual kicks in and we see virtual clones of ourselves. I laugh at the images as Alex looks like a girl and Jules a middle-aged man. Jaz has a jumpsuit on, ready for a workout. I wonder who I am? Spinning around I try to find a mirror. Instead, I catch a glimpse of my reflection in a suit of armour. *A Japanese tourist?*

“Where the hell did you get these avatars from?” I ask.

“Apologies. They are left over from another training session. You will just have to ignore them,” Ayanna says.

I can’t help myself and start sniggering, as Alex appears to dance around like a ballerina. Jules has a walking stick and staggers hesitantly, his avatar’s hair glistening white.

“What are you laughing at?” Alex asks.

“You! I think you would be great dressed like that for the real thing.” He strides towards me, but Jules puts out a virtual stick to stop him.

"Shall we concentrate on our surroundings?" he instructs. Ayanna appears in this ethereal world as herself (of course) and now directs us.

"Follow me and I will lead you through the rooms you will need to be familiar with."

The initial room disappears, and we now begin to wander past large iron gates, along a gravel path into the main house through a side door. This takes us into what appears to be a small cloak room. Another door opens and now invites us into the kitchen area. It has all the utensils you can imagine. The walls have old brass pots and pans hanging around, a shout back to the history of the place. Industrial cookers and wash areas are clean and gleaming. Knives are magnetised to the wall, beside fat fryers, and refrigerators.

"Plenty of useful weapons here," I say to myself.

"This is where the food is prepared and you will be taking the trays from here, through this corridor," Ayanna instructs.

We follow, making me wonder what we look like in the real world; probably staggering around like blind people. The corridor is inlaid with wooden panelling; paintings hang, along with inserts containing marble busts. All quite impressive. My virtual hands wander up to one of the statues and I get the eerie sensation of running my fingers over it.

Beyond this long, dark corridor, we enter a large banqueting room, with a stretched elongated table and elegant furnishings. The drapes around the windows hang like elaborate long dresses adorning a rather large aristocratic lady. Ayanna directs us to where the action will be.

"Through here you will be offering the guests hors d'oeuvres and drinks. As you were taught, this is the first contact you will have with the guests. We want you to be alert to any conversations and networking. Catherine and I will be acting as guests, so we will be observing, as well giving you backup. It will be imperative that you pay attention to our comms as there will be more than enough distraction."

I scan around the room, memorising the layout; windows and exits confirmed in case of a hasty retreat. I have been in too many situations where I had to adapt the plan to make a dash for safety. I doubt that the others have the common sense, nor the experience, so I'll have to be watching out for them too. Jaz bumps into me.

"Hey. Are you ok?" I ask.

"Yeah, just a bit woozy headed. I don't think these things really suit me." I sense she might throw up.

"Take a deep breath and calm yourself. You know how to do that, with all your yoga stuff."

"Hmm…you are right Maisie. I should, but my mind gets distracted when under pressure." That's for sure. I wave my hand around and eventually catch her arm.

"Here, walk with me. I can steady you."

As we walk the full length of this vast room, I notice something strange flickering in one of the corners. I blink, thinking that I'm starting to suffer the same nausea that Jaz is. *Am I getting a migraine?* It becomes quite distracting, and I pull on Jaz's arm.

"Hey. Do you see something over there? That flickering?" I ask her.

"No. What do you see?"

"It's like an image that comes and goes. Reminds me of that butler you used to get in the Tomb Raider games."

"I never played those sorts of games," Jaz says wistfully. I peer intently at the apparition. Letting go of Jaz, I wander over to check it out.

"Does anyone else see this weird thing over here?" I get a collective no, along with Alex taunting me, saying I am finally losing it. I hear a faint noise, followed by a voice.

Shaking my head, I think I *am* going crazy, as no one seems to be sharing this vision. I'm about to take off my headset when the voice becomes clearer.

"Maisie. Leave your headset on." My heart jumps through my head. I know that voice.

"*Mum!*" I nearly shout in excitement, but then realise that it can't be. She's dead.

"Maisie," it continues. "I have finally cleared all my data files and rebooted. I apologise that it has taken so long." *Anton*? Is this my AI buddy, my father created to be an assistant?

"Please keep this confidential between us, as it would not be prudent to reveal who I am at this establishment." *It is Anton*. But with my mother's voice!

"It would be best not to say anything as I will speak only. Now I am back online, I have had to make several adjustments while I am in the process of creating my communications channel to you." I stare at the avatar, which is now complete and appears to be an African male, dressed as a butler, with the voice of my mother, which is very confusing.

"As you can see, I look and sound strange. It is due to the deep clean I had to perform to rid myself of the hack from the man with no name." I nod. It brings back the dreadful memories of what happened in Versailles.

"Your watch will activate soon, and our lines of comms will be re-established. I trust you got my message about not trusting anyone, especially in this team?" Again, I nod. So, it *was* a message from him, posing as my mother.

"Good. You are involved in a mission which has the potential for great peril. I am not yet up to date with all that you may have been through, but I am reassured that you are still alive." Thanks, Anton. That gives me lots of comfort! Ayanna shouts across to me.

"What is it that you are seeing? I have some interference with the VR in that area of the room."

"Oh, it's ok. I think it must be a glitch in the Matrix," I say with typical sarcasm. She shakes her head.

"OK, let's remove the headsets and have a break."

One by one the avatars dissipate, leaving only my African butler. He smiles and waves.

"Be aware, Maisie. You are more integral to this mission than you realise." With that gem, he disappeared.

What? Why does he leave me with a puzzle? I am now left even more mystified as to what this is all about.

27 – PUNCH BAG

We are sitting in a semi-circle staring at a screen, Jaz shuffling around, distracting my pondering. *Anton is back!* But how did he manage to break into the VR show? His ability to hack into any security system is proving to be unrivalled. Now he is likely to be online again, I feel a sense of reassurance building. Finally, I am not alone in this mad world!

"So, as I have said, the operation is crucial to our ongoing security within NATO and the west in general," Catherine Short rambles on. "Your earpieces and tie cams will record every conversation within two metres. It will feed directly to our control room. Ayanna and I will be alerted to any movement of any illicit objects or files of interest which are to be recovered." She sits, a smug smile on her face. Strange how some people can smile without their eyes. Quite freaky.

"I am aware that operations can go south if unforeseen circumstances occur," Ayanna continues, giving me a secretive look. "If you suspect someone is acting strangely, you must report it immediately. This will give us time to react accordingly. Also, if the situation becomes too volatile, we will extract you as promptly as is feasible."

I glance at Jaz who has that look of mistrust. She must be brewing over the whole SAS connection with her mum's death. I hope she doesn't blurt it out, especially here. I kick her gently and distract her. She turns her glare to me.

"If you kick me again, I will rip your head off," she whispers. I frown and shake my head.

"Try that after I've trained you. Then we will see how much you've learnt," I spit.

"Jazmin and Maisie; do you have anything to share?" Ayanna asks. We straighten up and shake our heads.

"Nope…all good here," I say. Jaz nods and sighs deeply.

"Good. You can have the afternoon off," Ayanna adds.

"Or, if you want, a training session with Maisie; I'm sure she would be willing to take you on," Shorty interjects. I look around wondering if anyone *is* interested. Jules and Alex nod and Jaz cocks her head to one side.

"Now's the time Maisie G – let's see what you've got." Jaz's response sends a shiver down my back for some inexplicable reason.

"OK then. Let's do it."

We amble to the training rooms where I have done my solitary training since I've been at MI6. We get into comfortable clothing for the session and the three stand arms folded intently gazing at me. I am a little intimidated by this, especially as I was taught to be a ghost, anonymous in my life of despatching. Drawing attention to ourselves was something Olga would not tolerate.

"Maintain a low profile," echoes in my mind. Pushing that thought away, I explain what I will teach and what I expect from them.

"Jules; I suspect most of this will be second nature to you, being a black belt at Taekwondo?" Alex and Jaz turn their gaze to him.

"Man, you kept that quiet," Alex says.

"I knew you had something about you, Jules," Jaz says, her drippy eyes smiling. *More than you know,* I think.

"Yes. It is a skill I have not wanted to advertise. Purely for self-defence and protection," Jules sheepishly replies.

"Ok. Let's get the adrenaline going and we will do some stretches and then on to the punch bags," I say.

Twenty minutes later, we are nicely stretched out and stand in a row in front of the bags. I display some punches and kicks, making sure they understand the correct methods so as not to damage their wrists or ankles. Alex is up first and attacks the bag like a mad dog.

"Alex, slow down. Start slowly and then build. It's not going to bite you," I say. He pinches his nose and tries again. "Ok, that's more like it."

After a range of punches and kicks, one by one they assault the bag. Jules, as I thought, knew precisely what to do and finished with a flying reverse kick. Jaz however, hits with the strength of a sloth. Her movement is as slow as one climbing a tree.

"Come on Jaz, put some effort into it, girl." I'm resisting being too down on her. I know her emotions must be all over the place.

She positions again, with her arms raised and begins her comical jumping around. She launches into the bag, shocking us all with the sudden change in energy.

"That's it! Great, go for it, Jaz," I say with excitement. To say that a moment ago she looked like a wilted, soggy joss stick, the strength with which she attacks the bag is quite unbelievable.

Finishing with a flurry of punches and low kicks, she turns towards me purple and perspiring. Her eyes are raging, more than when she went berserk in our room. I sense we all shift on our heels as she walks past, expecting her hands to lash out.

"Well…that was…*interesting* Jaz. I think we should have a drink and then we can do some sparring." They all nod, and we find a space to sit and breathe.

"I get the feeling you had someone in mind when you were hitting that bag," I say, watching Jaz quietly fuming, saying nothing. "Alright, if you are on silent mode, that's fine. Just be controlled as we spar, or you might find yourself compromised and take a hit that you regret." She swigs water like we are in a western saloon bar and wipes her mouth across her arm.

"Maybe…maybe not," she replies.

I get the feeling that any one of us is going to be the punch bag in this arena. I prepare the guards on my stomach, and legs, with pads on my hands and select Jules first. I know he will be used to this sort of practice.

"Ok Jules. We will do a sequence of low kicks and then punches up to the midriff and then to the head. Try not to batter me." He nods and lines himself to my right.

He follows my instructions to the letter, and we present a perfect performance for the others to match.

"Alex, you can come next," I say.

"Great. Now I can show you what I can do to a squirt like you," he says. I grimace.

"Well, that's in the spirit of teamwork, isn't it?" I reply. He sniffs and runs his arm across his nose.

I know he is going to be rough from what he did with the bag, but his chaotic attack on me shows his faults and his clear misunderstanding of control under pressure.

"Alex, try to keep a pattern going. I don't want to hurt you by defending myself." He smirks and recoils for a second before launching into a range of punches.

My pads are beaten back, and I try to stand against the sheer force. I have to keep my position by leaning into his shots, which gives me an arm ache. He tries a shot over my guard to my head. I react and parry it away leaving his face wide open for a punch. For a split second I thought about not doing it. Then again, he might learn a lesson.

His legs buckle, his body staggering backwards. The blow from my right pad connected with his jaw. His eyes swam for a moment, not realising that he was in trouble. Falling to one side his dazed expression could be mistaken for a look of pleasure.

"I told you to be careful," I say, a little smug. Jules rushes over to him and helps him into a sitting position with his knees to his face.

"Here, have some water," Jules says.

"That was uncalled for," says Jaz.

"Better he learns here, than on the job. He was leaving himself wide open to several strike responses," I reply.

Jaz leans down to him and whispers into his ear. She looks up and gets herself ready. I notice a weird look in her eye, as if Alex's defeat has struck a nerve.

"OK Jaz. You have watched what Jules and I did; do you think you can copy?" She nods.

Starting slow, we go through the routine; with my encouragement she is reacting better than I expected. We continue with low kicks, reaching to the higher ones. To my surprise, she spins around and launches a high reverse kick to my head. I duck and straighten, wondering where she is going with this. Again, she sends a dummy shot to my stomach and spins again, this time catching my ear.

"Shit, Jaz! That was keen," I blurted out. She has an evil look creeping across her face and continues her silly prancing about.

"Too much for you, *MG?* Let's push it harder."

Without a second's breath, her punches come one after another. I get the feeling that these are aimed at me rather than the pads. An adrenaline rush floods my sight and I have to blink it away so I can now concentrate fully on this attack. Again and again, she presses me; high then low, dummy shots followed by opposite kicks. I don't know what is firing her up, but I know I have to be on point to keep on top of this.

I glance at Alex who is awake again and is smiling at my predicament. Did they have some sort of pact going on? Jules is standing to one side drinking as if he is watching a Sunday morning cricket match. Another spin and high kick crashes down on my shoulder. I need to bring this to an end.

Without thinking, I react and throw off my gloves and take a Jeet Kune Do stance and force my mindset to slow everything down. I watch in slow motion Jaz's jump and flying kick directed towards my torso. I sidestep and allow her to overshoot and direct a punch straight into her face. It didn't need a lot of force as I used her own momentum. Her groan is elongated along with the blood spray from her mouth, as she lands crumpled on the mat beside me.

I stand breathing heavily and try to make sense of what just happened. Everything speeds up and I kneel beside a broken Jaz.

"Oh Jaz…I'm so sorry. That all got out of hand," I say. She is sobbing quietly. I feel a rough hand on my shoulder. Alex pushes me to one side.

"Hey, Jaz. Are you ok?" He gives me a glare. "I knew you were a bitch. What did you do that for?"

"I had to stop her somehow. She was getting carried away." My explanation sounds hollower than it needed to be. Footsteps come in from the door and I see Catherine Short and Agent Delaware. She has a frown that would ensnare a crocodile and Delaware is fidgeting with his pen.

"What the hell is going on here?" she exhales sharply. "This is supposed to be a training session not a brawl." I step back and purse my lips.

"When you fight, the adrenaline can take over," I say. "It's difficult to keep under control, isn't that right Jules?" I look to him for some support. All I get is a weak nod. *Thanks.*

"Maybe this training you are giving is not working, Miss Greene. I suggest you go back to your quarters and rest. We have been informed that the operation is to be brought forward. We have one day to prepare." She scans the team with her slit eyes.

"Now is the time to prepare yourselves for your first operation. Make sure you are mentally and physically fit. We can't have any mishaps; is that understood?" She slaps her side, like she's about to gallop away on a horse.

"Yeah, and remember; your country relies on you," added Delaware.

No pressure then.

28 – BAD VIBES

The training in the gym has left its mark, not only on our arms and faces, but on our trust towards each other. I have not had any response from Jaz each time I try to chat with her. She sits nursing her split lip and keeps sighing. Alex and Jules have made themselves scarce as well. I need to talk. I wander off to find Ayanna.

This building is not as impressive as you might think. It's really like a glorified office block. After all, most of the work done here is shuffling files from one computer to another and communicating to agents around the world. Not that exciting.

I find Ayanna sitting at her desk, watching the gulls hovering outside her window on an unseen breeze. She turns and nearly knocks over her coffee, covered with a cooled scum.

"Oh Maisie; you creep about like a cat," she says.

"'Training I'm afraid. Ready to pounce before the victim knows what hits them." I raise my fingers in a feline way and hiss. "Have you a sec.?"

"Sure. What is it?"

"I'm really getting the jitters about this project, operation, or whatever…Can we go for a walk?" She nods and shuts down her computer.

"I need to get some air. There's a nice coffee shop over the Thames," I suggest.

We walk over Vauxhall Bridge, our coats billowing like sails in the stiff breeze. The same gulls seem to drift our way, as if they are on a surveillance mission.

At the coffee shop, Ayanna reminds me too much of Olga, as she settles down with her usual Arabica blend and pastry and stares at me.

"Ok, what are we talking about? Something that will reassure me that you are onside for this operation, I hope." I look across my coke, my lips skewing.

"The training session was a disaster," I admit. "I can't say that any of them appreciated it and I feel like I'm the odd one out."

"Well, you did smash two of their faces," she replies. "I know it seems contrary to what we are trying to do with you, but to be honest, I think it will have a good outcome." This comment forces me to frown.

"Really? Jaz is ignoring me, and Alex and Jules have gone walkabout. No one is communicating with me. How is that going to work out? Cooperation is what's required, and I seem to have shattered that."

"Don't beat yourself up; I know these kids better than you do."

"How well? Did you know that Jules, for instance, is *gay?*" I stare, wondering if that is crossing a line.

"Someone's sexuality is their own concern. Not for anyone to judge, Maisie."

"I'm not judging. But did you know that?" She nods.

"So, what about the cover up over Jaz's mum; why are you spinning that story? You know she knows." I continue to stare at her, trying to force a reaction. Her calm eyes give nothing away.

"What I am about to tell you…" she moves closer, checking side to side, "…is confidential. The communique that 'Trojan' was leaked to the wider security community, was diverted by Agent Delaware." She rests back on her seat, as if relieved to have unburdened herself.

I mirror her and sit back, thinking about what that really means. *If an agent from the CIA has blocked an important dossier, what reason could it be for?*

"Is he CIA?"

"Was."

"And now?"

"He is in a consultation position." Ayanna glances from side to side again, appearing to be uncomfortable.

"So, why is he interfering with official communiques which are confidential and crucial to world security?" I ask. She shrugs. "What does Shorty think of it?"

"She is unaware, as far as I know."

"Why haven't you said anything?"

"I am beginning to have my doubts about her too," she admits.

My thoughts go back to the archive incident when she was on her mobile phone.

"She was acting weird to be honest, when I sneaked into the archives and watched her scanning a level five security report." Ayanna winces.

"You can be a pain in butt at times, Maisie! How did you see that?" I explained. "Well … whoever she was talking to, must be in on a secretive operation that neither I, nor anyone else, has no prior knowledge of." Ayanna seems to retreat into deep thought and stares up at the ceiling. I slurp my drink.

"Have you a gut feeling about this mission, Maisie?" she finally asks.

"Only that it's laced with poison, and I'm concerned that we could all end up being dead." She glances to one side and sighs.

"If you can be upfront about this Sergeant Jane from the SAS, it would at least put me in the picture." I frown and wonder if this situation is becoming too complicated. Can I trust her?

"She…was wanting me to be tight lipped about her involvement because she also knew about the leak and had been alerted to the threat that this would pose to security. She said her role was to protect me." At this Ayanna tilts her head.

"From whom?"

"I dunno…the four apocalyptic horsemen, or whatever they call themselves."

"Bloody hell; I am now getting bad vibes about this like you," she says, her face screwing up.

"Good. I've been pissed off for being alone with that feeling," I say. She gives the faintest of smiles.

"Ok. Look, this is what we should do. I can set up a separate frequency to the radio mikes we will be using. Only you and I will be able to communicate, alongside the open channel the others will be using." Her face has changed to one of focused determination. "Keep this between us. If either of us see or hear anything that would jeopardise the mission, endanger any of the team, anything - then we abort, ok?" I nod.

"What happens to this item on auction if we do though? Isn't it so important that we can't fail to snatch it?"

"That's not your problem, Maisie. I am the chief operating officer of this mission. If it all goes wrong, it's on my head." I look at her and a well of sadness forms in my gut.

"You can't take the wrap for that, surely? Those in authority should be the ones."

"You would think so. But I have worked with these bureaucrats for so long, I see a different attitude. One of culpable deniability - that's what happens." I see pain flash across her eyes, an uncommon emotion for her. The usual unruffled calmness is melting like a chocolate egg in front of a furnace.

"If we have each other's back, then I am happy," I say.

"Yeah…maybe no one else has," she replies.

29 – FIRING UP

Our secretive chat has brought me to a dark place. My mind can only think of one hundred and one conspiracy theories, and I'm confused as to what my role in all of this is. Can Shorty and Delaware be in it for other covert reasons? How many agendas are at work here? I've got to get my mind straight and the only way I can cope with this turmoil is to go back to my training. I march back to the gym.

Stripping down to my black crop top and shorts I begin to go through my ritual. Breathing, stretching and then on to the rowing machine. This will at least bring me peace of mind and distract from my scepticism.

We only have one more day and then we are in the field, a live operation. I'm wondering who is coming out of this cauldron of crap – dead *or* alive. Ayanna has the weight of this op all to herself, especially if Catherine Short is scheming behind everyone's back. And what is Agent Delaware up to? Are they colluding for some reason?

I hit the weights and push up my usual limit of 100 lbs to 110. I must have the mentality to push harder and stronger if I need to draw from my experience. Pumping up helps release the endorphins, those natural kinds of highs, without any opiates. I push through a routine that lasts for an hour. Then into the shower. I briefly wonder if

I will get another visit from a creepy soldier. Maybe I'm just wishing it were a guy.

I've often wondered what having sex would be like. I would never let on that I'm a virgin as that would spark a flurry of ravenous males circling for a feed. Anyway, perhaps my strong persona effectively keeps any unwanted attention at bay.

I think of Freddie in Paris and want so much to contact him. I got the impression, though, that he was under strict orders from his ex-military dad that he should never cross my path again. But that is like a red rag to a bull. I am determined to hook up again, one way or another.

Finishing with a vigorous towelling down, I consider returning to the firing range. I must get my eye in and be ready. With Olga we did this at least once a week, to be ready for any unforeseen circumstances. Her training sort of created in me a robotic response to any threat. This has to be a positive in this situation. An attack could come from any angle.

The dispatches with Olga were simple, though. We would go in under cover, assess the situation with our pre-planning, and then dispatch and exit. *This* operation is messy. With no weapons at hand, it makes us all vulnerable. Also, the VR tour was too superficial; I needed a precise recon of the place. That's what Olga relied on me for. I'm good at it. Here, I'm relying on others who are dubious and potentially dangerous.

I check in with the firearms person and select a Heckler and Koch USP 9, with and without silencer. I want to feel the gun in my hands to let the kick back and power sink into my psyche, as I have a feeling, I will need this in case of an emergency. Not a weapon I have used in the field as Olga was the dispatcher; I was the cover, the backup, the *Talisman.* However, this time I need to be ready for whatever is thrown my way.

The targets roll forward and I request they be set at different distances, randomly selected. Also, fast moving. Rarely do your opponents stand still to be shot at. That only happens in movies, which I think is comical. They supply various people for collateral damage e.g., soldiers, police, citizens to fire at, as if it's a game. It's all for entertainment value, I guess. Real life does not give you the time nor the convenience of taking easy shots at people, and it's certainly not for fun.

I load and fire. This time I aim for headshots in the first round. I need to be sure that I'm accurate and deadly. The next magazine I load and fix the silencer. Again, the targets move back and forth, shifting side to side. The silencer has a different kick back. It stifles the gases, so it reacts differently.

So good to feel the heat and smell. It satisfies a deep longing and I had forgotten how much I enjoyed this. Another magazine empties and I assess how my aim was. I was disabling this time by firing at legs. No good to have an assailant running around, even if they have no weapon.

Next, it's the heart. *Crack, crack.* The target on the body gives you a rating as to the accuracy. I can see that mine is spot on. Ten is dead centre, but I'm aiming for the heart which on a body is not central, but slightly to the left of centre, behind the breastbone. This lowers my score but is accurate.

Satisfied that I'm as ready as I can be, I hand the equipment back to the attendant and wander back to my room, expecting Jaz to be still sulking. I smell the expected scent of Sandalwood wafting down the corridor. I poke my head around the door and put on a cheery face.

"How are you doing?" I ask.

No reply.

Not surprising, there was no one there.

I spin round and look down the corridor to where the lad's room is. I can hear chatter. It sounds quiet, repressed, secretive. I skirt along the wall as silently as possible, my Converse trainers sadly squeaking on the polished linoleum flooring.

Nearing the door, I lean into the wall, just enough to get an ear on the conversation. There seems to be some heated whispering going on. That annoying talking that usually happens when you are trying to get to sleep and someone is attempting not to wake you, but it pisses you off.

I hear Jaz speaking quickly and erratically for her, even more than normal. She sounds agitated. What are they talking about? Jules joins in. Seems like he's calming her down. Alex butts in and speaks too loud for the other two as they tell him to be quieter. I hear my name mentioned at least three times. Then Ayanna's. This is beginning to intrigue me, and I try to edge closer. There's a scuffling sound. A bag being opened, with a zip pulled.

I hear them jostling, passing something around and hear, *"be careful,"* and, *"make sure this is right."* Jaz tells Alex: *"it's your responsibility. Make sure it works."* Arrogant as ever, he gives a *"yep"* and Jules asks for whatever it is back.

Then, their movement indicates that they are about to break up this clandestine meeting, so I need to scram. I skip the other way down the corridor as if I'm returning from the canteen. Jaz and Alex come to the doorway and *embrace*! I'm shocked and can't believe what I'm witnessing. I dive into a cleaning storage area, taking me out of sight. I listen to the faint noise of lips pressing and kissing.

Wtf??

Jules comes out and scuttles off down the opposite way. I peep out and see he's carrying a holdall. There, next to our room, Alex and Jaz are embracing, his hands around her butt. *What the hell is going on?* Are they in a relationship? How many other things don't I know?

30 – FISHING

I've waited forever, surrounded by brooms, mops, and cleaning fluid containers, whilst this smooching session continues. Sitting on my haunches, I'm in shock to be honest. *Alex and Jaz are an item?* When did that happen? No wonder she was like a rabid dog in training. Alex, her boyfriend, was beaten by this other girl! I can't take any more surprises. And what was the secret meeting all about? Do I confront them, or let this play out?

"See you later," I hear Alex say. His shoes echo along the corridor indicating he is off in the opposite direction. I cautiously rise and peek around the corner. Jaz is waltzing into our room. I wait until she disappears and follow. I fiddle about anxiously, and I find a melted Snicker bar in my hoodie pocket and its contents ooze all over my hands. *Yuk!* But that'll do to get me through this light-headed feeling.

"Hi, Maisie. Had a good training session?" she asks, in an insincere girly voice. I resist smashing her face in.

"Yeah…it was good to fire myself up. I hope *you* are focused. Tomorrow, we go live. Your nerves better be under control." I lick the sticky chocolate off my fingers.

That expression, which until now I have assumed is dozy, drippy, and generally annoying, gives the slightest hint of deceit.

"Yep… I'm sure we will be ok. You have kicked my arse all over the place, so I feel toughened up." She gives a weak smile and turns to twiddling her smoking stick.

"You might find a few more surprises…*like me,*" I say, almost kicking myself for nearly giving away my own secretive spying.

"Oh, what are they?"

"As I have said before…adapt and live. I get the feeling that we are all going to have to do that."

"I suppose so. By the way, we are getting together for a prep talk with Short and Delaware tonight."

"Really? That will be entertaining." I stare across to her bedside cabinet. An array of clothes hangs out of the drawers, as if she is sorting them for packing.

"Are you going somewhere?" I ask, pointing.

"Oh, I'm just sorting through my stuff. I need a clear out. Might try a different wardrobe once this operation is over."

"Wow. More 'floaty' dresses and scrunches – how exciting." She glares at me. I am determined to provoke her. I'm not sure if she can hold her tongue or not. We will see.

"So, what has brought this on?"

"I dunno…just fancy a change. I think since my mum died, it has shaken me up to think that there's a big world out there, and I need to fly."

"Hmm…maybe by the seat of your pants, if that training was anything to go by."

"Let's see, *shall we?* I want to get away from this place when tomorrow is over. I've had enough of people bossing me around." She glances my way.

"You don't get it, do you? I have done my best to help you prepare for this operation. It's been hard not to squash any ambition you have, to be honest. MI6 are not the ones to help you." I sit cross legged on my bed, back against the corner. "You would do better behind a desk and do your GCHQ stuff." She shuffles a case from under her bed and lays it flat on her duvet.

"Maybe you are right. But I've learnt loads here and I'm looking forward to the rewards."

"Oh, what may they be?" I ask. She squirms giving away a hidden thought.

"I can't say…I don't know…something more, more satisfying."

"I get the feeling that you know, but you're not telling."

"That depends on how tomorrow goes," she says mysteriously. At this, I notice a wince, the smallest acknowledgement of a hidden agenda.

"Maisie. Just watch your back…like all of us. We are on the edge of something huge and none of us know how it's going to work out."

"See… that's what I'm after…an admission."

"Of what?"

"Guilt." Jaz's hand waves past a bottle of exotics smells and knocks it flying, emptying its contents over her case.

"Damn. Look what you have made me do."

"Not my doing…the hand that acts independent of the owner, leads to unforeseen consequences," I say, like some French philosopher. "Better watch *your* back, tomorrow."

This fishing session is over. I'm off to the canteen; Friday night special, cod and chips. That should get my body fit for a boring pre-op talk.

31- THREE MONKEYS

I'm sitting at the edge of the team, the others sat like the three emoji monkeys: see no evil, speak no evil and hear no evil. None of them are giving me eye contact. After what I half-heard in the corridor, I'm not surprised; I'm just angry. Jaz is chewing a rogue nail, Alex is snorting so much his nostrils are flexing like his abs and Jules is in a semi-meditative state, staring at thin air.

"This is it," Ayanna states. "We have the complete logistics for tomorrow. Catherine and I will be attending the gathering as guests. It has been confirmed it is a masked ball, so our identities will be at least under cover for the most part. However, this gives us a problem of recognition." She turns on a video. "Our intelligence gives us some help, as the conspirators are donning horse masks, believe it or not." I cough and neigh at the same time.

"Their cover represents, what we have discovered, is a group called the 'Four Horsemen'," Shorty continues. "Our intel confirms that they are interested in whatever the tech is on auction. If you can do your best to interact with these four, then our comms should pick up any relevant chatter."

I study the screen, noting the colour and shape of these masks. They are more gargoyle-like than horses. Memorable, all the same. I glance across to Ayanna who nods in confirmation that we are both in the know. The others look disinterested. Shorty carries on with her discourse, telling us that we too are to be masked.

I wonder what masks we will have. Marvel characters or War Hammer I would vote for, as the lads would feel like it's one of their games. Jaz, maybe the Scream mask, as she adores that. Me, I would want a plain old ninja mask. However, these would not suit the etiquette of the venue though, I guess.

"Your clothes for the waiter service are in the next room, along with your comms and masks, marked with your names," Ayanna says. "If you can ensure that you are smart and ready for five am in the morning. We have a few hours drive to the location." Jaz sighs and twiddles with her scrunchy.

"Any problem with the early start, Jazmin?" Shorty asks. Jaz shakes her head and sits more upright, although I notice a hesitancy in her body language. That's an abnormal response for her.

We pick up our masks which are the usual fancy, bejewelled masquerade types and wander through and collect our servant clothes. Isabelle is here, handing out our bow ties and neckties.

"The cameras are embedded in the ties and are remotely controlled so you don't have to do anything," she explains. "Here are the in-ear comm units. They will sit snugly in the ear and will again be activated remotely."

I fiddle about with mine and stick it in my left ear. Isabelle wafts a hand towards me. I instinctively catch it. She grimaces as my strong grip bends it back.

"Oh, sorry," I smile. "Instinct. Anyone coming in the hitting zone of my head..." She nods and requests that I unhand her. I release and walk away. Alex doesn't even chortle; his usual response. I give a hard stare forcing him to make eye contact. He purposely looks away. I spin round to see if I can spur Jules into action, but no - same response. What is wrong with them all?

"I suggest you try on your clothes tonight to ensure they fit and are comfortable. You will be wearing them for most of the day," Ayanna instructs.

We find different areas of the room to try on the said clothes. I change as quickly as I can. Undressing with others in the same place gives me insecurity as it has always been Olga and me and no one else.

The trousers and blouse fit beautifully, and the waist coat finishes off the look. The necktie fastens with a clip at the back, and I look at myself in one of the full-length mirrors supplied. The trousers are so well fitting they show off my butt nicely. Trouble is, I look like a Spanish guy ready to play some castanets and start dancing. The mask is green (which I thought was appropriate) and sits around my head with black elastic. One by one, we emerge like insects bursting from our winter cocoons.

Standing around, we check each other out and I make a mental note of who is wearing what mask. Jaz is red and silver; Jules is pink with gold and Alex is blue with silver. Mine being green, with a silver and gold pattern, has a certain flair. I hear a tut coming from one of the masks. I think it was Jaz.

"What?" I ask.

"Typical. You get the best one." It *was* Jaz.

"Well, red suits your face," I say. This has the makings of a scrap if I'm not careful. Ayanna interjects.

"They enhance your cover. No need to be petty, Jaz. They are serving a purpose. They also have the benefit that when we leave this operation, no one will be able to recognise you." She stares at Jaz, and I see her head droop with the reprimand.

“Ok. I suggest you all retire to your rooms and get a good night's sleep. The day will be taxing so I want you to be on point with what we are doing. Any questions?” asks Ayanna.

No one gives a whisper of an answer. I flinch as this is so weird it’s making my back crawl.

“What is wrong with you all?” I ask in frustration. Again nothing. “Ayanna…a word.”

We saunter off to a corner of the room.

“Look. What is it with these guys? I’m feeling edgy especially after the secret conversation they had.” Ayanna lowers her brows.

“What was that?”

"I heard them scheming something in the lad's room. They mentioned me and *you*." Ayanna glances across to where the three have congregated.

"I will try to get it out of them. Please don't jump to conclusions." She wanders off to the group. I watch with interest to see what reaction she gets.

They chat and Jaz glances my way for a second. I give a faux wave and smile. She then returns to her ignoring-me mode. Ayanna walks away, shaking her head.

"You don't need to worry. They say that because it's coming up to your birthday, they are going to surprise you with something." I nearly choke with laughter.

"Hmm…that is unlikely, as it's nowhere near my birthday." Ayanna frowns and runs a check on her tablet. She must have some sort of data file on me.

"Yeah…it is a bit odd. I'll make sure they tell me everything, so we aren't second guessing what they are up to." She moves away to find them, but like the shifting mist on a Scottish Loch, they have disappeared.

32 -LAST NIGHT

I wander back to the dorm with a strange feeling that tonight is not going to be restful. With Ayanna failing to get the full picture from the three, I am uncertain what to expect. Surprisingly, I find no scent of eastern promise wafting down the corridor, so I wonder if Jaz is there or not. I poke my head around the door frame.

"Oh…you are here. I am shocked that no joss sticks are smouldering."

"Well…it's going to be a rough night's sleep if you are coughing and complaining, so I thought I'd not bother." That is another surprise. Jaz has sacrificed her smoking and grounding habit.

"Ok, I am grateful for that. *Are you ok?* I get the vibe that you are all planning something." I'm not letting this go.

"Look; I'm cheesed off with this place and once this operation has finished, I'm going away. I haven't told Ayanna yet but I'm trying to keep a lid on my feelings." She gives her drippy look with a tinge of angst.

"I see…do you think you could enlighten me over the secret meeting you had with the lads? I'm intrigued." I stare hard at her. I'm not going to make this easy for her. She twitches and rolls her shoulders, moving away to pack clothes into her suitcase.

"That's private," she finally admits.

"What is it you have in that holdall?"

"What holdall?" Her movements become more erratic.

"The one that Jules marched off with?" Again, she gives signs of escaping the question.

"Just something…"

"What, Jaz? Does it have anything to do with me?"

"Not really…it's an insurance policy…of sorts."

"Against…?"

"Things going wrong tomorrow."

"Why aren't you telling Ayanna about it? She oversees this operation and needs to know everything that could jeopardise or surprise us." I feel my face becoming redder as we speak.

"It's…it's something that Catherine has asked us to do."

I stare at her face, her admission distorting it.

"What the f***! How come she has got the three of you to prepare something that the agent who is in charge knows nothing about?" I am about to explode. Jaz now collapses on her bed, her shoulders bobbing up and down.

"Jaz. Surely you understand that this seems odd." Jaz is now in full sob mode.

"I can't tell you…or anyone…it's too dangerous…to my family," she blubbers.

"What? How come it has anything to do with your family? Are they coercing you into this?" She nods reluctantly.

"Bloody MI6! I knew we couldn't trust them. So, can you tell me what they're forcing you to do?" She shakes her head madly.

"No…no I can't. You don't understand, telling you this has put my family at risk, even now." I hesitate to ask any more as I see that Jaz is slipping into despair.

"Ok…ok I get it. But will it create extra danger to all of us?"

"Only…*you.*"

Wow, that's reassuring. I sink onto my own bed and try to work out how much danger I could be in.

"Is Catherine going to do something, besides obtaining this data thing?" She is again reluctant to say anything else. I try to calm myself and breathe deeply.

"Ok. I'm not going to quiz you anymore. This really gives me the creeps, to be honest. I have to trust you all to watch my back. But this means I have to watch my own." I think over what Jules said: *'Heed the warning, Maisie. Heed the warning.'*

"I'm sorry," Jaz finally says and pulls up her duvet like a security blanket. "We have no choice."

I twitch with the implications of what she has said. The words of everyone who has warned me about this operation to trust no one, is echoing in my head so loud, I am needing some pain killers.

***

I decide to go for a walk to calm my thoughts. I'm considering going for a workout, but that will only stoke up my emotions even more. This is such a can of worms, an operation with so many landmines, any misjudgement will explode in my face. Should I see Ayanna? Should I send a message to Sergeant Jane? Shorty and Delaware are proving to be the unknowns in this tangle of mistrust, and we are on the verge of something so volatile, it's not just me that could be in danger, it's the rest of the world.

This is heavy shit.

I wander the corridors, the lights dimmed, shadowing a few officers who are working late into the night, probably checking up on foreign agents. The late-night vigil goes on 24-7. No one rests here, completely. National security must be maintained at all costs, and that with the alert late night staff of MI6.

I'm still limited as to which floor I can go to, so I check out the canteen and grab a coke. Not the best bedtime drink I should be having; gives me wind at the best of times.

There are random staff members scattered around, some bleary eyed, others in small groups planning the next mission into Africa or Asia, for all I know. Switching off from the hubbub in my solitary place, it gives me time to reflect over this experience at MI6. Has it been any good for me? I am not sure. The only good thing that I have enjoyed is having a friend in Ayanna, my sister-substitute, whom I still consider has integrity.

The main thing that bothers me is that if my parents were being investigated or undermined, then I am really no further in finding that out. Only that some people couldn't trust them. That still stings and I hope to find peace of mind when they are exonerated one day.

I fiddle with the ring pull which pings as I let go and flick it. What's this 'insurance policy', as Jaz calls it? Why would Catherine be threatening the team to act against Ayanna and me? It smells of a set-up, a cesspool of bullshit. Emptying the can, I throw it with satisfying accuracy into the trash. I want to see Ayanna, but she will be long gone home. I am not sure that the guards will let me out alone. What about the pen that Jane passed to me? It's fixed in a book that Jaz lent me.

I have to warn her.

That gives me determination to get her on board, so I march back to the dorm with renewed purpose. I must watch my back. The light is still on so Jaz must be awake. I peer around the open door. All I see is a lump in the duvet. She must have dozed off, hopefully full of regret over what was hanging over her and the lads. I carefully slide the book over and pull out the pen. Along with my phone, I skip out to the corridor. Intrigued to see if the lads are still awake, I stop by their door.

No sound and no light.

Regret doesn't seem to stop them sleeping either. I continue towards a quiet area, where staff chill out and read the latest novel or magazine that's made old style with paper rather than on a tablet or computer.

Sergeant Jane's pen looks like an ordinary Sharpie. I pull the lid off and instead of a writing tip, there is a button. I press it. The writing on the side illuminates with a blue flashing. Bluetooth, I'm guessing. I pare my phone and wait. A low beep confirms it's linked, and I type my message.

"Ayanna knows you are involved in the auction. Catherine Short and Agent Delaware are scheming something. The team is preparing for the event to blow up in our faces. Jaz tells me that they have an 'insurance policy' and it refers to me! Not sure what to believe anymore. Thought you should know. Maisie G."

I hope this gets to her. I send. Then it occurs to me that she was seen with Jaz's mum. Should I ask her for an explanation? She said this messaging was only one way, so I wouldn't get a reply, anyway.

More people drift past me, and I feel twitchy. This stress is making me sweaty and uncomfortable. Time to get some sleep. This could be my last night.

33 - EARLY START

My alarm alerts me that 4:30am has arrived and my head is thick with sleep. Wearily, I glance across to Jaz's bed and see she is well buried in her duvet. Kicking off my bedding, I roll to land on my feet. I throw a Converse at her. A muffled yelp is the reply.

"Hey! Sleepy butt: time to get ready," I say with a ruttle in my throat. She turns, one eye closed and the other not focused.

"Aww…can I sleep another hour?"

"No, you can't. We must be dressed, standing by the exit at five."

"Oh no…" she turns to hug her pillow.

I can't wait for her, so I get showered and tie my ponytail into a tighter French twist. The waiter get-up is slick and figure-hugging. Must be because all my blood has sunk into my legs and thighs while sleeping. I shake myself. A few stretchers and warm up exercises wake me. Jaz has finally dragged herself out of her bed and returns from showering looking like a rat emerging from a swamp.

"Come on, we have five minutes. Shorty will be giving us the tenth degree if we don't look on point." Jaz moves as if dumb bells are holding her down.

"Ok…ok, I'm getting there."

Six minutes later and we are standing in the twilight of the morning, the sunlight barely brushing the treetops with a golden glow. The lads have prepared incredibly well. Jules must have pushed Alex hard to get him here on time. Ayanna has that princess look, with her signature red lipstick, her hair tamed into cornrows, with beads. I can't help but stare at the complexity.

"How did you have time to do that?" I ask.

"Practice and dedication," she replies with a grin. "Ok everyone," she continues. "A minibus will take you to the location. You will be checked in as part of the catering staff. Be careful when you interact with others in the kitchen. We don't know if any of them are potential combatants. Do your job well and respectfully and avoid attracting attention to yourselves." She gave me a glance. I tilt my head and shrug.

Shorty strides across. Her hair is in a tight bun, with her usual two-piece suit affair, now in a pea green. Makes her face look paler than normal, as if she is about to throw up.

"Team. You are now entering the world of espionage. I wish you well with the operation. Agent Bolt and I will arrive in separate vehicles. Once we are settled in, your comms will be tested. As this is an evolving operation, pay attention to how we direct you. There are many unknowns at play." I look away and nod to myself.

"I have every confidence that it will be a success," Ayanna says, as a black Mercedes minibus pulls alongside us. We pile in and I notice that Jules deposits the mysterious holdall through the back door making me flinch.

Sitting in silence, we spread out across the seats, each having a row to ourselves. I press in my ear pods and select an upbeat playlist. I find this gives me that 'game on' feeling and gets me focused for action. 'Dark and Stormy' is the title, a mix of heavy dance, rock and alternative. Settling into my seat, I switch off all the conflicting thoughts that have invaded so much of my thinking recently. This is real, and I have to be prepared for anything.

Ayanna has taken our phones, as she doesn't want any distractions. My watch was allowed, which I am relieved about; I can still play music. Also, I am expecting Anton, my AI computer, to contact me anytime. He seems to be taking far too long getting his act together, I think. So, I allow myself to drift, as this is a two- and a-bit hours' drive.

***

The journey skims through the English countryside via motorways and dual carriageways, until we meet the windy roads I remember so well. Driving this way last year, I found that my parents had a house hidden in the Peak District. It was a pleasant surprise, but also shocking. Olga had kept this secret all my life. To find that I had family living nearby broke my heart. The chance meeting with my grandmother produces a warm comforting memory. I smile to myself. One day I will introduce who I really am; I hope it doesn't kill her.

"Ok team," Shorty declares. "We are nearing the location. Ayanna and I will be on the guest list, so will arrive and mingle. Make sure you check in with the administrator at the side door for all catering staff. You will need these." She hands out lanyards. They only show a barcode. No names. The catering business we belong to is apparently KWS - 'Kings Waitering Services'. Very royalist.

"These will gain you entry into the kitchen area. There you will wait until the call comes through for you to distribute drinks and the snacks. As soon as we arrive, we will check in with you. Make sure that your earpieces are fitted correctly. We will check that the comms are working once we are in the building. The cameras will be primed by our logistics personnel at MI6. They will be monitoring the situation, along with Agent Delaware."

We pull into a service station and Ayanna and Shorty get off the bus taking their gown clothes bags, along with any other accessories they need. I feel a lump forming in my throat. Not that I'm scared, but that kick of adrenaline I get before I engage with a mission or dispatch. I glance at Jaz. She is staring at the back of the seat in front of her.

"Hey," I say. "I really want to look after you today. You do realise that I have to be on point with whatever is thrown at me, though. If you get in the way, I can't guarantee your safety," I whisper.

She turns her head, without looking at me. Pursing her lips, she reluctantly nods. Alex gets up and walks towards me. I pull back and squint as the sunlight reflects off the window.

"Maisie…" He hesitates. "You and I got off to a bad start. I'm sorry that we did that. I get carried away with wanting to be the best. Your kick ass lifestyle made me jealous, I guess." I'm pushing myself back into the seat as I'm shocked by his admission.

"What's got into you, Alex? Have you been possessed by another person?" I ask. He smirks.

"Yeah, you could say that. I'm not usually that arrogant, really. But I needed to say that, before all this kicks off." He nods and wanders back to his seat.

I shake my head. Was this a dream? Alex is admitting his guilt. I can't take it in. Why is he saying that now? It's almost like he needed to get it out before we die or something. I turn around and try to get Jules' eye. He nods and smiles. This is confusing me. Are these dudes ok after all? I sit back and stare vacantly out of the window.

34 - STATELY HOME

My thoughts are swimming in a sea of uncertainty as we swing into a driveway with an ancient tree acting as a sentinel to the main gates. They are made of iron, blackened by years of painting and age. The minibus halts. Guards move in unison from the stone pillars either side and ask the driver for ID and who is aboard. They are heavily armed with submachine guns, Heckler and Koch MP5K.

He is given permission to pass as my stomach aches, a sign of some building anxiety. We wind along a dark drive, dense with shrubs and trees either side, up and over a small hill, down deeper into the estate, meeting a river, traversed by a bridge of sandstone. We get our first sighting of the house we are to operate in.

It has that ominous air of antiquity, with one half in ruins. Looks like part of it was an abbey before one of Britain's kings decided to divorce his wife and destroyed all the buildings that represented anything to do with stopping him. A lake flanks us to the right, with a large waterfall cascading down to another adjacent road. The minibus swings in front of the main building, making my heart miss a beat as the tyres crunch on gravel and brakes squeal.

The driver presses a button, and the door opens with ease. I am the first to get off and I straighten my waistcoat, rearranging my blouse as it's all scrunched up around my bum. I carefully check my earpiece is in place. Jaz is next, followed by Alex and Jules. I have an unexpected feeling of vulnerability and my heart races. Here we are, in an isolated location, with no backup and no supervisors. I hope that the others don't screw this up.

A young man dressed in a dark suit walks across to us and directs us to an arched wooden door. I glance around so I can get some sort of idea of the outside. I never know if that could be crucial later. The driveway sweeps around the front of the building leading to a side road. Not sure where that goes. The road by the waterfall disappears off into more woodland.

The house is made from the same sandstone as the bridge, and glows in the early morning sunlight. It is three stories high, with numerous leaded windows, the main house built in a 'L' shape. A stone balustrade runs along the roof, a tower fixed in the centre.

Following the man, we walk through the arched doorway, a guard with the same firearm standing beside it. These guards have standard clothing for a battalion of soldiers; fatigues and helmets. No recognisable markings anywhere. Anonymous. No allegiance on display, so Sergeant Jane should feel right at home here.

We are led to a desk with a bespectacled clerk sitting with a screwed-up face. She must have been sucking a lemon or noticed a nasty smell emanating from someone. She scans our lanyards.

"KWS stewards to the left please. Wait in the kitchen area until you are required," she says without any expression. I give her a good long stare. I am wondering if she would be someone I will have to deal with later or would she run a mile if all hell broke loose. She stares back with that look of superiority that is meant to put me in my place. *That doesn't work with me, lady.*

We walk like penguins through a familiar corridor that the VR sequence played to us, and I run my fingers along the real busts in the cavities.

"Please don't touch the exhibits," a voice from behind commands. I look round and see a middle-aged balding man, dressed in a brown tweed suit. His face gives me the impression he has had one too many drinks, being red faced and blotchy. I can't help but flick my finger across the next one. It prompts another grumpy noise. Jaz walks next to me and shakes her head. I assume she knows full well that my childish behaviour is not a good idea.

The kitchen opens before us, larger than I expected. The roof timbers reach high, vaulted up into the ceiling, like a church. It's airy and spacious. Brass cooking pots are pinned to the walls, representing opulent times of the gentry. They hang mocking the modern cookers and utensils beneath their watchful gaze.

The scent of baking and frying indicates that the cooking is underway and makes my mouth water. Kitchen heat forces perspiration to break out across my brow. I wipe it away, careful not to stain my sleeve. We are told to wait by a table where the silverware sits awaiting the food and drinks. Obediently holding our masks, we line up along a wall.

Alex brushes up against the sandstone, a smudge of rock dust smearing his back. He reaches over his shoulder to brush it off, without any luck. Realising his mistake, Jaz takes over and bats him down. I notice their eyes drift to each other, confirming their fondness, as they simultaneously smile. She rearranges his waistcoat and adjusts his tie. She will be jumping on him next.

"Easy tiger - no time for romance here," I whisper.

Jaz glares at me. Alex chortles for the first time in ages, with Jules lifting a finger to his lips. He is right, of course. We must act as ghosts in our role, and not attract unnecessary attention. However, the kitchen staff seem oblivious. They are too busy scooting around in a steam haze. Pastry, with a variety of fillers for these hors d'oeuvres, are manically baked and cooked. Such a mix of smells is making my stomach growl. Jules raises his eyebrows.

"Sorry…I should have had some breakfast," I say. He nods in agreement.

I take in the room, making a mental note of all the exits and any useful tools of the trade. Metal pots and pans, along with knives and hot surfaces are all useful in an emergency. They can be adapted from creating a delicate cuisine to slicing off an assailant's head. The kitchen area can be such a toxic mix of deadly components. I'm distracted, as we are asked to take drinks and welcome the arriving guests.

Masks on.

First contact.

This will be interesting.

35 - NUMBERS

We load our silver trays with a variety of glasses, containing pre-poured champagne, fruit juice, and cocktails. Jules leads the way. He has the presence and posture that we all should copy. Alex, however, still has handling difficulties and stumbles down the steps as he attempts to follow.

"Slow down," I say. "It's not a race. Take your time. You are not in competition with me now." He steadies his hands and nods. It seems this change in his character is more than temporary, as he falls into line and controls his impatience.

Walking carefully along the corridor, it opens out into a waiting area, bit like a huge cloak room, where the guests are entering through another arched doorway, but three times the size of the one we used. Probably a demonstration of the divide between the aristocracy and the servants.

Other stewards take coats, depositing them in a storage area, making note of their owners' numbers. No names here, as each person is offered a numbered token. All who enter are already masked.

A woman takes a drink of champagne from my tray and requests where to go next. I have to think back to the VR and glance around the hall.

"I believe it's this way madam," I say. She nods.

"I hear a hint of a foreign accent," she says. I am surprised she was so on point.

"You have a fine ear. I am part French, madam." I lied.

"More of an Eastern European accent, I believe." A well of anxiety wells up in my chest. This woman is too keen.

"I have a mixed heritage," I explain.

She nods and walks off. Phew, that was close. The man who was with her accepts a drink from Jaz and follows like a well-trained dog.

We keep our trays steady like statues with more guests arriving. I have counted about twenty so far. I glance across to Alex and Jules who stand out like bookends being more than six feet tall. I whisper to Jules encouraging them to stand apart as they could be too much of a focal point as people come in. I hear a crackle in the earpiece. It must be activating. A voice echoes in my head. It's Ayanna.

"Team. We are about to enter the house. Your cams and comms are activated. Well done so far. We can see and hear clearly. Keep it up." Nice pep talk. A bleep follows her chat and I hear her again.

"Maisie. This frequency is only for us. You will hear that sound each time I switch. Acknowledge by asking someone if they need the toilet." *What?* Ok. I pick on the nearest person.

"Excuse me; if you need the restroom, it is over there," I point, and the guest nods and takes a drink.

"Very good Maisie. I see that you are good at this."

"I can adapt," I whisper.

"Ok. I'm switching back." The sound changes as it reverts to the team comms.

"We are entering the hall separately," Shorty says. "We will be wearing our masks, but we will confirm contact when it's safe."

The stream of guests is gathering pace, with us having to refresh our trays several times. With practice, we all seem to be relaxing into our role. Jules and Alex standing so tall, attract most of the women, while Jaz and I are busy around those who act disorientated.

"Could you suggest a drink for a delicate stomach," one woman asks.

"I believe the gin, tequila and non-grain vodkas are better suited to a sensitive stomach," I say.

"Oh, that is most informative, dear. Thank you." She takes a juice instead. I raise my brows. No pleasing some people. I thought that sounded genuine too.

"Ok," Ayanna says. "The guests are congregating in the main room where the auction is going to take place. Catherine and I will be circulating. No sign of the four yet."

"Roger that," I hear Alex say.

"You don't have to say stupid things like that," I snapped, whispering into my hand.

"Yes, better to say very little," Shorty concludes.

We carry a fresh supply of drinks and follow remnants of the guests through to the main room. I watch the others wandering around looking for those whose glass is empty, offering a replacement. The earpiece bleeps. Ayanna is back on.

"Maisie. We have intel that a helicopter is about to land on the lawned area in front of the house. I suggest you work your way towards the door and greet whoever is joining us. Could be our marks." I confirm by coughing a *'yes'*.

Leaving the crowd, I wander back to the entrance hall. I hear the noise of rotor blades nearing the building. From that deep throaty sound, I can tell it's not a regular ride. I get eyes on the landing through a small window to the side of the oak door. Another staff member strides to the door, almost shooing me away. I resist the reaction to hit them with my tray.

The sound of the helicopter is deafening as the door opens, the updraft blowing leaves and other rubbish in. Another person scurries around clearing up the mess with a broom and dustpan. I keep my vision clear of obstructions and watch as a party of people disembark. I am shocked to see that it is no average helicopter. It's a Chinook. Army type personnel carrier.

These are used by the military, RAF and the like for special missions. I know they can carry up to 44 troops along with supplies, weapons, and ammunition. Behind the guests, a group of special force soldiers follow and create a perimeter around the helicopter. Wow! This is not what I expected. Ayanna bleeps again.

"What are you seeing? Sounds huge!"

"Yeah, a Chinook with a battle group on it," I say.

"What the hell?"

"I know. What the hell have we got into?"

"Watch yourself. These must be the people who have the items for auction. Can you spot any cases?" I glance around, trying not to appear interested as others are busying around the door.

"Yeah. Two cases are being carried in. They are chained to the carriers." I hear a crackle in the earpiece.

"Excuse me." A guest has crept up behind me. *I've got to be more careful.*

"Yes, sorry. How can I help?"

"Maisie - it's Jane," she whispers. I glance around making sure no one is within hearing distance.

"Oh…I wondered when you would appear."

"I got your message. We have intel that someone in MI6 is about to sabotage this event and obtain this item of interest. Watch your back. Now I know who you are, I can support you." If my face was visible, she would see a grimace. This conversation is being relayed *to MI6.*

"MI6 knows someone is here from the SAS but has no ID on you…and… this conversation is being patched through to them as we speak…*sorry.*" Jane slaps her hand on a window ledge.

"Now they will have recorded my voice too, *damn*."

"Look…if we are in this together, why is that a problem?"

"Some consider me a rogue soldier, with a disaffected unit." She glances back and forth as if weighing up exits. "I am going to make myself scarce. I don't want one of your people taking me down." She turns and marches towards a door, away from the main hall.

Confused by this new revelation, I turn back to the main entrance as the helicopter guests stride through. Instantly I recognise the face masks.

They are the four horsemen.

36 - FOUR HORSEMEN

Stumbling back over someone who was cleaning up the mess the whirlwind had created, I compose myself and ask if they would like a drink. The shorter of the four replies with a raspy accent - Northern Irish, I reckon.

"You can get me a champagne darlin'. The rest of the crew can have juice," the woman commands.

From the tone of her voice, I can sense that she is the chief. I remember Shorty giving a look of disgust when describing this person; *Moiran Cafferty*.

I recall their other names: *Erin Bogslava, a Slovakian; Henri Fontaine, a French national.* Ok, so I'm no mathematician, but that is only three; so, who is the fourth? There are obviously four people there, two men and two women, but I can't be certain, as they are dressed in trousers and a variety of patterned waistcoats. One has a top knot, dark hair; another has blond hair in a ponytail; the last has shaved hair at the sides with a coloured chevron streak running from front to back. The Northern Irish woman has bright ginger hair in dreads. I think without the masks they would look scary enough. On the nape of each neck, I see a tattoo - *a horse with a thistle!*

A prickly sensation rises up my back as I turn to refresh my tray and grab the requested drinks. I return a little out of breath, sweat forming under my pits.

"Thanks darlin'. Now where would the auction be?" I point. They nod and take their drinks with them. I quickly alert the rest of the team.

"The four horsemen have arrived," I say.

Without any warning, I get an earful of hissing and crackling nearly forcing me to take out the earpiece. *Ow. What was that?*

"Hello," I whisper. No reply. *Has comms gone off?* I tried again, with no answer. Great! I will have to find them. Walking through the gathering, I pick out Alex and Jules easily. I can see they too are glancing about, confirming theirs are off too. Where is Jaz? I have been so busy I have lost all contact with her. I continue to wander between the guests. Still no sign of her. I sidle up to Jules.

"Have you seen Jaz?" I ask.

"No. I thought she was with you. Have the comms gone off?" Jules asks.

"Looks like it. Do you know where Ayanna and Shorty are?" I ask.

"They are the ones over there, by the suit of armour."

I glance that way and see that Shorty is conspicuous because of her height and making it look like she is scratching her ear. Ayanna is drifting away from her, walking back to the kitchens. I follow, catching up with her in the corridor. Touching her shoulder, I was trying not to freak her out. It didn't work. She yelps.

"It's only me," I say, trying not to snigger.

"Bloody hell, Maisie," she says. "You and your sneaking around. The comms have gone off. Looks like someone is using a jamming device." She looks around. Anxiety is probably racing across her face hidden under that mask.

"We are blind, so I must rethink how we proceed."

"Did you hear that the four are here?"

"No, I didn't get that."

"I've ID'd Moiran Cafferty, I reckon. The others, I can't be sure, only that they all have horse and thistle tattoos on their necks."

"Oh, that's convenient. Makes tracking them easier."

"If these are the ones you showed us, then who is the fourth person? There were only three in the briefing." Ayanna raises her hand to her mouth.

"That is what we need to find out." *Obviously…*

"And …did you hear my chat with Jane?"

"No. She is here as well?"

"Yep…but that will be a relief to her."

"Why is that?"

"Something about being disaffected; rogue soldier."

"Oh great…that's all we need. I hope she keeps out of the way. So, we will have to work closer than before. I will go and let Catherine know. Be careful. If they have prepared like this, then we might have more surprises." She squeezes my arm and walks back to the main hall.

Alex and Jules pass her, and they have a brief chat. They continue towards me, and we head back to the kitchen.

"So, we are blind and deaf," Alex says.

"Yeah...have to use our spider senses now," I reply.

"So, do you know where Jaz is?" asks Alex.

"No, none of us do. I'm worried she may have had a panic attack and hidden somewhere," I say.

"She's stronger than that," Alex states. His affection for her is overriding the obvious.

"Well, now these four horsemen are here, we have to be on point with what happens. We will have to stick close to Ayanna to get our instructions," I say.

"So do we carry on taking drinks around?" asks Jules.

"Yep, just mingle and get as close to the marks without drawing any attention to ourselves," I reply.

We wander back, with replenished trays and circulate, asking if the guests want a refill. The room is full of people and the level of chatter is increasing as it tends to when everyone is trying to talk at once. I slip in between two women who are dressed in shimmering satin robes, coloured in a rather gaudy rainbow pattern.

"Any more drinks?" I ask.

"Not for me; what about you, number 66?" The woman sniggers. A number instead of a name amuses her.

"Oh, that would be wonderful. Champagne - the delight of the soul," number 66 replies. She takes it from my tray, her head tilting forward, so her eyes can see over the ill-fitting mask.

"I do believe you are one of the prettiest waiters I have come across," she continues. "Maybe we can meet up after this event." I catch sight of her winking.

"No thanks. I'm quite happy being this far away from you," I answer curtly. She pulls back, almost spilling her drink.

I slip away with as much speed as the tray allows. I have to find the four horsemen.

This phrase is beginning to grate, as they are not men but a mixture of women and men. Sometimes the modern day wokeness becomes a pain in the butt when using old fashioned terms.

I sway between the crowds, now well over a hundred people. From the mix of accents, I wonder if this auction has attracted a worldwide audience. I hear that Northern Irish accent again and zone in on it.

"Make sure that you have prepared the finale, Henri," I hear her say.

"Of course," I hear the French voice reply. Now I know who that is. He has the blonde hair. Another one speaks. This time it's the Slovakian, Erin Bogslava.

"This has more participants than we expected. Will be fun!" she says. Her head has the shaved sides and colour. From what Shorty said, she looks far younger than she is, having a kill rate that would rival Olga's. I will have to watch out for her. Still the unknown one has not said anything. I make an approach.

"Would you like a drink?" I ask. The person lifts a hand and wafts me away. *Rude.*

"I think that means no, darlin'," Cafferty replies. I nod and walk past them. Perhaps they can't talk. A mute? Or maybe protecting their identity?

I continued to Ayanna, who was sipping her drink, bathed in the sunlight from a stained-glass window, sitting on the wide window ledge. The split dress reveals her smooth dark legs. I nod. She nods in reply.

"I have ID'd the two other marks. The blonde one is Henri, and the coloured hair is Erin. They said something about a finale… Still no idea who the other one is. Didn't even offer a chat." Ayanna moves in closer.

"Well done. Alex and Jules are circulating with food, so go and fill up. Have you seen Jaz? I have lost contact with her." I shake my head.

"I'm worried she might be in panic mode," I say. "She disappeared just before the four came in."

"Try and find her. I don't want her causing any distraction."

"Ok."

I wander back to the kitchens, brushing past the four, hoping to catch another morsel of information. The fourth one, turns his back on me as I approach. I assume that he is very unhappy about anyone getting too close or finding anything about them.

This one is a mystery.

37 - DUST TO DUST

I arrive at the kitchen with a buzz of activity as staff are racing around baking pastry and filling the side dishes, ready for us to take around. Without anyone seeing, I snatch a few snacks and stuff them in my mouth. I nod to a young man with his head covering tilted to one side. He has the appearance of a sailor having been on one too many binge sessions.

Suddenly I'm less hungry. Sweat is dripping off his forehead directly onto the food making me gag. I can do without that. Glancing away, I turn my attention to the rest of the kitchen commotion and find it almost therapeutic. The busyness of others can have a calming effect on me; quite strange.

My thoughts start to drift, and Jaz's absence begins to gnaw at me. I skirt the outside of the kitchen, making sure she isn't hidden away in any recess. Nope. Not here. I walk through a constricted corridor with a stone staircase winding up, left of the kitchen. Perhaps this would be worth checking out. I take a quick look around, checking no one is seeing my detour, and skip upwards.

The small steps make me almost trip as I am running too fast, trying to make as little noise as possible. The stairs abruptly come to a wooden door. I listen carefully. There is a shaft of light edging around the gap of the frame. It's unlocked as I gently push. A god damn awful creaking sound echoes from it like a door in a horror movie, as I quickly scan the room.

It is full of old musty smelling furniture and drapes. The dust has settled so long in here that everything is cloaked in grey. *There* - I see evidence of an entry. *Footprints*. They look recent and relatively small. My heart races forcing me to keep my guard up as I don't want to be surprised by a ghost jumping on me, or worse still, one of these unknown combatants.

I stand rock solid, listening hard for any movement or sound. It's so eerie. Old places like this give me the creeps. Too many late-night movies reminding me of the unexpected, or wizards summoning up evil demons. There's no sound, except for my breathing, so I turn to head back to the kitchen. Then I hear it, the faintest noise. I swing around.

Before I can react, a figure is racing towards me. A blow hits my head and I crash onto the wooden flooring. Dust explodes around my face, making me cough. Another blow comes hard onto my back. I am trying to activate my head into action, but my sight is swirling. I force myself to roll away towards the door, raising my feet up as a protection. My foot gets another blow, at least saving my head.

A burst of adrenaline allows me to spring up and I twist, spinning my leg out, hoping that it either hits this person or distracts them long enough for me to compose myself. It does neither, as it hits some furniture, sending a jolt through my body. I hunch up in reaction to the pain. At least my sight has recovered enough to see the next assault coming.

The figure is now flinging something at me. I have time to drop and almost do the splits, something I never achieve completely in training, as my flexibility is not what it should be. The object smashes onto the door sending fragments of glass all over me. I roll again and get myself fight-ready. Quickly assessing the distance, I swing out my foot to hit the person's legs. This time, I contact flesh and bone; I hear a yelp as a fibula cracks.

The crash of the person is quick and unhindered, as they fall through a glass top table. The dust cover envelopes their body as they disappear in the hole they made. A hazy cloud rises majestically creating fragmented shafts of light to blaze through the room. The sound of silence contrasts the frenetic fight I have survived. Quite surreal. I shake out the mess embedded in my hair as I slowly walk over to the cloaked body.

I carefully pull back the drape. My heart was racing, as I half expected it to be Jaz lying here. It wasn't. Thank God. It *was* a female though. Still and breathless. Red drips from beneath the tabletop and I then see the wound which finished her off. Part of the glass embedded itself through her gut. Not what I expected.

So, what were you here for? I look around the room and spot where this person was hiding. I stride away from her body and pull back the furniture that hid her secret work. On a side table sits a device, housed in a black case. Part computer, part jamming equipment - I had seen this sort of stuff used by the FSB when Olga and I had got involved with an undercover dispatch of a warlord in Chechnya.

This must be what jammed our comms. I study the screen and see various frequency waves pulsating, I guess obstructing any other frequencies. I wonder what I should do. There is no time to ask Ayanna, so, I just do. Is there anything we could glean from capturing this kit? After a second of thinking, I shake my head. Nope. It's going to be toast. I am about to pick it up and smash it, when I hear the door creak.

I fall back under the cover of the drapes. I hear heavy breathing. Then a yelp. I know that sound.

"Jaz! Where the hell have you been?" I ask, swiping back the drape. She stares at me.

"Did…did you do this?" she says, her voice shaking.

"Yes…I didn't have any choice. It was me or her. As I keep saying, 'adapt or die'." Shock is freezing her expression.

"Where have you been? We were looking for you. Are you ok?" She shakes her head.

"No…this whole thing is too scary. I can't cope. I had to get away, so I went to the loo, to get myself together."

"I thought it would be getting to you."

"And then the comms went off…my head went all crazy; felt alone and scared. And now this…" she points.

"It's ok…I've found the reason," I say, pointing at the jammer. Then, I wonder something. "Hey, you are good at hacking and computers, yeah?" Jaz shrugs.

"Yeah, I suppose."

I stride across to her and put my arm around her.

"Come over here; I want you to see what you can do with this." I sit her down in front of the equipment.

"Could you control the jamming and get intel on the source? Better still, find out who is behind it?" She shivers and then nods.

"I would think so."

"Great. Look, stay here and see what you can do. I'll tell Ayanna what you are doing, and I'll lock the door, to give you some safety." She glances at the body now drowned in a reddish-brown drape.

"What about that?" she points.

"Ignore her…dust to dust and all that."

38 - GAME FACE

I need to smarten up after that encounter, so I find the loo. I'm digging glass out of my hair and brushing dust and dirt off my clothes. I wash my face, and then stare at myself. This has really fired me up. Any near-death experience makes me more alive than before. I am so thankful that I have survived so many, it makes me happy to be on this earth. That's why I am determined to get this operation over with and do what needs to be done. The mirror reflects my game face.

A guest wanders in and I quickly replace my mask. They give an up and down look, which makes me self-conscious. Perhaps I have missed a smudge. I swing around to check. I must have snagged my trousers, as a rip runs along my butt. *Shit.* The woman comes up to me, and I back away.

"It's alright dear. It is such a nuisance when clothes are not as resilient as they should be. Here, I have a small sewing kit in my bag. Always carry one for emergencies." She pulls out the small kit from her sequin covered handbag and proceeds to select a dark thread and needle.

I must admit, anyone with a weapon, even as small as a needle, I am usually wary. This lady, though, seems genuine enough and I allow her to sew my 'accident' together, whilst she chats away about her home in the Cotswolds. This surreal moment lasts about ten minutes, whilst other guests come and go, giving their own clothing mishap stories. Finally, she claps and congratulates herself on a job well done. I say thank you and quickly exit.

I grab a tray of food, swig back a juice and make my way back into the main hall trying to compose myself. Alex sees me and wanders over.

"Where did you go? Ayanna and Catherine have been looking for you and Jaz. They were getting worried you had both disappeared," he says.

"Don't worry. I've found Jaz and got her onto working out how to unlock the jamming. I had a small fight." He studies me as if I'm making it up. "I know, it's crazy, but my first kill has happened."

"What?" His voice sounds like a shrew.

"Shush, you idiot. I will tell Ayanna and hopefully we will get some intel on who is behind the jamming - and who is running this show."

I wander through the room, unloading the food as I go. I try to walk past the four again. The cases they brought in have been unshackled from them and are laid on a table, still closed. A general hush descends on the gathering as a woman and man begin to talk through the PA system.

"Excuse me everyone. We will begin the auction in ten minutes," the man says.

"If you need the restrooms, the catering staff and stewards will be able to help," the woman says, her voice laced with a thick South Afrikaans accent. "May I remind you, that when we start, the room will be locked down, due to the nature of our auction today. Thank you. Enjoy the food and drinks."

This spurs me on to find Ayanna. I need to update her. She is now in conversation with one of the marks. It is Henri, the blonde ponytail. I nudge her as I walk past. She turns her head and accepts a canape from my tray. I allow her to continue as that might be a useful conversation. Jules, I see hanging around Shorty, so I keep moving towards them.

"So," I say. "I appear to have found the reason for the jamming." Shorty nearly chokes on her caviar.

"What…what did you say?"

"I have found the jamming device… and dealt with the person." She again coughs and drinks her juice quickly.

"*Maisie…what have you done?*"

"I thought we were not using names, *Catherine?*" I can tell her face is colouring up under her mask.

"Don't answer me back. It is crucial that we are in control of the situation." I nod.

"Yes…that's why Jaz is on the task of deciphering the equipment and reversing the jamming of our comms." She plonks her drink onto Jules' tray, causing him to correct the imbalance.

"You are not in charge here. What do you think that will achieve? We need you to keep to the briefing."

"Well, I thought that Jaz was more useful with her hacking and computer skills than out here, as she is freaking out about the whole operation. It will keep her occupied." Shorty moves towards me in a threatening manner.

"Get back to your job and stop interfering. Where is Jaz anyway?" I shake my head.

"Out of harm's way. The three of us can cope. I'm hoping that comms will be back on soon." I stand my ground. She backs off and marches off towards Ayanna.

"Do you think she is pissed off?" I ask Jules.

"Err…*yes*. You aren't in charge Maisie. We aren't privileged to have all the intel on this operation. What if you are causing a problem?"

"Whatever she has said to you guys about me, ignore. Don't you see that she has another agenda? Ever since she admitted that she had doubts about my parents, she has had it in for me." I hesitate. "So, what is in that holdall? It's nothing to do with my birthday, that's for sure." He looks away and shakes his head.

"Thought so. All of you are under some sort of coercion. Well, whatever it is, I will not be the pawn in her game." Satisfied that I have made my point, I wander again, offering food until it runs out.

Guests are walking and rushing about to make sure they are not missing a piss stop. Staff appear with stacks of chairs and begin to arrange them in rows facing a raised table where the cases lie. The hall is now evolving into an auction room, with the PA system set up as the focal point.

I watch as the four set themselves on the front row and settle. The unknown one pulls out what looks like a handheld laser, as the light flashes across the front table and then shuts down. *I wonder what that is for.* Ayanna, having finished her chats, is heading for me with a determined stride.

"Catherine has informed me that Jaz is unjamming the comms. How did you find that?" she asks, with a mix of annoyance and surprise.

"It was an accident. I was searching for Jaz and found this person in a room. We fought and I won." She froze as that sank in.

"You've had an encounter with someone? You do realise that will ripple down to whoever is controlling this affair."

"Yes…obviously. But I made sure that Jaz is safe. She was freaking out. And she is great with tech, so using her for breaking into this system will be a bonus, don't you agree?" She tilts her head.

"No wonder Catherine was fuming. You still have that annoying independent streak. Well, I hope she is ok, and that this operation doesn't go belly up." She turns to the main doors for the hall. "Those doors will be closed as the auction begins. We have to ensure that two of you are outside as well as one of you is inside. I suggest that Alex and Jules stay outside, and you remain here, ok?" I nod.

"Wouldn't miss it for the world." Ayanna shakes her head. We part our ways. I quickly refill my tray with a mix of drinks and food and station myself near the doors. Alex and Jules walk past me and nod.

"See you on the other side," I say.

A one-minute warning is given, and people begin to take their seats. The general noise level is reducing along with the activity, creating a change in the atmosphere. I sense we are entering the next phase of this operation. My own excitement is rising as I want to know what all the fuss is about. I am also fascinated to see how much money is going to be bid for these items. The people I have spoken to don't seem like the millionaires I would expect. However, with the international mix of guests, it could be that these are only the representatives of bigger 'cheeses'.

Someone brushes up against me. I check them out. I hope it's not the woman who fancied me. I look deeply into the eyes of the mask. I blink. This is not what I expected. My heart races. Blood rushes to my head. I feel my legs losing their strength. This was one person I didn't bank on seeing anytime soon.

39 - MAN WITH NO NAME

"Nice to see you again," says the voice that has haunted me for months. "You had better take a seat Miss Greene. I want you to watch what happens today and thank your parents for their legacy."

I feel a sharp prod in my back. From the feel of the barrel, a 9mm handgun is forced into my lower back. A shot from that position would shatter my vertebrae and cripple me for life. The one with the firearm forces me onto an empty chair. The man who took my mother's sapphire in Versailles, sits next me, grinning.

"This must be a surprise, you and I, meeting so soon. I am guessing you are not here alone," he says. "I wouldn't alert any of them as that would only make your situation worse. Also, I don't want any more of my people getting killed, as you are in the habit of doing." I glance his way.

Is this really the same man? His accent is rich with British aristocracy and the eyes are burning as when he gloated over the sapphire divulging all its contents into his computer. I look away, wondering if Ayanna and Catherine are nearby. With everyone seated and looking forwards, it's impossible to locate them. I turned back to him.

"So, what have you got to do with this auction? I thought you had everything you needed after stealing my mother's sapphire." He gives a stilted laugh.

"So, did I. Until I studied the contents of the data. I mistook your mother's ingenuity as ignorance. The jewel did indeed start to give up its secrets, but your parents had built in a failsafe. It can only work with the correct keys and most importantly, the right person." I snigger. Mum and Dad had prepared so well to protect these secrets.

"That's a shame isn't it. I'm so pleased that even in death, they have stopped morons like you causing so much destruction." I get a jab from the person behind me. I feel it leaving the imprint of the barrel end on my back.

"Don't push your luck, Miss Greene. This time you will not get away like you did before. Harmony's death was of great sadness to me. You *will* pay for that." I flinch at the memory of killing her in Versailles.

We are distracted by a man coming to the microphone. He does the customary tapping and asks for everyone's attention.

"Welcome to this special auction. We are aware that the objects on sale have an enormous value and so the bidding consoles we have provided, will check the assets you have declared to pay for your successful bids and confirm that you can afford them." A wave of muttering flutters through the hall. The man leans over to me.

"As you can see, we have been thorough with our surveillance and preparation. That's why your comms were jammed so there's no outside interference." *Oh, you do think of everything.* I'm not letting on that there may be a surprise waiting for him.

"Let's sit back and watch the show. I'm expecting the bidding to produce a good return today," he says and rests back against his chair.

I stare at his face and wonder how he has eluded every intelligence service. This man, with no name, appears to have more control than is due to his status. Neither MI6 nor Anton, my AI computer, have anything on him. It will be the greatest prize of all to find out who he is.

The man who is taking charge of proceedings begins to explain what will happen next.

"We have five items up for sale. As you are aware, these have greater value if bought together. However, if bought separately, I would suggest that the eventual buyers will need to join forces to fully benefit."

This speech leaves me wondering what on earth are in these cases. A screen is lowered behind the speaker and blinds miraculously descend over the windows, creating a cinema like atmosphere. A video begins to play. It is narrated by some English dude, describing the route capitalism has taken the world and that a new course must be championed. It takes digs at the USA and UK and the damage it has done to society worldwide.

I can't help but yawn as this history lesson is making me bored. Another jab in my back. Are they making sure that I'm awake? The man continues to grin, and I spot a glint of gold from one of his molars.

The rambling video then takes a turn for the worse. The narrative is now about how change will come, and that the guests of the auction are in a unique position to embrace that change. By bidding for the items, they are essentially investing in a new world order. I glance back at the man.

"You can't seriously think that these people have a chance of changing the systems and cultures of millions of people just like that?" He turns, his grin broader.

"Miss Greene, you, and the rest of your security organisations, are purely attempting to keep a lid on change. It's not in their interest or their governments, to allow it. It would not be good for business. A shift in the status quo would dissolve centuries of bureaucratic rule. So, I, along with others, are going to initiate that change." He now exchanges his grin for a smug smile.

"By killing millions of innocent people," I add.

"That is the consequence of change, Miss Greene. The machinery of that new order has to pave the way…"

"...through a graveyard of unneeded death," I finish off.

Another jab.

"I see that you have no stomach for the inevitable. Sorry to hear that. However, you will not need to agree with me, as you will not be around to witness it."

"Are there no limits to what you will do to achieve that?" I ask.

"Certainly, there are always limits. One has to decide where they lie." He directs his attention to the speaker as he is priming the guests to prepare for the bidding.

I feel my legs and arms tensing up. What happens next is not under my control. I have to think and act as calmly and decisively as possible. It may be my last chance.

40 - AUCTION ACTION

The cases are brought to the front table in a ceremonious manner, as if the British crown jewels were being presented. The guy with the laser swivels off their chair and walks over to the first case. They twiddle the laser between their fingers as if they are performing a magic trick and then points the green light to the case. There is a whirring noise. The guests closest, raise their heads straining to get a glimpse of what's inside. The lid opens with a muffled expensive clunk. The person lifts it, allowing a glow of light from the interior.

"I would advise people to stay at a suitable distance from the contents whilst they are unsealed. We don't want anyone becoming too eager to be contaminated," the man gleefully says.

*What the f*** is in there?*

"Can we start the bidding at 10 million?" the speaker continues. Hands begin to raise.

"I would advise you that your electronic devices are to be used for the purpose of bidding. This is *not* the Antiques Roadshow." A ripple of laughter runs along the rows.

Behind him, the screen displays numbers as the guests are putting in their bids. The starting price is exceeded immediately, and within seconds the price has gone up to 55 million US dollars. I can see why the numbers approach is clever as it keeps the anonymity of the bidders.

"How do they know what they are bidding for?" I ask.

"The format is intuitive. We have designed it, so the guests are given the details on a computer screen sent back to whoever is directing the bidding. These guests here are merely puppets for the real bidders."

"So, everyone is anonymous. You like this idea, don't you. No one knows who *you* are, either." He returns another smug look.

"Annoying isn't it, Miss Greene? I took a leaf out of your mother's book, for that." At the mention of my mother, I feel anger surging through my veins.

"What do you know about my mother? It was a load of bullshit you said to me in Versailles."

He shakes his head.

"Believe what you want; she and your father essentially made all this happen."

I screw up my face and resist punching him. Unfortunately, I know that the gun placed in my back would blast a hole through me before the blow would make contact, so I force myself to relax. The screen continues to scroll up with the bids, as they are now in excess of 110 million.

"Who will benefit from this sale? Your retirement fund?" I ask. He sniggers.

"Of course, they will pump up my investments, but what I am more interested in is the power that it will bring when the politicians of this world recognise, they have no authority or ability to control. That will lie with me." Another twisted smile creases his mouth.

"This is what my parents were preventing, not initiating. You are manipulating their legacy for your own greed." I feel like spitting at him. Again, I have to resist.

"Quite right. I have no loyalty to their ideals. I have my own, progressive plans." He turns to the person who keeps jabbing my back and whispers.

They wander off, leaving me thinking that I could act. Except, for one thing. The man now holds a 9mm with his right hand, tucked under his left arm, pointing straight at my gut. I'm too close to get a blow effective enough to misdirect any shot. I have to sit tight.

"Oh, there we are. The first lot is bought," the man says. I hear the auctioneers gavel smacked down.

"Sold to number 78 for 125 million US dollars," he states.

"A good start to proceedings," the man says.

"So, what was that?" I ask.

"Depleted uranium along with some other nasty ingredients."

"To make a dirty bomb, I assume," I say.

"You are partially correct, Miss Greene. Your mother was successful in evading the capture of the vital mix, which when added to the uranium, will create a catastrophic release of toxic gases. Very useful for adding to a city's sewers or underground railway system."

"So, basically you are funding terrorists," I say.

"Change is brought by those who are prepared to barter with life, to produce new life," he hisses.

"Absolute crap. You are nothing but a capitalist in another guise. It just means you are the one profiting from it. Don't give me that shit you are supporting a better system. Every system is corrupt - it has men and women like you in it." He glares at me and produces a phone.

"You see this," he turns the screen to me. "All I have to do is give the message and your silly little friend gets her throat cut." I hesitate before staring at the screen.

I can't see who it is at first; then I recognise the hair, the scrunchy, the pale face. Then I know it's Jaz.

41 - LOYALTY

I shiver to see her panic-stricken face, paler than normal. Sweat is dripping off her forehead and those scared eyes are full of tears. I feel helpless. I have no way of freeing her. The man must have directed his thug to go and find her.

"You bastard. Let her go." I know this is a futile demand. I have no leverage.

"That is not going to happen, especially while I have you where I want you. So, sit back, behave yourself and she will be safe - for the time being." He sits back and nods to the auctioneer.

"The next lot is a pendant of great beauty and hidden value." *That can't be what I think it is?*

"Can we start the bidding at 5 million?" the auctioneer asks.

"Really? You have the pendants from my parents and Harmony's parents?" I whisper. The man hesitates and looks to be moving to either jab me with the gun or strike my head with it. He then relaxes.

"Don't speak Harmony's name in vain, *Greene.* Her parents and I were great friends and partners back in the day. The betrayal of their trust sickened me when your, so called, good agent parents, let them loose to the wolves." I have to resist my own kick back at his reference.

"You seem to have a lot of hatred for my parents. Is that why you and Catherine Short are colluding?" I ask this, knowing I could be off the mark, but want to draw his secrets out. He stares at me through his dark purple mask.

"And why do you think I would be working with an officer of MI6? I have my reputation to think about." He grins and turns his attention to the bidding. It has reached 17 million.

"And what reputation would that be?"

"One of anonymity and off the grid. I am but a ghost in the machine. No one knows who I am, and no one will. Along with this sale, I will vanish into the mists of history, after securing the most violent transition to the new world order."

"Sounds very grand for a psycho," I spit. "So, you have no loyalty to anyone, except your own delusions?"

"Loyalty is a fragile construct. When tested, it is found to be corrosive and unreliable. I do not trust in loyalty."

I breathe in deeply. This has to be the man's weakness. He doesn't trust anyone, like me. So, his isolation makes him vulnerable to anyone else who would want him out of the way, or despatched. Surely, he cannot survive in this state for long, especially if he means to destabilise the world order.

"If you go ahead with your plans, a huge target will be put on your head. There will always be someone coming for you." He turns to me again and the grin morphs into a sneer.

"That is where you are mistaken. I am all things to all men. No one can trace me." He nods his head, and a person strode over, taking his gun. "Sadly, our chat ends here. I must go and prepare for the finale. Farewell Maisie Greene. I am happy that we met. Your parents would have been proud of their heir and how they weaponised you." At that comment, I'm left wondering what he means; *because I am an assassin?*

The person sits beside me, again pointing the gun at my gut. I study their face. It is long, ending in a pointed chin. The lips are covered in some sort of lip salve, painted with a dusky salmon pink. I assume a woman but looks are deceptive these days. Dolphin earrings dangle from their ears, encrusted with diamonds.

"I like the earrings," I say. They turn and a grin appears, revealing a diamond embedded in a front tooth. "You must have paid a fortune for that. I doubt you can get that on the NHS." The grin returned to a feature-less expression. "Is that what pays for *your* loyalty?" They sigh deeply.

42 - ANTON

The bidding continues regardless of my predicament. The pendant is now at 23 million US dollars. Displayed on the screen, I recognise it and wonder who wore it. My mother or father? Or Harmony Chase's parents? I still don't understand why they are so important. Do they hold some key information that needs to be unlocked too?

I shuffle around as I feel hemmed in. I'm trying to get my head into some sort of action plan. Sitting here, doing nothing, is beginning to aggravate me. I can't rely on Jaz being safe, as now the man who has no name is here, I am anxious that his tactics will be brutal and uncompromising. My guard flinches at my movement and tells me in a gruff, feminine voice to keep still. That is a sign they are far from happy about babysitting me.

The man who has no name walks across to the right of the hall and he bows down to speak to someone. From now on I will make up a name, as it makes him a legitimate target. I thought for a second and came up with the perfect one - '*Loser*'. Not that brilliant, but it is what he is going to be anytime soon, as far as I'm concerned.

The person cranes their neck to look across towards where I'm sitting. I instantly recognise the mask.

Catherine Short.

No great surprise that he should talk with her. So, they are in this together. But where does that leave

Ayanna? I still can't see where she is. What threat does this mean for all the rest of the team? I feel my arms tense again. I am angry that I left Jaz exposed and that I didn't push harder over my suspicions about Shorty. I glanced quickly around the people sitting close to me, judging what the fall out would be if I took on my guard. I don't want anyone else getting shot.

It's a tough decision; I am in close proximity to at least three others and a deflection could see any of them sent to the meat grinder. The woman tells me to keep eyes front. I bite my lip and slow down my breathing. It's a technique I learnt from Navy seals to slow down my heart rate, ready for action.

My response has to be fast and furious. I have no idea if anyone else has a weapon. Would that mean a big shoot out and no means of escape? My eyes are clouding over as my anxiety peaks. *Focus, Maisie.*

A crackle comes through my earpiece and makes me snap out of my self-doubt mode. I glance at Shorty who is now walking along the outside of the gathering with Loser. I study her mannerisms to see if she has received the same interference on the comms. No sign of her touching her ear. I hear it again. I focus on the head of a man in front of me. His hair is jet black and sleek, so much so, oil has dripped onto his collar, creating a smeared stain.

A garbled voice begins to come through. I check to see if my guard has heard any of this. *Still looking straight ahead.* Another louder whining noise stings my ear. I wish I could take it out. It's giving me a headache. Then, I heard it.

"Anton here. I have finally got my communications sorted. I apologise that it has taken so long. Maisie, are you safe?" *How can I answer that?*

"You may or may not be in a position to reply. I am currently breaking into the building's security system. If they have any CCTV, I will make my own assumptions from that." *Good lad.*

"I have been busy in the meantime, getting up to speed on your MI6 mission. After my initial warnings, I will update you on specific threats." He begins to reel off what I suspected all along.

Catherine Short is working as a deep cover operative for an unknown organisation. Her analytic skills were being used to infiltrate MI6's operations regarding 'Trojan'. Anton tells me that her betrayal of the security services has left them severely compromised. I have a ton of questions to ask him, but that will have to wait.

"...And pendant four, goes to 112 for 32 million dollars." The bang from the gavel makes me jump. I spin round and see the guard is temporarily distracted by the murmuring from the bidders and a general shuffling of bums on seats. Anton interjects with a suggestion.

"I see that you are temporarily stationed in the main hall. If you can disarm the guard sitting next to you, I suggest you make for a door which is hidden behind a red velvet curtain to your left." I glance across and locate it. "Take care in proceeding through the door, as there are two other guards adjacent to it."

What does that mean? Either side or just beyond it?

Whatever, I'm going to have to act fast. I glance back at my guard and consider that a solid punch to the face and downward jab of my arm will dislodge the gun, hopefully falling kindly for me to grab it. Anton comes back with another monologue.

"It is with regret that your team is being held hostage at different locations around the building. How you free them is very concerning as any alert that you are now released could set off a ripple of retaliation." That's what I fear. It could be toast for all of them if I get this wrong.

A general moving of bodies erupts as the auctioneer suggests a stretching of legs. This has to be my moment.

Those sitting closest to me, stand up, surrounding me with a human hedge. The guard is distracted and glances around. I execute my plan.

A quick punch to the jaw and left ear, followed by a downward jab. The person shudders sidewards, and the gun is dislodged, falling across her lap. I grab the .9mm and swipe her again with the barrel. She whines with the impact and rolls onto her right side. People seem to think she has stumbled and offer to help her up.

This distraction plays well for my escape as people gather around her. I dash to the red velvet, hanging tantalisingly for my escape. I brush it to one side and grasp the door handle. I take a deep breath and open it. As Anton said, there are guards standing aimlessly at the other side. I act as quickly as I can. I kicked the nearest one in the stomach and detached the semi-automatic from its belt, allowing it to clatter to the floor. The next one I hit hard to the head, whipping with a handgun. They both fall conveniently to the side of the corridor, heads smashing on the stone wall. That was easier than I expected.

"Anton; I'm in the corridor. Where do I go to rescue the team?" I hear his gravelly voice directing me left and then right, along a warren of passageways. This old house has so many secret corridors, I could easily get disorientated.

"Continue along this corridor and the first wooden door to the right has the team members Alex and Jules, I believe."

"Thanks for coming back online, by the way. I was wondering if you ever would. So, you were trying to warn me from the start. Who was the woman who got killed in London?"

"An associate of your mothers, from long ago. I had a reference that enabled me to contact her and convince her to approach you. I had to imitate your mother, I'm afraid, to arrange that."

"That's why she said it was from my mum," I say, as I wind through the passageways. "Sad, she had to give her life for it." Anton agreed, declaring regret.

"Be careful…there are laser triggers at various points around the building," he suddenly tells me.

"Ok, that sounds high-tech. What have they got to protect?"

"That is unknown. Proceed with caution." I will.

At every turn along these corridors, I check to see if any guard or lasers are ready to ensnare me. I made sure the door I originally came through was wedged with the two guards, so that will slow any chase from the hall.

I reach a turn in the corridor, and I notice a glimmer of green spread across the lower section of the stonework. It shimmers as dust kicked from my walking floats upwards. I drag my hand across a window ledge and throw the collected dust. I see the lasers plainly now, split into criss-cross streaks.

"Is there any way to cut the power to these?" I ask Anton.

"I will search the power sources located in the building," he replies. "It is very elusive so far to my hacking. They have a sophisticated system," he said with slight annoyance. That must be a first for him; however, I know he likes a challenge.

I pace up and down, feeling agitated. I study a low window and see that the lasers don't cover that area. I push the catch and the lead casing creaks and groans as I push harder. Scrambling through the gap, I tear my trousers along the original mended section. *Blast* - so tight they are going to be hanging in tatters from my butt soon.

I'm on edge thinking about Shorty - I wonder where she's gone. And Loser? I will have to be careful now I'm on the loose, as they will have alerted the guards to snuff me out. *I have to find Jaz and the others quickly.*

"I see that you have chosen an alternative route," Anton burbles.

"Yes. I can't hang around waiting for you. Where does this courtyard take me to?"

"Follow it along the wall and if you can, find another window and enter the building beyond the laser protection zone. The stairs from the corridor will lead to the room where Jazmin is being held." *Excellent.*

"I've missed your chatter, Anton. Good to have you back," I say with more than a little relief.

"Always an honour to serve the Greene family, Maisie."

43 - UNLEASH THE JAZ

I find a window that is easier to dislodge and crawl back into the building. There is no sign of any guards. The stairway that Anton suggested is ahead of me, so proceeding carefully, I keep glancing around, both for guards and any surveillance cameras. If Anton sees things, then so will they. Nothing in the corners of the walls. Perhaps there is nothing in this wing to protect.

The stone steps grate on my shoes, gritty from generations of wear. I climb slowly. It appears to be a symmetrical mirror image of the other stairs I climbed to find the jammer. A wooden door is ajar, and I hear voices. There's a screech. *That's Jaz!*

The other voice continues to threaten her. Something about keeping to the arrangement. This makes me wonder if Jaz is really on side or not. In either case, I have to rescue her. Then I can see what *'arrangement'* she has.

I prepare the handgun, checking the safety is off. The magazine is loaded with 13 rounds so I'm happy it will do the job. I approach the doorway low and quietly. The gap is just enough for me to see around. There's a piece of broken glass lying in an alcove. That will do nicely. I position it to get the best reflection.

There's another woman, about my height, but broader, wielding a gun at Jaz who sits, tears streaming down her face. This at least confirms to me that she is still under some sort of coercion. From here I reckon I can open the door swiftly and shoot the woman without damaging Jaz in any way. It's a risk. It's bound to alert any guards nearby, but I have to act.

Bang.

The door slams to the side, making me jump and almost scream. The woman leaps at me, with her gun ready and threatening. I instantly roll, getting jammed against the wall. I raise my handgun and fire. The blast of hot gas kicks my hands back, as I get sprayed with blood splatter. She falls on top of me, her head bashing against the wall.

For a moment, my head is swimming, my breathing erratic. I have to shake that off. Her body is heavy, sprawled across me - I push hard to roll her away. There's a yell and I watch Jaz running straight at me, a club-like weapon raised.

"Hey…it's me, *Maisie*," I say breathlessly. She halts and stares.

Her face is glowing, with raging eyes, like the bedroom fight we had but multiplied six times over. She gradually lowers the improvised weapon and continues her enraged glare. I turn my handgun away from her as I watch her face morph into the usual drippy expression, followed by a torrent of tears.

"Oh Maisie…I'm so sorry. I thought you were another killer. Although you are… not that sort…" she rambles.

"It's ok, it's ok," I reply, getting up and taking the club from her. "Breathe, breathe. Take it steady. You must control yourself. We have to find Alex and Jules, who are also prisoners."

She looks up as Alex's name is mentioned.

"Is he ok? Where is he?"

"I'm not sure. Anton is helping me find them."

"Who's Anton?"

"Oh, my AI friend. He's very good at intel." She narrows her eyes, a look of disbelief etched across her face.

"Can he be trusted?"

"Yes, absolutely. I found you, didn't I? Come on, we need to move as this fire fight will be alerting their guards into action." My thoughts jump to the woman's comment.

"Before we go, what is this 'arrangement' she was talking about?" Jaz purses her lips.

"It doesn't matter now…" she says, talking to herself, more than me. "I was forced to make sure that you were neutralised." I flinch. "You know, stopped from interfering with what was going on. Catherine had threatened us all with jail and worse if we didn't agree."

"*Bastard,*" I spit. "Why? She is a piece of shit."

"Sorry Maisie. It wasn't what we wanted. After my mother died, she said other members of our families would be under threat if we didn't comply." I pace the floor and kick the lifeless body.

"Ok. Can I take it that the arrangement is now over? Null and void?" Jaz nods. Her face changes to one of determination.

"I'm with you on that. How they have treated us and now all this, I'm not doing what she wants anymore."

"Can I trust you with a gun?" She nods and holds out her hand.

"I'm about to unleash the true Jazmin," she says. "I'm ready,"

"Great! Then we will have to be careful as we find the lads. Then we can work out what to do next." Nodding again, she checks the gun.

"Remember; don't point that at me, or I might have to take action." She allows a grin to flash across her face.

Tracing along the corridors takes forever, as we constantly check for CCTV and guards. The series of interconnecting passages, make this warren confusing. Anton tells me it was part of the abbey, a place for contemplation and rest. At the moment, that sounds ironic.

"How did you get out, Maisie?" Jaz whispers.

"Anton came back online and showed me the way. Gave me the guts to break free from the guard." She nods.

"How long have you known this, Anton?"

"Only since last year."

"I am fascinated by a computer that actually interacts with you. When all this mess is sorted, you will have to show me his programming."

"I'm not sure I would know where to start. It was designed by my father." I resist my gut tightening. "They were amazing parents."

"It was a shame you don't remember them," Jaz says softly.

"Yeah. I'm starting to get some memories, only patchy though." I stop. There's a scuffling sound further down the corridor. "Two, maybe three running this way. Take cover."

We dive into a stone alcove, pinning our bodies as deep as we can. The noise of boots and rattling of utility belts increases. I nod to Jaz, who is holding her weapon downwards, with straight arms. Within seconds they are on us. I don't have any faith in our hiding place so, I indicate I'm going for the shot. Surprisingly, Jaz leaps out, making my heart race.

She said that she was about to unleash '*the Jaz'*. That was an understatement. Firing at will, she launches into a full-on assault. Her gun is cracking repeatedly. I follow a microsecond later and watch as three guys with automatic weapons are jerking back and sideways as Jaz's bullets strike them. It's all in slow motion again, as I roll along the gritty floor, my hands pushed out in front, firing at legs and arms.

We both lay for what seemed ages, breathing heavily. I scramble to my feet. I nervously glance over the bodies and check that there is no response. Between us, we made toast of the guards, bullet ridden and dead.

“Well, Jaz. I am impressed.”

“I didn’t think I could do that in a million years,” she says, her breathing heavy - adrenaline firing up her eyes.

“Neither did I; you certainly unleashed the Jaz. But we had better get going, as that fire fight will unleash everyone.”

44 - TEAMWORK

Anton directs us up some more steps to where a short corridor splits off to three rooms. He says that Alex and Jules are in one of them. Not very helpful, so we must guess. I sidle up to the first one and listen, Jaz copying on door two. We look at each other and shake heads. Silently, we skirt over to the middle door. Anton suddenly perks up and gives me an update on the auction.

"The auction appears to have taken a turn for the worse," he informs. "I have heard that the bidding has ceased and there are multiple screams coming from the room."

"That sounds interesting. What is causing the commotion?" I whisper.

"There was some chatter amongst the guards that whoever is in charge here, has closed the bidding and locked down the room. People are getting anxious."

"That doesn't sound good. I hope Ayanna is ok. Do you know where she is?"

"With everyone masked, it is difficult to get a lock on her whereabouts."

"Well, let me know. She is part of our team, and we all need to get out," I say. Jaz pulls on my arm and points.

Through the doorway we hear some comms chatter from the guards in the room. It is relaying the assault on the ones we downed and warning them we are on the loose.

I sidle up to the door and wave at Jaz to follow. Indicating with my fingers, I count down to our explosive entry. *3,2,1.*

The door swings inwards and slams against a cupboard, surprising the occupants, three of them holding semi-automatics. My heart rate jumps as they respond at different speeds to our arrival. The first raises his weapon and in an instant, I spot the safety is on. He points and tries to fire. Realising his mistake, he flips the switch. It has given me enough time to fire into his torso, thrusting him away and down from us. Jaz fires at another one and hits him straight between the eyes. The final one has reacted by surrounding himself with Alex and Jules, bound and gagged to chairs. He points and fires.

I collapse to the floor, pulling Jaz with me, as the bullets whip past our heads, smashing into the wooden door. I see a gap between the guys, and I fire, hoping not to catch either of them. Three shots simultaneously rip into the guard jolting him sideways, the blood splatter covering Jules and Alex. They both shake their heads.

I run over to check the guards are immobile and turn to the lads. They looked flushed and agitated. I pull the gaffer tape from Jules's face. He yelps.

"Thanks Maisie! And Jaz - you were both amazing," he gasps. Jaz runs over to Alex and pulls his mouth covering off, perhaps too slowly, as he moans.

"Jaz...you could have done that a bit quicker," he complains. Then a smile breaks across his face. "Thanks, lovely. You are a star. Get us free. I'm ready to kick some butt."

"I think you need to hear us out first," I say, cutting the bonds. "Shorty is in collusion with an unknown organisation who are running this auction. She is an undercover operative, given the job of divulging information on a mission called 'Trojan'. We have to assume she is armed and dangerous." I watch as the implications sink in. Jules raises his hand, wipes the blood stains from his face, and looks directly at me.

"Maisie...I have to...we, have to apologise. Our mission was to stop you from interfering with this operation. I see now that we were being used. I am so sorry." His regret is etched across his eyes. Alex nods.

"Yeah, we were forced into it by Short and Delaware. They threatened us." I nodded and said it was ok.

"I forgive you. But the time for celebrating is far from now. We have to assess the situation and get a plan. My assistant, Anton, will help us get around the building. We then must ensure that Ayanna is safe too. I haven't seen her for ages."

"Who is Anton?" Alex and Jules ask in unison. I explain briefly and encourage them to concentrate instead on locating Ayanna. Neither of them had seen her, which is worrying. Either she is being held too, or she's in hiding. Anton kicks back in.

"The auction room is now in uproar. The proceedings have been interrupted by four people acting in a threatening manner," he describes. "The man with no name is demanding that the audience be still and listen to their demands."

"So, Loser, as I now call him, is taking charge and holding these guests as hostages. That's unexpected," I say.

"Also, the man, you call Loser, has demanded that you surrender yourself, otherwise guests will be sacrificed for the cause, whatever that may be," Anton says. I relay it to the team.

The others look at me and Jules and Jaz shake their heads. Alex copies a few seconds later.

"That is not going to happen, Maisie. We are not going to abandon you to these mashed up cretins," Jaz says reassuringly. I smile.

"Thanks guys. We will have to improvise before he carries out his threats." I suddenly remember about Jane and wonder where she is.

"We do have another aid with us too, one you know nothing about. Sergeant Jane McAlister, from the SAS is somewhere here." They give a variety of sceptical looks, with Jaz looking particularly worried. "She has been assigned to keep me safe, apparently. So, I am hoping that we can use her muscle too."

"Are you sure we can trust her?" Jaz asks.

"Yes, I'm sure, Jaz," I reply, hoping I am right.

Alex shakes his head.

"SAS are involved too? This is mental. What have we got into?" he mutters.

"Yeah, it's crazy, I know," I reply. "Come on. We must get going and see how to free these guests, even though they all seem to be involved in terrorism." Anton interjects.

"There is a team of guards heading your way. Be prepared. I estimate five to six, heavily armed," he says.

"Ok. We have to move. Anton warns me that an assault team is on the way," I gasp.

We each select a handgun and semi-automatic rifle, ensuring they are fully loaded. I nod to the team. At last, this teamwork feels like what we should have done all along.

45 - SAPPHIRE

Anton directs us along a set of corridors, by the cloister area. Through the windows, the gardens look immaculate and calming. If only my head and heart could reflect that. I am leading our team into battle and it's giving me reflux. Jaz is acting like a new person, striding confidently beside me, trailed by Jules and Alex, who are in super awareness mode too. We arrive back at the laser protected area. I warn the team to be wary. We halt halfway down the corridor.

"What is being secured here, Anton?" I ask.

"From my hack into their systems, I have found a central hub of communications housed here. It gives signature echoes of your mother's sapphire." My back bristles.

"So, it *is* here then. Do you know why the other brooches are necessary?" The team gawp my face as I burble on, and anxiously glance around.

"I am still unsure as to their significance, but they may well be a form of keys," he says.

It makes me wonder if my parents had a control mechanism for releasing the information on the sapphire. The man said there was a fail-safe.

"Do you know if this Loser is in league with the four horsemen?" I ask. Alex stares at me.

"Four Horsemen of the Apocalypse?" he interjects. I gaze back at him.

"Have you heard of them?" I ask, surprised.

"Yeah…it's a great game. I've played it over the last year. Graphics are amazing. End of the world stuff." I shake my head.

"Thanks for that insight, Alex. *Not relevant.* This is real and it *could* be the end of the world as we know it, so concentrate, *please,*" I ask.

"Anton, what is the failsafe? Have you anything on that?"

"That is unknown. Again, access has been denied," he replies.

I am distracted by the sound of military tactical boots marching down the corridor ahead. I instinctively glance around for some cover. But there is none. We are sitting in the middle of a shooting gallery, and the guards will pick us off like ripe cherries.

"Go…GO!!" I shout, directing them round the next corner. I catch sight of a team dressed in fatigues and body armour running towards us as we round the bend. A recess to the right would give us an advantage, so I point madly. Out team fall into it and take up defensive positions to the back and front. Alex is grinning. Jules is sweating but composed. Jaz is staring wildly. I think that the danger is sinking in.

"It's ok, Jaz. Keep that breathing calm and we will get through this," I say. She nods.

"Alex. Be careful. I know you think this is a game, but it's a deadly one. Don't get yourself shot. We need you."

"Thanks Maisie. I didn't think you cared." I smile. I do and I don't. It's best for all of us if we survive.

A flash catches me by surprise. First approach is under way. A grenade to disorientate us. Smoke fills the corridor followed by shouting to lay down our arms. I nod to Jules and Jaz. We lay close to the floor and aim. The battle begins.

Firing at will, we spray the corridor hoping that some will hit their mark and deter any further advance. A series of shouts and yells confirm what I hoped for. The expected return fire was *not* expected. They must have heavier weapons because the stonework is exploding like firecrackers, shards spraying over us.

We roll back in for cover. I check my rounds and flinch at the amount. I shake my head to Jules who acknowledges what I am saying. We all seem to be short on ammo.

"Anton. Have they disabled the lasers? They are passing through that area, and nothing is happening. Can you reactivate them? I'm not sure what that would do, except start an alarm, but it's worth a try." He replies that he can. I hear an alert call.

"Reactivated."

This is followed by yells from the assault team and a scuffled shouts as to who switched the lasers on again.

Then it comes. A symphony of horrific noises burst along the corridor. Fizzing and burning, followed by shouts and screams of pain. I push my head out to see what is going on. To my shock, the soldiers are being dissected by red beams cutting through their bodies. I am gagging, as the blood bath looks unreal. Jaz follows my lead and seeing the mayhem, can't help but throw up. This is not like the films she watches.

Jules and Alex now gather around us. Alex instantly yelps with some sort of twisted pleasure and Jules grimaces, holding his hand to his face.

"That is so cool," Alex says. "I never thought I would see that for real."

"You are one sick boy," I say. "That is disgusting…and what's more, it could have been us." I spit out the bile in my mouth and reluctantly thank Anton.

"Well, that sorted that. Thanks Anton…not what I expected. Anyway, does that enable us to get into the comms room, now?" He confirms he can control the lasers, so yes.

We compose ourselves and run quickly down the once secure corridor, wading through the killing field. The door is locked. I take my handgun and shoot into the lock, blasting splinters over us. It gives and I slowly push it open, waving to the others to keep low and alert.

The room is darkened, except for a central platform where a blue light sends a spiral of flashes to the ceiling. As it circles, dancing patterns are created around the walls. My heart jumps as I recognise this as my mother's sapphire. It sits in a revolving housing, with a white laser fired into the jewel. I am mesmerised by this light show. Jaz breaks my gaze.

"What is that? Looks like something out of a sci-fi movie," she says.

"Yeah, it is the wonderful creation of my mother and father," I say, with pride.

"Over here, Maisie," Jules whispers. I stride across to a computer screen. "It seems to be compiling lists of information. What does that represent?"

"I have no idea. I think this contraption is extracting information out of the stone. I know it holds sensitive and secretive stuff. It's got to be the reason for this operation. The other things on auction must be connected… to do with making this dirty bomb, I guess."

"This is real spy stuff, Maze. I'm impressed," says Alex.

"*Don't* keep calling me that, Alex," I snap. "Anyway, it's not something to gloat over. We have a responsibility to stop whatever is going on here and get out safely. Jules and Alex, watch the door. I'm going to see if I can break the jewel free." Jaz looks at the screen again and holds my arm.

"I have a worry about that, Maisie. The protocol is complicated from what I can see and taking it out of the housing before correctly shutting it down could damage it." I take note of what she's saying, knowing her computer skills.

"Do you need to play around with that?" I ask, nodding at the keyboard. A grin flashes across her face.

"I would *love* to," she replies and sits down, typing in her ultra-fast manner.

I return to the sapphire and stare at its beauty and ingenuity. My heart is full of admiration for what my parents have created, laced with a pang of worry. If my parents passed this onto me for safekeeping, it's down to me to make sure it doesn't give up any more precious secrets.

46 - PRESENCE

Jaz merrily types away on a thin keyboard, resembling something out of Star Trek, trying to decipher the action of the laser, whilst my eyes are transfixed on the beauty of this gem. The blue fragmented shafts of light swirl around the room creating a montage of morphing patterns. As I move closer, I feel a weird sensation in my chest. At first, I thought I was becoming overwhelmed with emotion at my parents' ingenuity. However, the closer I get, I'm increasingly feeling sick.

"Be careful, Maisie. Something really weird is happening. As you get closer to the gem, the readings on this screen are going crazy," Jaz says. I glance back at her and march over to see what she meant.

"Look - this is what just happened as you approached it." She points at a graph. I don't understand what I'm looking at.

"So, what does it mean?" I ask.

"No idea. It's acting as if you are attracting something from it," she answers.

"Maybe it's like when I first came into contact with it," I muse. "I put it around my neck, and it started to ask for a password. Although, it was for my mother's eyes only, apparently." Jaz pulls a quizzical look. Then a light bulb moment races across her face.

"An Interactive Data Transfer Device, IDTD," she says mysteriously. "Wow!"

"*What?*" I ask.

"It's a theoretical device that stores data in a digital format, fixed into an object. This must be one of those." Her eyes light up, as if fireworks have exploded in front of her. "They activate when linked to the DNA of a person, or people, and can only be unlocked by their presence."

I feel more and more uncomfortable as she is describing this futuristic mechanism. Is it responding to me standing next to it?

"So, when I put it on, it recognised my DNA? That *is* sci-fi!" I replied.

Stepping towards the sapphire, I have sensation of conflicting pride and anxiety. My parents have created a futuristic device that until now, was thought as a scientist's dream. It slowly becomes clear why so many people have been telling me I am so important to this operation. My very DNA must be built into the gem.

"When I gave the password, *I am your talisman,* it activated the data transfer," I say to myself, but overheard by Jaz. She sits more upright.

"I am loving the serendipity of this, that we should come across such amazing tech." She turns to me and grins. "I am super excited about chatting to Anton. He sounds so cool!"

"Does this mean that without me, the gem is useless?" Jaz nods.

"Apparently, *you* are like a failsafe; the one that holds the key to it." She beams as if receiving a well-earned prize.

"Ok. If that's the case, why have people tried to get rid of me all this time? Without me, this is useless," I ask. Alex pipes up.

"Perhaps, they either didn't know you had such power, or…you were just another pain in the butt, that needed removing from the face of the earth." He grins.

"Thanks Alex, I was missing your sarcasm," I reply.

"Don't you think we need to get out of here soon," Jules asks. "I have a feeling that more guards will be raining down on us." We all look at him and nod.

"So, what do I do about this?" I say, pointing at the gem.

"Ask it something," Jaz suggests. I pull a puzzled expression.

"Ok…hmmm…*switch off*." Nothing happens.

"Maybe you have to use the password first," suggested Jules.

"Ok… *Maisie G - I am your Talisman…*" I say with a silly deeper voice. Suddenly, the gem changes colour to a deeper blue and the white laser switches mode, scanning it with a broader beam.

"Oh wow…that's freaky," Alex says.

"Keep going," Jaz encourages. "Command it to stop or something."

"Sapphire stop!" I say with authority. Nothing.

"Sounds like you need certain keywords, like *cease*, *proceed*, *make it so…*" Alex says, chortling. I glance at him and give a sneer.

"That is quite relevant," I hear Anton tell me.

"What? Are you agreeing with Alex?" I shake my head.

"Try - deactivate, or disconnect," Anton continues.

I speak the words, sceptical about the whole thing. Then, the light changes and the laser powers down. The housing that was revolving, halts and the gem rises. The clasp flips open, beckoning me to release it.

"It worked!" I shout with more excitement than I thought possible and reach across and pull it free. I carefully place it in my waistcoat pocket, covering it with a tissue.

"Great - now can we scarper?" asks Jaz.

"I have bad news…" Jules says, with an ominous tone. "No one is going anywhere." We swing around and gawp at him. He stands across the doorway holding a semi-automatic with the safety off.

47 - TRUST NO ONE

For a moment, lasting far too long, we are staring at Jules, trying to work out what he is meaning. My back bristles. I can literally feel the hairs on my neck stretching out as far as they can. I reduce my eyes to slits. Is he telling us this because we are surrounded, or has he suddenly become our enemy?

"What are you saying?" I manage to gasp.

"You are to stay here…" he replies. "... until they arrive."

A cold shiver runs up my back - a frown creases my face. Jaz and Alex are subdued, bemused as I am. My hand twitches, making an involuntary move to my handgun. Jules raises his weapon towards me. I see he is not messing around.

"Don't do anything, Maisie. I told you to heed my warning," he says with a tone I have not heard before. His whole demeanour is different, as if he's morphed into another person.

"Dude - what is wrong with you?" asks a confused Alex.

"Nothing. I had to wait for the right time to see what released the gem. Now I have the answer, my employers will be pleased," he replies. We keep staring at him.

"You can't be serious," says Jaz, with a quivering voice. "Not after all we went through. Catherine was adamant that we should neutralise Maisie and not kill her." I look across to her and grimace. Is she still onside with me or not?

"Catherine Short has nothing to do with it, Jazmin. She is a pawn in a bigger game. I was placed alongside you all to get into a position of trust and be patient." He flicks the barrel of his weapon across away from where we left our semi-automatics.

"Place all your weapons on the floor and kick them over there." He points. Carefully we drop our handguns on the floor and obey. He waves again, making us walk over towards the door. I hear a crackle in his earpiece.

"Congratulations Jules," I hear a person say. "You have unlocked the mystery of the jewel and caught the big fish. Well done." I fidget and can't resist giving Jules a sneer.

"Secure them and obtain the jewel," they say. Jules nods and waves to me.

"Maisie - the sapphire." I reach into my pocket and slowly draw it out.

"Now carefully, roll it to me. Don't try any fancy tricks. I know your abilities, but you don't know what I am capable of." That comment forces me to raise my eyebrows. I roll it, falling just short of his position. Jules shakes his head, as if he could guess my ruse. I tense my muscles.

He takes a step forward, keeping eye contact and reaches out with his foot. A momentary glance is all it takes for someone's concentration to wander and that can be their downfall. Jules pulls his foot backwards, making his balance change. The weapon is slightly lowered and away from us. The sapphire causes his foot to slip, and his weight is now to his left.

All these factors come into play when deciding the right time to attack. I have to use every ounce of experience to make those life and death decisions, and this is one of them. I breathe slowly and deep. Fixing my eyes on his face, I build up the power release to be quick and effective.

I jump forward like a stone shot from a catapult, my arms raised and ready. My foot kicks up and flicks out at his right hand, the trigger hand, hard and low. His reaction was quick as I expected. The fight in the gym made me fully aware of his reflexes. He sees my attack and tries to pull back. His weight is not balanced. The gem causes him to twist, as it rolls under his foot. These shoes don't help either, giving very little grip.

His weapon fires and sprays the room, thankfully away from the other two, shattering the computer screen and other equipment, sparks flying everywhere. In the mayhem, I stay focused and kick out at the buckle that secures his weapon. It unlocks and the sudden release makes his hand droop. Another kick to his stomach, followed by a series of punches to his head made him stumble backwards. The semi-automatic spirals away from his grasp whilst he attempts to correct his stance.

I can't give him time to recover, so I continue my attack, unrelenting. Another knee to the groin and then punches into his kidneys. Most people would have given up by now. My breathing is rapid and sends a red swirl through my sight. He regains some composure and rolls away from me. I see his hand reach for one of our discarded guns. I see it raised ready for firing straight into my gut.

Then, I hear a shot, the searing heat of the discharge next to my ear. I stare at the face of Jules, into those usually soft brown eyes that captivated me so much when we had our heart to heart. They reflect sadness and regret, slipping away from reality into another realm. A tear forms in the corner of each eye and rolls sympathetically down his cheek. Then, the eyes roll upwards, showing white with red veins and … death.

It takes a moment for my breathing to correct itself. I'm kneeling beside Jules' lifeless body in shock. Blood is smearing the floor around his body, creeping out like an oil slick on the ocean. Shaking my head to get some focus, I turn round to see a handgun quivering, grasped by Jaz, her face ashen and tears rolling.

I carefully take the weapon from her and rise to hug her. Her body is shaking as I embrace her. We need a second to take in what has happened. Alex is steadying himself against a chair, unable to look at anything. His head must be in a whirl too.

"It's ok, it's ok," I say softly into Jaz's ear. "You had to do it. Thank you for saving *my* life this time." Her crying is making her hot and sweaty.

"I'm sorry…so sorry Jules," she weeps. I hold her tighter.

"You did the right thing. He was against us, hanging us out to dry," I say, but my stomach has a huge hole filled with regret.

"I was told to trust no one. I think that proved it. Except for you guys," I say with a smile, tears wetting my cheek. We reach for each other and bear hug.

48 - MONK'S ESCAPE

Standing together like this brings me a quiet confidence that I can trust these two. We found the mole in the team, and he lies unresponsive, in a sea of red. I feel a pang of hurt though, due to my unguarded affection for Jules and that he duped Alex and Jaz too. No wonder he was always so quiet. He didn't want to give anything away or maybe become too attached to us, knowing what his mission was. Alex finally speaks.

"I can't believe that he was hiding in plain sight all this time. I thought we were mates." He shakes his head. I think I spot tears forming in his eyes. That's a first.

"I know," I say. "I was warned that someone in the team was untrustworthy. I just didn't know who." Jaz and Alex both look up and then away from my gaze.

"Sorry Maisie - we made it hard for you to trust us, especially after what Catherine forced us into," says Jaz awkwardly. I allow a smile to break the tension around my jaw.

"I was once told by a Catholic priest that forgiveness is the most difficult thing to choose - it's that feeling of injustice, you are compelled to deal with yourself." This prompts Jaz into weeping, more a release of tension and shock, I guess, than my religious musing. "So, as hard as I find it, I'm choosing to forgive you guys." Before they can answer, I hear shuffling of boots outside the room. I nod to them.

"I think our escort has arrived," I whisper. "Time to get focused."

Alex strides across to the semi-automatics collecting them and hands one to me and then Jaz and says sorry. I smile in return. Jaz similarly repeats her regret.

"That's ok. Now we must adapt - and live!"

I pick up the sapphire and tuck it away in my trousers. This is going with me. I'm not losing it this time. The sounds of boots halts just beyond the door. I see that the lasers are activated, the green strands criss-crossing the corridor.

"Anton. Are you still with us? You have gone quiet."

"Affirmative. Their audio feed continues to be interrupting my access to you, but it has now been restored."

"Are these lasers still active and in your control?" I ask.

"At present, the control is see-sawing back and forth between me and the other administrator. I shall endeavour to overpower it."

"Ok. While they battle with that, is there another way out from this room? Do you have the schematic of this area?" He says he does and indicates an exit through a wall.

"How do we go through that? It's blocked up." I am standing in front of what was once an ancient doorway, now filled in with stone.

"Place your hand on the stones and find one that gives. That should release the mechanism." I obey whilst asking Alex to mind the main door.

I feel around each stone, first by the left and then the right-hand side. This takes far too long, as I hear the guards' agitated voices trying to get the laser to shut down. Alex appears to take matters into his own hands and pokes his semi-automatic through a gap and fires. I spin round, frustrated with his impulsive action.

"What the hell are you doing? That only confirms we are armed and still here." I feel my blood pressure rapidly rising.

As if in confirmation, a torrent of bullets crashes around the door, splinters flying everywhere, making us dive for cover. Alex looks across and mouths sorry. I go back to my prodding and finally something gives. A creak and groan, followed by a grating sound of stone against stone, greets my ears, as the hidden doorway is revealed. I push hard against sandy rock.

I poke my head into what looks like a tunnel. A musty smell wafts out, along with cold clammy air. It must be an escape route for the monks of old, perhaps one of those priest holes where they hid in times of persecution.

I wave madly to Jaz and Alex to follow me. Once through and closing the stone door behind us, we carefully tread the ancient way of escapees, feeling our way along the cold damp walls. The stones are dusty and gritty, fragments getting lodged under my nails. I hear Jaz's breathing becoming laboured. I guess she is heading for a panic attack.

"Keep breathing deep and slow, Jaz. Remember your yoga," I say.

"Yes…I must control my breathing," she pants.

It doesn't help as this tunnel is getting darker and darker. I press my watch for the faintest of lights, which helps a little.

"I will increase the illumination," Anton pipes up, and duly the watch face brightens.

"Where does this lead to, Anton?" I ask.

"It will terminate at the outside of the house, near to a maze. Caution must be taken, as your escape and subsequent termination of Jules has alerted the whole assembly of guards. They will be searching for you everywhere."

That is expected. We must also be mindful that Ayanna is still trapped and Sergeant Jane, the SAS woman, is still around. I don't want them to be caught up in all this too. But where are Shorty and Loser?

"What's going on in the main hall? Are they still being held hostage?" I ask.

"They have been locked in. The four people, who you have named the Horsemen, are lecturing the assembled audience, with a certain amount of intimidation."

"Any sign of Shorty and Loser?"

"None. They have successfully avoided surveillance." Hmm… not surprising.

"Well, keep checking and let me know if you find Ayanna and this Sergeant Jane McAllister. They've disappeared."

"Of course, Maisie."

Jaz grabs my arm and stumbles towards the watch light.

"Oh, how long are we going to be in here? I'm getting panicky," she says.

"Not long - we are nearly there. I can see a light ahead."

As if answering my optimism, I spot a sliver of light running vertically in the distance. It spurs me on, and I break into a canter, pulling Jaz with me.

I reach out and feel a handle. Rough and heavy, it takes all my effort to shift it - a little. Alex catches up and asks if he can have a go. I step aside, resisting the feeling that this is another one of his challenges.

The groan of rusty iron on iron, the grinding of years of disuse, echoes along the tunnel. He jams his weight under the mechanism and pushes harder. I see his face turning a shade of purple as he powers up his arms and hands. With a wrench and a final shove, he manages to free the door, and gives a huge expulsion of breath.

"There, that's got it," he says, putting his hands on his thighs. I slap him on the back.

"That's a challenge I'm pleased you won," I say, grinning. He laughs and returns the slap, this time, with kindness.

49 - DECISIONS, DECISIONS

The rush of air and freedom is overwhelming. Sweet air replaces the dank, with blinding light overwhelming the dark. We spill out onto a paved path, in partial shade from the house. The exit emerges from under some sort of overhanging stairway. I glance to the left and freeze as I see several guards and soldiers wandering around the front of the building. I push the others back into the alcove.

"We can't go that way; it leads straight into a battalion. We will have to make a dash right," I say.

Checking that way seems clear, we ensure that no one from the front can spot us. The huge gaping hole where a stained-glass window once proudly sat, allows the sunlight to blaze through, like a massive search light. We cling to the stonework like mountain goats, the maze that Anton referred to, coming into view.

Anton called it a maze, but I can't be more underwhelmed. It's only about waist high. I was expecting something we could hide in! In the centre, an old well stands and beyond that, a stone terrace, and railings. There doesn't appear to be any guards, so we carefully run along the outside of this lattice pattern of box hedging (how I knew what it was, I do not know!) and carefully head for steps leading out of the maze. The aromatic fragrance of herbs is released as we brush past, making Jaz sneeze.

"Shush," I say, somewhat frustrated.

"Sorry… I'm allergic to these plants," Jaz replies. Alex chortles to himself.

"What's up with you?" I ask.

"I was just thinking; Maze within a maze…" and sniggers again.

"You are a moron at times, Alex," I say. "Come on, we will see where this takes us. Anton, which is the best way out of these gardens?"

"You are in the rear of the house, so I suggest you work your way past the large pond ahead of you, through a tunnel and back to the front," he burbles.

"Ok."

I race ahead checking to see if anyone is over the small rise before us, whilst telling the others to fall to the ground. I crawl to a better position and scan around the lake. It's small and rectangular, with grass areas surrounding it. I spot the tunnel to the right.

"Come on guys, we need to get over there," I say pointing. Weapons low and ready, we start at a slow canter, then speeding up. As we near the tunnel entrance, I hear chatter. It echoes through our escape route.

"Sector 5 is clear. Do we go into the lake area and check there," I hear. *"Affirmative."*

Alex, Jaz and I instinctively run up the bank over the top of the tunnel. We crouch and wait. Boots crunch on gravel and two heads emerge, along with bodies dressed in combat gear. I have to make a decision; jump them and hope that no one is at the other end?

They stop and look around. I hear nothing else nearby. I nod at Alex. He knows what I'm meaning and like a giant ninja drops feet first on top of one of them. The contact of over 200lbs is devastating and the guard collapses with a yelp and groan, as I hear vertebrae break. I follow as the other one is turning to engage with Alex and leap onto his back. I twist my legs around his neck and with all my strength, snap his neck. He crumples under me, and I roll off crouching. We fist bump each other, relieved that it worked.

I look up and wave to Jaz who is frozen in place behind a tree.

"Come on, we need to keep moving," I say, although I have no plan as to where we are going.

We run cautiously through the tunnel, our shoes slipping on the loose gravel, echoing annoyingly. We halt at the end. I duck down low and look through the foliage either side of the exit. The left leads to more gardens, surrounded by tall walls and a gate. Exotic trees line the sides of the path. Ahead another path leads off alongside another stretch of water. To the right, the path goes around the side of the house.

"Ok, Anton, where to now? We have no plan; how do we get out of here? There are loads of pathways."

"You have some decisions to make, Maisie; either exit the compound and house, making good your escape, or prevent the mounting catastrophe in the main hall," he says with a sense of doom.

"And what is that?"

"The Horsemen are threatening the auditorium with death as you are on the loose and they want the sapphire. The man you call Loser is preparing some sort of toxin, which if released in the room will effectively kill them all."

Wow! The weight of all this responsibility is on *me*. I can't believe that I've been dragged into this position. Again, dispatching with Olga seems so much more attractive.

"Have you found where Ayanna is?" I ask tentatively.

"As yet not precisely. If she was left in the room with Catherine Short, then I am assuming she is still ensconced in there." That gives me a sick feeling in my stomach. I need to get her to safety as well.

"As you say, Anton, decisions, decisions." I turn to Alex and Jaz, explaining the situation. Both look subdued; they have their own choices to make.

"Look guys, I know freedom is so attractive at the moment and I'm not wanting to put you in any more danger, but I really need you to be with me on this," I say, resisting a begging speech. "If we scarper, then loads of people will die. If we get a chance to free them too, and kick this Loser's butt, then how much more satisfying would that be?"

I read the hesitancy written across their faces. I quickly glance around, as this is taking far too long, and I don't want any guards creeping up on us as we debate. Jaz is the first answer.

"I am scared and tired and … pissed off," she says. "Maisie, I'm sticking with you, as on my own I'm a mess and you bring the hero out of me…so…I'm coming with you." I smile and nearly choke up. Alex glances at Jaz and then at me.

"Yeah…you are a crazy bitch, but like Jaz, you bring something out of me that I never had…that's a sense of loyalty. So, let's go and kick some butt!" I pull them both to me and we hug.

Decision made, we make a pact to watch each other's back and dive into the unknown.

50 - GUARDIAN ANGEL

Skirting along the wall, we hesitate, as the path widens to an area of grass and opens to the rest of the house. I'm anxiously scanning the windows as anyone could be watching. If we are going to save those trapped, we must find a way into the house again without being detected.

"Anton, is there a door close to the main hall, but quiet enough for us to sneak through?" I ask.

"If you can get around the small garden to the left, a door is situated a little further along. This will take you back into the cloister area and then you must find a passageway which leads back to the outside of the main hall."

"Thanks."

I look at Alex and Jaz. They have no idea what we are throwing ourselves into. Yet I feel they have turned a corner and grown with all this trauma. When I said about grapes being squeezed - this is it!

A weird noise distracts us. Jaz points at a large bird.

"What's that? It's so beautiful!" she says, transfixed. Another cry from its mouth seems to be alerting everyone, giving away our position. The long tail feathers are raised in an arc of patterned brilliance.

"It's a peacock, Jaz," I say. "The house and park must have a flock of them. He's doing his best to attract a female, I guess, with that display." Alex gives me a quizzical look, as if I shouldn't know all these details.

"I learn from the internet, Alex. You should try it sometime, instead of playing games." He screws his lips up as if he was going to have a go at me, but then resumes his focus and nods instead.

I turn to concentrate on our next manoeuvre. We must get round the house without setting any alarms off or attracting any guards. Until now, we seemed to be lucky. The trouble is, I am expecting it to run out soon.

We carefully run to the end of the small garden and keep glancing this way and that. My nerves are really on edge. The wide-open grassed area is giving us no protection at all. Keeping to the house wall and under any windows is as good as it gets. I hear a crunch and then a muffled scurrying noise. I spin round and fix my eyes on a group of guards approaching directly towards us. This group has heavy weapons, easily out gunning us. I feel a panic rising. Instinctively I pull the others back against the wall. It has all the makings of an execution.

They see us and immediately point their weapons, five men in combat gear, automatics primed and ready for blasting us. Alex does what I feared and crouches as if he is in one of his games and is preparing to shoot when the stonework above our heads explodes, raining thousands of fragments over us. I think that was a warning.

"Don't do it Alex. This is a no-win situation," I say.

He snarls like a dog pulling on a lead, annoyed to be held back. Jaz tries to hide behind me, which would give no protection at all, unless I was wearing my bullet proof all-in-one suit. I reckon that would even fail with this assault.

"Hand over the sapphire, Greene," the lead soldier spits. "You have five seconds."

"Or what?" I ask, knowing full well the reply. He fires another round, blasting the ground in front of us, throwing up dust and grit into our faces. We grimace and raise our hands as a weak defence.

"I don't have it…another person has it," I say, attempting to delay the inevitable. He shakes his head.

"How many times have you tried to misdirect us? Now the gem, or we simply take it from the remnants of your corpse." The rest of his troop engage their weapons and spray the ground and the fragments hit us with venom, stinging my legs.

I have to make a judgement and it's one of those life and death things which I hate. To date, I have been able to dodge death, but my belly is giving me, not only butterflies, but a herd of elephants. What makes it worse, is I have Jaz and Alex to consider. I have dragged them into this situation, and I am heavy with regret. I gaze at them both, now almost pressing against each other for a last contact, a final touch of affection. I spin back to the soldiers, my eyes reducing to slits.

"Ok…I do have it. So…*come and get it.*"

I pull it out of my pocket and throw it high into the air. My slow-motion gaze tracks the soldiers as this distracts for a second. I reach for my handgun and raise it as I duck down. At this distance I have a fifty-fifty chance at hitting two of them before all hell breaks loose. My mouth is dry, my sight slightly blurry. I have time to say a quick prayer.

The first round goes off. I hit one in the chest, the biggest target, but the most protected. He staggers backwards. Another crack and the one next to him I manage to catch his shoulder and he spins to the left. The other three are now in execution mode and I can almost sense the triggers being compressed.

To my utter shock one of their heads explodes in a spray of red and white as it shatters. It has the effect of covering the other two in brain splatter, the shock racing across their faces. Another crack. The one to the left is thrown backwards as if he has been pulled back by a rocket, landing in a heap of tangled body armour and blood. The remaining soldier looks up and away from us, ready to fire at whatever is threatening his existence. He fires high and towards a square tower above and right to our position. I see the spray of bullets hit the stonework, the head of someone disappearing.

I will myself to grab one of our semi-automatics and roll into a forward stretch and fire at will. The last man standing, realises too late his doom and tries to re-align himself to fire back. I hit his legs with a quick burst. He crumples, yelling. I finish off by a single shot to his head. It throws him backwards. He's done. The other two I previously shot, are now being blasted by this unknown from the tower. They stand no chance and are finished in seconds.

We take a moment to shake the adrenaline from our heads and I reach Jaz and Alex. I shake their arms and instinctively check for any wounds. They are free and ok, thank God.

I peer up towards the tower as I'm wondering who our guardian angel is. A head appears again along with what must be a high calibre sniper's rifle. I squint to make out the face. *Sergeant Jane McAllister!* It was her. For a second, I wondered if Ayanna had got free. Earlier Jane had made herself scarce and now has thankfully come to our rescue on cue. I throw a thumbs up and mouth thank you, although from this distance, it would look nonsensical.

She disappears, wanting to keep her position as secret as possible. I force my mind back on track, as we now have the task of finding a way to get inside, not get caught or cornered, and set 130 people free from Loser and his horsemen.

I run over to where the sapphire landed, collect it, and push it deeper into my pocket. I wonder how many more times I will have to use it as a distraction. We run to a door, which I expect is the one on Anton's digital mind and try the handle. It gives and my heart flutters. We have weapons at the ready and slowly make our way through the corridor to the cloister area.

“Which way do we go from here, Anton? Left, or right?” I ask. He advises left and to follow the corridor along through a series of rooms and then up a set of stairs to the main hall.

“That’s bound to be guarded like Fort Knox, isn’t it? Can you see anything that would help us?” He says not, as there is no CCTV. “Great! Come on guys - we are blind from here on. Keep a watch out for any noises, signs of anything out of the ordinary.” At that, they both shrug, as if none of this is ordinary.

I agree.

51 - NEW MASKS

Tracking through this warren of rooms and corridors is leaving me confused as to which part of the house we are now in. At each junction, we madly look around, expecting another battalion to be waiting for us. Anton constantly burbles in my ear about the consequences of the sapphire being stolen by Loser, as he now understands what triggers the release of its information.

"You will have to be mindful of your pivotal role in the events that are unfolding, Maisie. Your DNA was infused into the gem's data, so any further extraction will require your presence and action," he explains.

"So, everyone keeps telling me," I say, smouldering in frustration.

This had me wondering about what my mother and father were really up to, before they were killed. Why did they put my DNA in the stone? It's as if they knew exactly what was going to happen to them - and me. I know Olga had promised to care for me in the event of their deaths. But why did they seemingly sacrifice themselves? It sends a shudder along my spine. Alex grabs my shoulder, distracting my thinking.

"I can hear what sounds like chinking, can you hear that?" he says. I listen hard. I sometimes miss things, as I have had so many blasts near my ears, I wonder if I am losing some top end hearing. Jaz nods, as she hears it too.

We are in a long corridor, with paintings and showcases, displaying antiques from the previous owners, one being a poet, I suspect, from all the books on poetry on display.

The sound becomes clearer, and we steady our pace to a crawl. I bob down at the next corner turn and glance around. I see a table, or trolley being gently pulled along by guards wearing protective suits. Is this the threatened concoction to terminate everyone?

"I don't like the look of that. It could be the toxin Loser is cooking up for the guests. We can't go all guns blazing as we could set it off and kill us all," I say. Jaz shudders. Then, she says something sensible.

"We need gas masks, surely. If they are suited up ready for it, then we need to get the same." I look at her in wonder. The drippy girl is coming of age.

"Yes, Jaz, very true. If we can find where they store the suits, we can enter the room incognito and that would be a brilliant cover," I say, impressed.

"So where are they going to be?" asks Alex. "Can you ask Antonio?" Anton immediately rebuffs that mispronunciation and asks me to correct Alex, causing me to smile.

"It's ok, Anton. He likes to provoke. And, as he asks - any ideas about the suits?" I say.

"Check the room along from yourselves, as I believe that is a likely location from where the toxin is being prepared."

We skirt along the wall and reach the door, breathing deeply, but not too deeply as this gas or toxin may be hanging around. I peek through the gap by the hinge. I see suited people wandering around. This is tricky. What if we were exposed before we get the suits? I nod to the others, and nervously push the door wider and creep in.

The room is criss-crossed with pipes and distillation tanks. This could be misinterpreted as monks making their own brew, which they were famous for, except these are clothed in hazmat suits, not in monk's habits. Our presence, fortunately, is totally ignored. I see a box with spare hazmat suits and nod to Alex to grab it. He does, with the gentleness of a *baboon*! The box collapses, flinging the contents across the floor.

The three people, who were previously oblivious to our sneakiness, now turn and launch themselves at us. I stand my ground, issuing a series of punches and kicks, sending one of them spiralling into a set of equipment. Alex launches into a brawl with another, and I can't help but watch how he does it. Resembling a street fighter of old he has his fists high and dances around, waiting for the person to throw the first punch.

"Oh, get on with it, Alex," I shout.

He glances at me, suddenly remembering the training we did and throws a low kick and then blocks the persons fists, he smashes them firmly with a one-two punch in the suited head. They collapse, unconscious.

“That’s better,” I say with a smug expression.

Jaz is attacking the remaining person with her usual ferocity, and I have to restrain her as they are down and out, even though she is hammering their head with her foot.

“Save your strength. We will need it.” She shakes my hands off and nods, staring wildly.

We pull out the suits, sliding them over our clothes, making them tighter than they should be. They are a dusky blue, with a darker blue trim. The masks are generic safety masks designed for toxic spills and hazardous waste. Once we fix everything correctly, which takes forever, we each carry an item from the room looking as if we are on a mission and make our way towards the exit route that the others took. I am hoping, this works, as the mobility in these things is crap.

We waddle along the corridor, nervously passing some guards who are not suited, but give us a wide berth. They have been warned I guess that anyone suited up is a potential hazard. Alex nods as if he’s a mate. I prod him and whisper,

“We are acting out a role, not becoming pals with them.”

He nods and waves. We catch up with the first crew pushing the trolley and slow down, creating a single file of doom carriers. They wait a while causing me to get hot and sweaty. My mask keeps steaming up; I'm wondering if I have it fitted correctly.

Finally, the crew ahead of us are ushered through a door. We dutifully follow, surrounded by guards, jarring my nerves. We found ourselves back in the corridor which leads to the main hall, where we were distributing drinks and food. How things can change in a few hours.

52 - UNVEILING

The doors to the main hall are securely closed and guarded by two burly men, this time not dressed in fatigues, but in suits, wielding impressive looking M27 assault rifles. I am thinking that this bunch likes their weapons, parading them with pride. The guys ahead of us halt and wait, so we do the same. I try not to catch anyone's eye as it could blow our cover.

A nod from one of the guards is given and the lead hazmat moves to the door as it opens, pushing the trolley along as if he's presenting a birthday cake, instead of the canister of death. Certainly not a pleasant surprise treat for anyone. We duly follow and enter the hall.

I feel the tension increase as we walk in. The guests are all lined up against one side, with the chairs stacked to the other. Their faces express a range of anxiety; from ashen, scared, terrified, to disbelief. I overhear one saying, *"I didn't believe he would do this,"* almost collapsing.

We halt at the front of the hall from where the auction was being directed. Loser stands with hands on hips, the four horsemen pacing around him. None of them have gas masks or protective suits on, which I find odd. They have discarded their other masks as well. I can't help but stare at them. I want to take in as much detail of these faces as possible.

For the first time I can study the man with no name. 'Loser' has an ageing face, lines radiating from his eyes to his cheeks, his eyes piercing arctic blue. Frown lines crease his forehead, with a receding hairline. His nose is punch-flat, the end slightly turned upwards. A thin grey goatee covers his chin. I don't know if Anton is getting any feed from here, but if he can get an accurate video of that face, we might be able to get a fix on him.

The four surround him with semi-impatient stances, pacing around as if they are late for a meal appointment. I zone in on Moiran Cafferty, the one who asked for the drinks and seemed to have superiority over the others. Now unmasked, her dreads are hanging as a random frame around her face. She is relatively young looking; I'd guess mid-twenties. Her freckled face makes her look quite the girl next door, except for the snarl that screws up her face. She has a petite nose and large greenish eyes. Mascara is heavy around them, giving the impression she is giving a death stare.

Henri Fontaine, on the other hand, looks quite pretty in comparison. His blonde hair tied in a ponytail makes him look playful. His blue eyes are less aggressive, and his pale skin is softer. He has a typical French hooked nose, which is the only feature that gives away his heritage.

Erin Bogslava is, as Shorty described, very youthful, almost making myself look mature in comparison. She is shorter than the others, and everything about her is petite and cute. Her eyes are small and dark brown, her features in proportion with her child-like head. Her hair style is the only give away to her aggressive nature, half-shaven with red dye, and zig zags along the sides. I have made a mental note to watch out for her.

So, coming to the final horseman, who has no name yet. His Southeast Asian features are just that - they give no clue as to where he comes from. That round face with a constant steely stare and jet-black hair tied so tightly his scalp looks like it's on a torture rack. I expect his fighting skills will be a match for me.

Now I have assessed each one, I am impatient to find Ayanna in this rabble. It has to be my priority to free her and then we can escape this madness. I glance carefully at the guests huddling together. The condensation in this mask is making it difficult to see Jaz and Alex, never mind spotting Ayanna. My own breathing is becoming laboured as I wonder if I have set the apparatus correctly.

I fiddle with the headcover, trying to be discreet. Alex turns and sees my unsuccessful adjusting. He reaches across and twists something and instantly I feel the humid air inside the suit change. The visa de-mists and I can once again see clearly. I nod in thanks. He turns around to face the front. I now notice Jaz is wavering. I hope she isn't having a panic attack.

I was about to reach out to her when the Loser asked for the toxic agent to be brought to the front. We dutifully walk forward, wondering what on earth we are to do now, as I'm sure the real chemical brothers ahead will raise the alarm and ask what we are doing there. I nudge Jaz and Alex, pointing to them to turn left, away from the front, hoping this will make us less conspicuous. As we walk past the horsemen and Loser, I furtively glance up at them. Maybe unwise as I get eye contact with Cafferty, and she stares at me.

"I thought we were releasing one toxin today? Who are these guys and what have they brought in?" she asks Loser. I look at what's in my hands and what the other two brought along. They are canisters which I thought were props for our cover. Loser glares and storms across to us.

"You idiots! Why have you brought the Sarin as well? I didn't request that. Take it back to the lab immediately," he rants.

I hesitate, as this will defeat the reason we came in. We can't leave without Ayanna. I look up to Loser and wave the canister around. It seems to make him nervous. Perhaps we have a bargaining chip. I nudge Alex and Jaz, trying to get them to turn and follow me. I have an idea.

I meander towards the crowd of unwilling onlookers and force a route through them. People volunteer to move out of my way; they probably think I am about to contaminate them. I glance about trying to get a fix on Ayanna. Everyone is maskless so it should be easier.

The commotion is too much for some people and they start a chorus of shouting and screaming. I notice that Loser is starting to lose it and marches across to where we are going waving his arms around.

There, by the window recess, I spot her. She is pale and her mascara has run; looks like she has been in tears. I increase my pace, as I feel Loser is about to pounce on us.

"Ayanna - it's me Maisie," I whisper. "Come with me, *now.*"

I watch her face drift from surprise to unbelief, then to hope. She nods and drifts in behind me. Loser is on top of Alex and pulls his shoulder back to face him. My heart misses a beat as I think this is going to be the end of our rescue.

"You shithead! What do you think you are doing? Get out of this room, *now,* before I keep you here for the end show," he spits with anger. I am praying Alex doesn't go ballistic and swipe him, or we will be ending the show right here and now.

Thankfully, he has the wisdom to just nod, and we dovetail into one line and head for the door. Jaz clangs her canister against a chair, making everyone jump in terror standing close to it. She says sorry, which I thought was ironic.

Our escape is so close now. I reach for the handle and turn it. Behind me, a voice grates and bellows across the room.

“Hold it, you three. I want to see who you are.” It’s Cafferty, her Irish accent rich and damning. We halt and turn to face all four of them staring straight into our masks.

53 - NO HIDING

I stare back at Cafferty, her eyes almost pressing up against the mask visor. She is searching for something to confirm a feeling, a hunch. I have had the same experience when trying to suss someone out. This is uncomfortable; her stare through that dark mascara sends the message she's working for the devil.

"I know those eyes," she says. "I saw them on the way in. Yes…the drinks - it was you!" I flinch as she is so on point. I almost feel like congratulating her and presenting the canister as a prize.

"I didn't know you were part of our team - *or someone else's."* She quickly grabs the canister and rams it into my stomach. I react far too slowly, and the impact winds me instantly. I crumple and cough, spraying the inside of the mask with spit.

"Trying to scare us with a bit of Sarin, are we, little shit? Well, I can't have you messing with our plans, can we."

She turns to Bogslava and nods. As quick as a flash (or the Flash) she produces a knife and slashes Jaz's suit, diagonally. I freeze, half expecting Jaz's bowels to gush out. Thank God, it was only suit-deep and no blood. I see Alex flinch and pray to God he doesn't engage, as guards are ready with their weapons. We are vulnerable and almost immobile in these ridiculous costumes. Jaz has frozen to the spot, and I hear the faint sound of humming.

"What have we here?" Bogslava laughs. "Sounds like a merry tune," she says in a harsh accent. "Perhaps you do a little dance too, sweetheart." She prods her stomach with the knife. Fontaine squares up to Alex, who I thought was going to tower over him, but I'm surprised that he can easily eyeball him.

"Oui, this one too is a petite bebe," he says in a French accent and smirks, drawing out a small device from of his waistcoat. He jams it into Alex's groin. His reaction is instant, and groans as whatever he has jabbed him with takes effect. I think it might be some sort of stun baton, but in miniature. Alex falls to his knees, and Fontaine kicks him in the chest. He collapses at Jaz's feet.

"Well, whoever you are, there is no contest; I am getting bored," says Cafferty. "Guards! Take these rats out and dispose of them." The doors open and the two guys whom we passed on the way in, grab Alex under the arms and drag him out. Jaz is pushed along with him. I am just about getting my breathing steady when Cafferty comes right up to my mask again.

"On second thoughts, I want to play with this one - just take the other one. I'm sure that we can have a bit of fun with you darlin'."

I notice that while this charade is going on, Ayanna has positioned herself close to a suit of armour. She has carefully drawn the sword from its scabbard, cleverly hiding it under her dress. She sidles up to me and Cafferty glares at her.

"Where do you think you are going?" she rasps. "Stay there and enjoy the show."

I'm certain that I don't want to stay around for whatever they have dreamt up, and I shuffle in between Ayanna and Cafferty, trying to hide the sword.

"Hey, pretty thing. Don't you bother trying to help anyone, you are up to your neck in deep shit now," she says with amusement.

She looks back to Loser who has joined the four. He now asks for me to unmask and show myself. This is not playing out well for our escape. Once he knows it's me, he'll make sure I won't be going anywhere - *ever again*!

I take as long as possible to take off my helmet and gas mask, whilst thinking what on earth I can do as a counterattack. I swivel round to eyeball Ayanna; she nods as if she has a plan. I slowly lift and then lower the helmet, my black hair sticking to my face. I casually rearrange it so I can see the expectant eyes of my assailants.

Loser immediately begins to laugh and turns to the crowd.

"Well, well, *Maisie Greene*! Back so soon. I was wondering where you had gone. Ladies and gentlemen," he says, turning to the onlookers, "here is the reason for the show we have arranged for you all. Her parents are the ones who created this toxin, so I am pleased that their daughter has joined us to test it out." He finishes with a swirl of his hands.

Cafferty nods to Bogslava to drag my ass to the front of the hall. Her grip is quite extraordinary. So petite, yet so powerful. I see why her kill rate is so high. I stagger alongside her, making it as difficult as I can to move me around. The suit isn't helping either. It's like being in a space suit, without any zero gravity to float freely.

"What do you mean, my parents created this toxin? You vomit a load of bullshit!" I say with annoyance. He gives a guttural laugh.

"So much you don't know, Miss Greene," he says, smirking. "They were aware that this information was so deadly that they hid it from MI6 and any other organisation. That's why it's with great joy that I can reveal it to our guests."

He follows Bogs and me to the front. I twist my arm trying to get free of this imp, but without any success. I feel like her fingers have fused with the suit. Loser climbs the stand and turns to the audience. He indicates to Bogs to set me down. She lets go.

"Greene, get out of the suit. We would hate for you not to feel the full effects of the toxin," Cafferty spits. I awkwardly pull it off my clothes which are now sweaty and clammy. Fontaine picks it up and sniffs it. *What the hell?* Is he some sort of pervert? Loser addresses the crowd, waving his arms theatrically.

"Now to all here and as a signal to those who are your superiors, this is what we can achieve, not only here, but on a worldwide scale," he explains. "This is a showcase, if you like, to convince you of all the power that I, *we*, have at our fingertips." He motions to someone, and a video begins to play on the large screen used for the auction.

It portrays a group of people in a room not unlike this one, but without the ornate surroundings. They are agitated and scared, which is amplified by shouts and whimpering from the assembled guests here. Then, without any warning, individuals on the video are wiping their noses and murmuring, turning to screaming. Others are holding their heads and placing hands around their ears. There is no sound of anything being released, but it's obvious that a serious toxin is attacking them.

The guests around me are gasping and cringing, some wavering, as if to faint. I find my mouth is dry as the reality of Loser's threat is more than a promise; he's demonstrating what death is going to look like.

54 - NO CONTEST

An overwhelming sense of hopelessness is one I have come to accept as part of living. If I expect a good outcome and don't see it realised, then I am disappointed. If I am wallowing in despair and the situation turns out better, then I have won a prize. This is a way I have tried to learn to overcome fear and anxiety. However, I can't say that I know what to expect out of this situation. I know that I want to live. Yet the odds are stacked against me, allowing clouds of doom to rise over my optimism.

I can't remember ever being in this position before. This crushing responsibility for others, whom I have grown to care for, is foreign to me. I only had Olga to watch out for previously. This mix of personal survival and selfless consideration is an unfamiliar challenge. I find myself grimacing, as I analyse options to get out of this alive. I am coming up short, with every plan.

The video continues to display the horrific work of this toxin. Someone narrates explaining how it damages blood cells, corrupting their integrity and basically exploding everywhere in the body. I find myself cringing along with the rest of the crowd. It is not a pleasant death, if there is one.

"I thought a prelude to the proceedings of today was in order and this theatrical demonstration was for everyone's education," Loser says, with a smug expression. "I trust that you now see what I have is deadly and effective. You have been bidding today for the ability to control this toxin. I have shown you that only one with the foresight and vision could ever oversee its use." He waves his arms around and performs a mock bow. The four horsemen snigger and slow clap, encouraging the guests to follow. As you can imagine, there was little enthusiasm for the applause.

"Miss Greene," he continues, "has thoughtfully joined us as we conclude the auction. She has the last item on sale today. I would encourage you all to be alert to the bidding process, as you are now bidding for your *lives*." He takes a step back, as if he is encouraging me to take centre stage. I glare at him.

"What the hell are you on about?" I ask curtly. He opens his hand.

"Pass over the sapphire, Greene. It will all become clearer," he says with a low intimidating voice. I reluctantly give it to him.

From behind the staging, Cafferty brings out the other case that she and the others brought in. She asks the unnamed one to open it. He duly pulls out his laser wand and points it at the case. It opens with a clunk. Loser walks over to it and places it inside.

"Your parents were clever; I'll give them that. This gem has all the information on the whereabouts and logistics of security forces of the countries that were in collusion with NATO. Their names, locations, weapons etc. are all hidden inside this exquisite gemstone. Now for this to work," he says turning to the crowd, "you will have to bid for its data. The one who bids the highest will have full control and have access to the world's most detailed reference to armed forces anywhere. This in turn can be auctioned to the highest bidder in non-NATO nations. You see, it really could be a great cash builder." He laughs.

"The toxin to be released today will effectively eliminate all the other competition. So, you have a choice: bid or die." He walks off to the side of the staging and smirks at Cafferty, who returns his evil grin.

I can't help a shudder running up my back. I have to do something. This auction is purely for his cash cow, and I don't think that he cares anything about the data. He is effectively getting rid of all *his* competition. This plan has to fail. I can't let it follow through. I glance around the room, trying to locate Ayanna. I was hoping that Sergeant Jane would be on hand again, but I doubt she could break into the hall.

Ayanna is to the left of stage and slowly moving around to where the guards are positioned by the doors. The bidding process cranks up, and the screen is alive with bids coming in thick and fast. I notice that the amount is crazily high; *$350m already!* I suppose when you have the money and your life is at risk, then you have to use it.

Shifting my position, I stare at the four, wondering who in a fight scenario, I could tackle first. I haven't seen any skills from them so far. I can only assume that the Chinese guy will have martial arts sewn into his DNA.

Bogs will be hard as her reputation for killing is well known. Cafferty and Fontaine are the big unknowns. Then there is Loser. I haven't fought him either. A wryly old agent of some sort will be trained to a high level, I guess too.

My instincts will have to lead me, as assume that I must be more than a contest for them; otherwise, we are all toast.

55 - SURPRISE, SURPRISE

This agitation is making me sweaty, as I try to force a decision as to what my next move should be. There is so much fire power in the room. I would be dead before making any difference in the balance of probabilities for a successful escape. I glance from one horseman to the next, then to Loser. Now is the time to do something.

The bidding is frantic, and I can almost taste the fear rising in the room. Now well over $500M, Loser is licking his lips I guess in anticipation of a long stay in the Caribbean. Perhaps he could join the Virgin boss next to Necker Island. I doubt they would be good neighbours, though.

My attention turns to Ayanna, as I am hoping she has a plan which I can dovetail with. She catches my eye and deftly nods. I'm watching as she slowly slides alongside one of the guards at the door. His resolute staring ahead is distracted by her, and he points his gun to tell her to stop. She raises a hand as if complying.

I am willing her to act but doubtful of the outcome. The four walk around impatiently, their eyes glancing over the crowd. Cafferty stares at me and I feel those harsh eyes tracing my gaze across to Ayanna. Is she following an invisible trail to where I'm looking? I can almost see her calculating the connection between us. This woman is one frightening cookie.

Abruptly, she marches towards where Ayanna is standing. My heart flutters, as any secretive plan that was forming, looks like it could be thwarted. With her moving away from the front, the others are distracted and shuffle around. 'Loser' is also tempted to look away from me. Time to make a move.

Anton, for whatever reason, has fallen silent, which is ironic, as his help would be so useful at this moment. I glance at my watch, not to check the time, but to see if any text or message has appeared without me knowing. There is something and I strain to read, careful not to show what I'm doing.

"Be aware that others are on your side. Get ready for a surprise," it reads.

Well, that is weird. Is that from Anton, or some other person? I look up and see that Cafferty is almost on Ayanna, who has spotted she is advancing towards her. The auctioneer is getting very animated as the bids are racing towards a billion dollars. 'Loser' wanders my way.

"I appear to have won the jackpot, Greene. So thoughtful of your parents to have left me this legacy," he scowls. I sneer back and wish I could smack that face so hard.

Then, the lights suddenly die, along with the bidding projection. The mike crackles and sharply cuts off. I watch as Loser along with the others are looking around in shock and surprise. This has to be my cue for derailing this event. I quickly look around, zooming in on the nearest object I can use as a weapon. I rip the mike stand from its moorings and whip out the wires; the plug ends will be great as weights to crash into someone's head.

Fontaine is closest to me, so with my improvised weapon, I whip the spiralling wires across his face. It sends a satisfying yell from his mouth, along with a burst of red from his crooked nose, as he collapses off the stage across the case with the sapphire.

"Smell that, jerk," I spit.

The semi-darkness is helpful to give cover but useless for me to see fully to attack, so I am struggling to focus on the others.

A crack and yells from the crowd echo through the hall as the main doors explode in spectacular style, blowing the guards forward and away. I catch the glimpse of Ayanna using her sword to take advantage of the change in fortunes, forcing it through the nearest guard's chest. She grabs his rifle and fires immediately at the other guard, blasting him.

Not wanting to take any chances, I quickly run to the case where the sapphire is housed and pull it out. I have to make sure this is secure, knowing what it holds. My decision was flawed, though, as Bogslava, races head on at me. Managing to push the gem into my waistcoat pocket, I duck, trying to shield myself from any attack.

Her kick comes hard and viscous to my side, followed by punches and elbows to my head. Rolling with the first barrage, I refocus as quickly as I'm allowed, as she is on me again like a rabid dog. I manage to take a stance and adopt my Wing Chun mode and block her thrusts. I have to be so on point, she is fast and furious, and surprisingly strong for a midget. We trade punches and kicks, parrying each other's moves. This is exhausting and these clothes are not helping; so restrictive, the shoes not giving me any grip.

She jumps and whirls around like a firecracker, so fast I'm mesmerised by her display of martial arts. In happier circumstances I would dearly love to have sparred with her and had a few drinks afterwards to get to know her better, but I fear that will never happen. I think she wants me dead.

Defending myself takes all my energy and I feel like it's ebbing away quickly. Having but a second to consider a different approach to stopping her, we manoeuvre closer to the case that Fontaine collapsed over. I grab it, rolling Fontaine away and use it to shield myself. Bogs' punches are coming thick and fast, unrelenting even with the case, the power behind them constantly pushing me back.

I stumble and drop it. I see her leering down at me and as a last-ditch attempt to down her, I give a swift kick to her left patella. She lurches forward, unable to redirect her pre- programmed attack and takes the full force of my kick. She screeches and falls to the side of me, as I take full advantage and punch her cleanly in the throat.

She rolls away from me holding her knee and throat gasping for air. I don't have any chance to finish her off though, as another attack starts to rain down on me. I swivel and get kicked in the face. It smarts and forces me to roll over the top of Bogs. It's the Asian guy.

He stamps down on my belly, and I yelp in pain. It winds me and I can't move as I'm wedged between Bogs and a stack of chairs. He comes at me again with another stamp, his heel aimed at my head. I pull the case across the unwilling body of Bogs and position it like it defended me earlier. I feel the force of his attack push it hard against my chest as I hold it fast. At least it saved my head.

I throw the case wildly at him, but he just glances it away like a paper aeroplane. Forcing myself up, I take a defiant stance and stare at him. My head is swirling with emotion and adrenaline, making my vision blurry. I have to defend myself and create a moment to attack. My body is suffering though, telling me to give up and rest, but that isn't an option. *Adapt and live* - that's always been my mantra and that is what will save me now.

56 - FIGHT NIGHT

There is no way I am taking this amount of pounding and getting away with it. I have trained all my life for these sorts of scenarios, but real life throws those unexpected tests which push you to your limits.

The Asian guy is a ruthless attacker. I can judge by his stance that his Kung Fu training is of the highest order. I shake my head to focus on whatever comes next. I'm hoping my own stance will indicate my intentions too.

We face each other, eyes locked and determined. With the chaos whirling around us, it's as if we've been transported to another dimension. Weapons discharge is exploding all over like fireworks, begging for my attention but I must focus on this immediate threat. In the dull light, his eyes are locked onto his prey - *me*. When you eyeball someone like this, it feels that you are being sucked into their brain, their world, and your soul is being extracted. I must maintain a strong will as I refuse to be intimidated by him.

Suddenly he launches into an attack and fires his punches and kicks quickly and accurately. I screw up my face with concentration to protect myself, repelling away every assault. Ducking and dodging, I delay my own attack as I have to assess him and work out where his weakness is. Everyone has one, but they can be well hidden if they are masters of their art.

He produces a weapon serenely and effortlessly in the middle of the attack. It was a concealed knife, drawn from his clothes and slashes out at my face. I bend backwards watching the blade drift over my nose. Swivelling, I snatch one of the mikes stand to use as defence. The knife slashes from the right and clatters against the metal, my heart missing a beat as it slices *straight through it*. A blade with that sort of cutting power is very special and rare. A cold shiver runs up my back. *What do I use as a defence against that?*

Leaning forward, slashing from side to side, he pushes me backwards. My foot hits the wall and I realise that I have nowhere else to move. He lurches at me, and I delay my dodge as late as I dare. In slow motion, I watch as the blade slices through my hair and then catches the top of my shoulder, cutting the waistcoat. It continues its journey embedding in the wall. My moment has come.

Having dropped his guard, his throat and torso are exposed. I tense my arms and legs, using the wall as a launch pad, aiming at both parts of his body with a double punch. My fists contact the flesh of his throat and his tense abs with all the power I can bring. His forward momentum has doubled my impact, making the resulting thrust devastating. He crumples up over me, as I sidestep and his face smashes into the stonework. The flesh of his cheek erupts in a spray of red, as it breaks and separates in explosive fashion. A yell comes from his dislocated jaw, confirming he is not a mute.

He lies unresponsive at my feet.

Satisfied that he won't be any threat to me, I gaze across the room, taking in the rest of the mayhem. The darkness is creating a claustrophobic feel to the place and it's impossible to focus on individuals. The flash from guns firing gives frozen cameos of faces in shock and terror. *Where am I going to find Ayanna?*

The main doors have been split and are hanging broken, allowing the only light to cascade into the hall. Other guards have entered and are firing at will, which is terrifying everyone. I catch sight of someone low and defensive, firing back at the advancing guards. That has to be her. I weave my way through the swirling bodies of alive and wounded, forging a path to where I think she is.

"Ayanna," I shout. A face turns, but not who I expected. *Catherine Short?*

"Get down, Maisie," she shouts back. I obey and crouch beside her. I can't help but stare at her.

"How come you have changed sides?" I hiss.

"You are not in the circle of trust that I am," she replies, mysteriously. "It is not about sides, but about maintaining cover for the operations I am involved in which are now wrecked because of your incompetence." A rain of bullets smack into the furniture we are hiding behind. I duck my head.

Her self-righteous answer makes me want to grab the rifle and show how *incompetent* I am. I feel a rise of anger strangling my throat.

"Where does that leave me, then?" I ask. "I am obviously not in your *'circle of trust'* and this whole event is going ballistic. I am not sitting around waiting for your undercover ops to work its way out." I look to the side and roll away from her.

"Where do you think you are going?" she screeches.

"Far away from you - you *charlatan*," I rasp.

I see her face briefly giving one of disdain. Am I bothered? She is still not trustworthy as far I am concerned. So, I have to adapt and get all those I feel protective towards, free. But where is Ayanna? And where are Alex and Jaz? I hope they're still alive.

57 - UN, DEUX, TROIS

Searching for a weapon in this light is a major problem. Dead or wounded people are strewn across the wooden flooring like confetti, making the location of anything useful impossible. I spot one of the guards who was unfortunate enough to clamber through the door early, laying across a sofa, who would at any other time be relaxing, taking in the view. This moment, he is sprawled, with his chest in tatters and an AR-57 lying at right angles to his body. This will do fine.

Grasping the weapon, I quickly check it's loaded with enough rounds to make some headway towards the door. Guards have stationed themselves behind makeshift barricades dotted all over the room. This gives the feel of one of those laser quest games, where everyone is hiding in different places in a dark smoke-filled dungeon. However, I have no coloured lights to tell me who is on my team. This could be tricky.

I know where Shorty is, but where did Ayanna go after the big bang? And who was it that initiated it? My text warned me of an assault, but not who it would be. Maybe it was Sergeant Jane and her SAS pals. It had all the hallmarks of their entry. Also, why isn't Anton giving me any updates? I need his intel.

My watch buzzes. I glance down and see another text. Anton must have read my mind. He is telling me that Alex and Jaz have entered the fray and are fighting guards outside of the hall. Amazing! I'm so glad to hear they are ok. I quickly duck down behind a large cabinet, immediately riddled with bullets.

"Anton. Why are you texting and not talking? Can you hear me?" I whisper. He texts again.

Apparently, the audio is unresponsive via the Bluetooth earpieces, that's why he's texting. Very teenager-ish.

"Ok, so where is Ayanna? I have located Catherine Shorty, who appears to be on our side again. I don't trust her though. You said she was in league with the Loser guy, but she said that it was deep cover, so I don't know what to think." My ramblings have distracted me for far too long. I get the whiff of some after shave I recognise.

Turning too slowly, my head sharply pounds with pain. I roll away from the source and look up into - *Loser's face!* He is holding a metal bar. I guess that's what contacted my head, but I'm not in the right frame of mind to guess, as I start to lose consciousness. I feel another strike across my face, this one waking me up again. *Oww...* I want to sleep, but he drags my body up to his sneering face.

"Greene - you are a fucking pain. I am about to tear you limb from limb, so say your prayers." His words echo in my woozy head as my arms are feeble and don't respond to any encouragement from my will.

He drags me across the floor by my feet, my head bouncing over bodies and scattered furniture. I see a whirl of faces in various states of terror and death, as if it's a ghoulish parade of my own demise. Through a doorway I am wrenched, away from the noise of weapons and people screaming. It's almost calming. Until I feel pain striking through my leg. *Is that a knife he has dug into me?* I let out a scream.

"Good. I'm glad you are still awake enough to suffer," he spits. "All the trouble you have caused, you deserve to know how much I have had to endure over these years waiting for this moment of redemption."

I am crying in agony, totally uninterested in this diatribe. I clutch the leg where the pain is worst. Twisting it, I'm trying to reduce it as much as possible. It doesn't seem to work; it's excruciating. Pressing hard, I stem the blood flow, adding to my torture. Looking into his sneering expression, I shake my head to get some focus back.

"What… what the hell are you on about now?" I splutter.

He kicks my leg adding to the torment.

"Your parents…they were so self-righteous, so full of themselves. They didn't care about other agents or friends. Everything they touched turned to ash." He walks away from me and pulls out a handgun. "All this work they did for MI6 was a charade. They had designs on this toxin, long before any of us realised what was happening," he continued, checking the magazine.

I pull myself up against a wall, my vision switching between blurry and clear. Glancing around, I seem to be in part of the cloister corridors. I recognise the windows.

"Their attempts at keeping this information to themselves was for their own gain; a bargaining chip, if you like, if MI6 turned on them. You see, my role was to ascertain their loyalty, their reliability." He turns to face me and fires. My heart shudders, as it ricochets off the stonework, next to my ear. It throbs painfully, and my hearing has been thrown into the depths of the sea.

"I was engaged in a deep cover operation, before Trojan ever emerged," he continues. "Other agencies, mainly the one you and Olga so adeptly worked for, were seeking this information. They had designs on controlling this toxin as it would mean their influence would be boundless. There would be no limits to their reach."

His monologue falls on deaf ears (literally) as I attempt to control my pain, my threshold now well beyond what I would have thought possible. I shuffle around and tie a piece of my torn waistcoat around my upper leg.

"Having discovered this, I was, shall we say, 'turned' by the potential fortune that this control would give. I was seduced and intoxicated by the wealth and influence it could give me." He walks across in front of me, waving the gun around.

"The assassination of your parents was a death nail to my plans, though. The agency that sought it, thought that dealing with the source was the best way to stop it from going to the highest bidder. They put the hit out on them. It was ironic that Olga was the one chosen for it." He smirks and fires again, this time the right side of my head, fragments of stone stinging my face.

"The information was lost, as far as everyone knew. But I always believed it would reappear, with someone, somewhere. Like a lucky penny, it would fall into my lap, to be resurrected." He sits on his haunches and stares at me.

"You, my girl, are my insurance; my route to fulfilling my plans. Except for one thing…I didn't realise that your father would have created a device that would be controlled by your DNA. Quite magical, but very annoying. So, I have to make a judgement call - do I keep you alive and make the sapphire divulge its contents or just make as much money as I can and then disappear, leaving no trace of the toxin and therefore no one to use it?" He shakes his head and stands.

"Decisions, decisions…" he walks away from me, tapping the barrel on his cheek. "Un, deux, *trois…*"

He spins around and points the gun directly at my head. I don't have time to pray.

58 - CAVALRY

I screw my eyes up and wait for the bang and bullet of death smashing through my skull. It doesn't happen. Another loud bang does, though, to my left. A flash grenade explodes almost on top of me, which adds to my trashed hearing. I roll uncontrollably to my right side away from the blast. Smoke fills the corridor, along with dull echoes of shouting and firing of weapons. Spitting out dust and stone fragments, I scan around for somewhere to hide. My leg is so painful, trying to run or even walk would send me into dreamland. I'd probably collapse.

A niche in the wall will do and I drag myself, keeping low, out of any crossfire. Through the haze, I watch a troop firing towards Loser's position, but can't spot him anywhere. I crack my jaw trying to get some hearing back again. It's slowly responding, but everything is still dim. A person dressed for the masked ball slides across to me. It's Jane.

"Maisie! You're alive, thank God! I thought we may have lost you in the mayhem," she says. I give an involuntary smile.

"Not done yet, Jane," I reply. "I guess this is your crew coming to the rescue?"

"Yes. We had difficulty getting past the guards leading to the hall, but we fought through…lost a few though," she says, with sadness creeping across her lined face.

"Did you get Loser?" I ask. She gives a quizzical look.

"I don't know who that is."

"That's the common thread here…no one does!" I replied. "He was here a second ago, about to fire a bullet through my head. He seems to have vanished."

I scan around now the smoke is clearing and see three others, dressed in dark fatigues, with the SAS logo on their shoulders, standing guarding back and front of our position.

"We will find him. If we recognise him from the main hall, we will get him."

"Good luck with that - he acts like a ghost." She smiles but then looks anxious. My leg is pouring with blood.

"*Medic*!" she shouts.

A team member races over and starts to assess the damage. My leg is bandaged and wrapped tightly. They pull out various stuff from their bag, but my concentration is wandering. It's abruptly brought back into focus again as she stabs my leg.

"Oww!" My protest was as weak as it gets. I then begin to feel a warmth rise as the effect of the syringe is working.

"Thanks," I finally say and the medic smirks.

"Ok. We need to extract you out of here," Jane continues. "Debs will lead you out of these cloisters to a safer place." She nods at who must be Debs.

"What about Ayanna and Alex and Jaz. We can't leave them," I say, somewhat slurred.

"We will do our best. It's a mess everywhere. There's no clear way to help everyone. You are our main priority."

I should feel smug to think that the SAS have me as their prime concern, but I can't help feeling a tug of loyalty for my team.

"We must get them out as well. I'm not leaving them to this bunch of deranged idiots," I protest.

"Yes, understood." She relays my concerns into her comms, and it screeches back.

"Also, we have to get rid of this toxin or we will all be toast." She gives me a frown and nods.

"Do you know where it is?"

"Last seen in the main hall, as the four horsemen and Loser were threatening everyone." She again repeats my words, and a reply is sent.

"I think we must neutralise that first, even though you are in dire need of medical help," she says. I nod and try to get to my feet.

It's like climbing a cliff face, as my leg is not acting as it should. I think whatever the medic pumped into me, has numbed it. I force it to move. Jane gives me a scowl.

"This will not be good for you," she says. I nod.

"Probably not, but we have to get this toxin destroyed. I'll ask Anton what to do about it." She gives a look of surprise.

"Who is he?"

"Someone who is helping me." I'm not in the mood for long explanations.

"Anton, are you listening?"

A muffled sound echoes through my earpiece.

"Yes…it's…difficult…to…break…through…the interference," he says, straining.

"What do we need to do to contain this toxin?"

"I need… to have the exact …components of it… to give an accurate answer." I shake my head in frustration.

"This is no time to be picky about the facts, Anton! We are in a massive mess if we don't neutralise it. Come on, there has to be a quick solution." I think my anger is forcing adrenaline through my veins as my body is coming alive again.

"With any biological bomb… a high degree of heat… will be required to… incinerate it completely," he finally concludes.

"Ok…" I say to Jane. "Do we have anything that can burn this bastard to dust?" She looks at me and thinks. A disappointing shake of the head pours proverbial water over my fiery determination.

"There has to be something. *Come on*...let's get to the hall and see what is happening." I hobble along and Jane grabs my arm.

"This way, Maisie," she says. I must be completely brain dead, because I have no idea where I am going. "We will guide you," she says.

Anton chatters to me again, coming up with a plausible idea.

"I have been delving into the possible outcomes of any toxin released. It would appear that your parents have taken precautions against any biological weapon being used in their absence."

"Ok, that sounds interesting," I reply. "And...?"

"The sapphire may hold the answer, Maisie." Oh, that's not what I expected.

"Your DNA appears to be a catalyst to its operation. Therefore, it is reasonable to think that you have control over anything it will have a connection to."

My dull thinking is taking time to catch up with his assumptions, and my less than hundred percent energy is dragging my down my optimism.

We are shuffling closer to the hall, sounds of firing resonating along the corridor. Jane holds me back as we approach a corner. She waves the other two to scan the area. They dutifully raise their weapons and sweep the adjacent rooms and corridor. Anton had better be right about this.

59 - RISK IS NOT A GAME

Jane and her SAS team drag my ass along the corridors towards the main hall, although after what I've just been through, it isn't the place I really want to be. We pass scores of dead guards, both in fatigues and suits, lying scattered all along the route. I casually picked up a sub-machine gun from one of them as insurance.

Jane pauses as she hears something, which my wrecked hearing misses completely. We all crouch, but my leg forces a shout of pain. Jane muffles my cry with her hand. *Thanks, but I really didn't mean to make a noise.*

"Open the doors - we have to evacuate, *NOW!*" a person screeches. If my hearing wasn't so poor, I could have sworn that was Cafferty. That Irish accent penetrates *even* my dim head.

Jane grabs my arm and forces me to hide behind one of the team. Another one scuttles along to the corner of the corridor to check the scene. She waves and gives various hand signals which mean something to the SAS but nothing to me. Another one of the team joins her and bobs down. There seems to be a hiatus; no one is moving. We hear a voice shouting again.

"Damn fuckers! Get the toxin aboard now; stop pissing around!" I hear.

The DF's must be the SAS, as Debs turns and grins. I don't know how many there are in this team, but the three here must have backup of more elsewhere, as I hear firing and explosions further away.

"Have you located Alex and Jaz?" I ask Jane.

"Yes… and no," she replies. "They were in the fight at the main hall doorway, but we lost contact with them as we forced entry." The tone of her voice signals regret.

"Oh no, I hope they are ok," I say. "Anton - can you locate Alex and Jaz. I'm worried they may be captured, or *dead*." My heart flutters.

"It is confirmed they have been quarantined by a group of MI6 operatives who are now active on the scene," he chirps.

"Wow, I didn't realise we had others on site. They are safe, aren't they?"

"As far as I can tell," he replies. Jane gives me a quizzical look.

"How is this, Anton, able to locate them accurately? Even we don't have any feed on their whereabouts," asks Jane. I smile.

"There's not a great deal that Anton does not know. It's complicated but reassuring," I say. She shakes her head and turns to watching the other two down the corridor.

A burst of fire rattles the windows and stonework, forcing them backwards, finding safer cover. They return fire. Jane talks to her comms, and she receives an update.

"It appears that your Anton is correct - a group of MI6 operatives have descended and are working alongside our unit. Your friends are safe and secure." She's interrupted as another message crackles through.

"OK. Team, we have to make a way through to the Chinook; *we have a code red,*" she says urgently. Turning to me, she explains.

"Apparently the conspirators are attempting to escape with whatever they threatened to release on the gathered people. We have been ordered to stop them," she says, breathless with the anticipated assault. I try to get to my feet ready to follow, but Jane tries to delay me.

"I don't think you are in any fit state for a fire fight. I'll get you somewhere safe. Leave this to us." I stare in defiance.

"I am not sitting around and missing the chance to finish off this job. Who do you think I am?" I ask.

"I know Maisie, you are a tough cookie, but I don't want you getting hurt anymore. You have done enough. Leave it to the professionals." I wince at this comparison of my own status.

"Maybe you are trained for this sort of thing, but I have been trained since I was a little kid. I do not sit out and let others do the work for me," I say, feeling flush with annoyance.

I get to my feet and walk, although awkwardly, towards the corridor exit, dragging my injured leg. Jane rushes alongside, grabbing my arm.

"You are a damn obstinate girl," she says, handing me another gun. "Just make sure you keep well clear of any assault we execute. I don't want you caught in the crossfire." She smiles and rests her warm hand on mine. "We could do with a recruit like you on our team one day." I return the smile and shake my head.

"I think I've had enough of being put into teams; I work better on my own," I answer.

We skirt around the corner and check no one is waiting. It appears that the evacuation is fully underway as no guards are in evidence. Reaching an outside doorway, the team assesses the danger and do all their hand signals. Jane nods to me that we can proceed.

I notice a case lying alongside the door. It has the look of a weapons case, maybe something the guards have left behind in the chaos. Curiosity draws me. I reach out and lift the lid, hoping that there is no boobytrap waiting to blow up in my face. The hinges creak and the smell of accelerant escapes the case, as I reveal the prize. The rest of the SAS team continued through the door, leaving me wondering how I could use this lethal weapon.

Anton had advised me that the toxin had to be destroyed with extreme heat. Could this generate enough if used? I'm not sure.

"Anton - I have what looks like an RPG 30. Can it be used to incinerate the toxin?" I ask.

"If you were to add another accelerant to it, such as aviation fuel, that would be adequate," he says cheerfully.

That has to be a solution, I am thinking, as I hear Jane calling back to me; the Chinook is preparing to fly. The thudding noise of the rotors begins to pick up speed. Staggering to the doorway, I see that opposing guards have stationed themselves around the base of the helicopter and are holding their ground. Jane and her team have taken defensive positions behind stonework porticos and are returning fire.

Through a side window in the chopper, I catch sight of those dreads and 'Loser' staring at us. My sense of outrage is building as this person is escaping again, along with his merry band of conspirators, the four horsemen. The injustice builds in me. I have to do something to stop this man once and for all. He has caused me so much pain and headache over this last year. Accusing my parents of all sorts of atrocities and colluding with other organisations. *I have to stop him.*

A rain of bullets crashed about my head, forcing me to dive onto the gritty surface of the car park. Spluttering, I lift my sight to see the Chinook begin to lift off, despite a hail of outgoing fire from the SAS team. It must have some sort of enhanced armour, as the bullets are bouncing off the fuselage.

I watch as Loser and Cafferty wave in derision and arrogance, as they rise effortlessly from the grass, loose material flying back at us. My head is pounding as my blood pressure responds in anguished hesitation. Madly, I scan the car park area for something to inspire me to act. I spot several trial motorbikes parked up in front of the old part of the abbey. A plan shoots through my head. I scuttle towards Jane's position.

"Have you any grenades? I need as many as I can get." She grimaces.

"What the hell are you going to do with them?" she asks.

"Create a firestorm," I say, smirking. Jane instructs her team to pass over any grenades they have.

"I also need your belt."

"I am getting a bad feeling about this, Maisie. What are you planning?" she asks. I ignore her question and ask if the team can give me cover.

"I'm running over there." I point to the bikes. Jane shakes her head.

"There is no way you are getting that far, even with two good legs. It's suicide!" I nod in agreement, but either it's my superior optimism or the drugs I've been pumped with are driving me to do it. I drag the case I found and hand it over to Jane.

"Here this will give us all the distraction we need." She looks at the contents and smiles.

"An RPG 30, nice one. So, I guess you want me to use it as you hobble over there?" I nod wildly. I can't help a manic grin crease my face.

"It's likely that the Chinook is equipped with chaff flares or some protection device, so it won't penetrate its defences. But it will be enough to change its course," I say. Jane nods and reluctantly says she will do it.

"Just be careful, Maisie. I don't want to add you to the casualty list." I smile.

Eyeing up the run (or hobble), my heart rate is pounding my ears. I will only have one chance to execute this.

A risk I know, but risk should be my middle name.

60 - STRING OF PEARLS

The length of time that it took from where I was in relative safety, to the wide-open space of the car park, was vastly underestimated. I don't know what I was thinking. It was further and more difficult, as my gammy leg was dragging me down too much. Even with the cover of the SAS team, I was showered with ricochets from bullets spraying around my head and feet. Fortunately, none hit me.

The nearest bike was waiting patiently for my arrival and I'm hoping that it will be a willing participant in my plan. I strap the grenades in a loop around my torso, tightening the belt. I don't want these coming off too soon and blowing me to bits. The bike thankfully has a key slotted in the ignition. Someone was expecting a quick getaway; however, my plans are scuppering that.

I switch on and rev the engine, at the risk of attracting more fire. Jane sees my predicament and nods. I give a thumbs up. The Chinook has risen to the height of the building and makes a turn. My calculated plan is that when the RPG explodes, it should direct the chopper away and over the lake. *I hope.*

Revving the bike and spinning it round on the gravel, I eye up my trajectory. If my thinking is correct, the Chinook will bank to the right. A raised section of land offers a ramp and is my only hope of succeeding with this mad scheme. I wait for the RPG to fire.

Swoosh, crack; the accelerant fires the rocket straight and true. As I expected, flares exploded, scattering around the fuselage, to confuse the warhead. *Duff - Duff - Duff,* they belch, like dragon's breath. The RPG now distracted veers off to the left and explodes in front of the Chinook, causing it to make a defensive manoeuvre.

As predicted, it begins to fly towards the lake. I rev as high as I can without spinning it out of control and release the clutch. I find the gear change really difficult as my leg is still playing stupid, but I force it. I am in full flight and the rush of air is flapping my hair around my face, distorting my vision.

"Get out of my eyes," I cry pointlessly.

I hit the bank with force, my body lurching forwards as it mounts the ramp. I can see the Chinook through my unwieldy hair just ahead of me. Twisting the throttle full on, I launch myself into the air.

That feeling of weightlessness is exhilarating but also scary, especially when I'm heading for huge rotor blades. I somehow have enough time in my slow-motion mode to unstrap my grenades and swing the string of deadly pearls at the helicopter.

The bike is so high that to my horror, I am travelling over the top of the Chinook, the tyres striking the blades of the front rotors. It has the mind-numbing effect of tossing me forward. I have a nano second of thought that I was going to be sliced into pepperoni. The string of pearls twists and turns as it descends onto the middle section of the fuselage, hooking onto a comms wire.

The bike gets mangled up in the blades and I hear a mashing of metal as it gets spat out. *I am* still flying; how I'm not sure, but my heart is screaming as I am descending rapidly towards the lake surface. It flashed through my thoughts that I hope the lake is deep enough for me to land with more than a fifty-fifty chance of surviving. Also, I have a flashback of the Olympics that to hit the surface of the water safely, you have to enter it with arms outstretched and be vertical, or the impact would smash me to pulp.

Whatever happened next, I can't tell. I blacked out.

***

I find myself splashing around in a watery grave, arms flailing as usual, trying to stop me from sinking. These shoes are determined to make me sink further, as the silt is dragging me down, so I kick them off and attempt to doggy paddle to what looks like an old fortress. I pull myself up onto a stone platform and lie, breathless and exhausted. Looking into the blue sky, I notice a dark shadow looming over my haven. Glancing across the lake, a fireball has exploded and now ditched itself into the water, smouldering, a cloud of foreboding smoke rising.

I can only assume my mad scheme worked. Shaking the water out of my ears, I prop up on sensitive elbows to take in the full picture. There is no recognisable sign of the Chinook, just debris scattered over the lake surface and some on the banks. I sigh with relief that I am still alive, miraculously. Also, I'm hoping that I did enough to neutralise the toxin, otherwise, the whole area will have to be quarantined.

Checking my ears and eyes for any signs of bleeding, my thoughts race at the possibility that some could have escaped, and I would be infected. What an irony, if after all this, I was the one that died from a toxin that my mother and father prevented the world from having. Please God…no.

61 - TEAM WORKS

Again, I lie on my back barely able to raise my head, I am so drained. My leg is pounding again; the drugs are wearing off. I try to bring my breathing back into order, but my heart is racing like a cascade. Sounds of scuttling behind me are not enough to make me move, so I'm hoping these are friends not foes. Perhaps they can't see me anyway. The scrambling noises stop.

"She's over there," I hear someone shout. I have been spotted.

"*Maisie, Maisie,*" a voice calls, one I know so well.

"You are alive, you crazy bitch," Alex says. His head blots out the blue, and I'm looking up into his mouth of gleaming white teeth, amplified by his dirty face. I can't help a splutter and try to laugh but it hurts.

"What did you expect? Adapt… and live, eh?" I gasp. I hear another voice I welcome.

"*Maisssssiiiie!*" Jaz's expressive nature is working overtime. She kneels next to me and hugs my tired body, which has no energy to return it.

"Ok, Jaz - I'm pleased that you are alive too," I say.

"Oh my god…when I saw the helicopter explode, I thought you were gone," she says, now with tears streaming down her cheeks.

I prop myself up again and study them. They both look like extras out of a Rambo movie, with streaks of dried blood smeared across their faces, with ripped clothes, and weapons in hand. I afford the luxury of a chuckle.

"Well, well. We made it as a team, in the end, just as Ayanna wanted." I pause and then think, *where is she?*

"Yeah, it was her heroic fight in the hallway that saved our necks. She was like The Witcher, swishing that sword around with one hand and using a sub machine gun in the other. I've never seen anything like it," Alex says. "Except for one of my games…"

"Yeah, ok. We are not going down that path thank you," Jaz interrupts, putting her hand across his mouth. I laugh and try to get up. One leg allows me to kneel but the other one is really complaining. They both come either side and loop their arms through mine.

"Thanks guys. You are amazing too. I heard you were in a fire fight. Then MI6 came along. What did they do?" I ask.

"They arrested Catherine Short and said that Delaware was in detention after they found out about his plan to release the toxin in London." I stare at them.

"What? He was planning an attack on London. Was he the mastermind behind Shorty's deep cover?" I ask.

"No one knows, but they are pretty clear on his involvement with this Loser guy, who I hope you have incinerated along with the toxin," Jaz says.

I gaze across the lake now subdivided into smaller smouldering wrecks drifting towards the waterfall, hoping that she was right. Several bodies are floating along with the debris, so it won't be long before the casualty list is known.

They lift me gently as I limp back along the lakeside. We stagger to the bridge over the waterfall, watching larger pieces of wreckage caught in the drainage grill. It's a grizzly sight, but I study any body parts that are caught up in the wreckage, hoping to confirm they are all dead. Sergeant Jane distracts me as she runs over to us.

"Oh… my…God!" she says. "How you did that, I will never know. It was awesome. My team wants to give you an award for bravery. I'm inclined to give you a clip round the ear," she says, grinning.

"I think that's what we gave this lot," I say nodding to the floating gallery of silent enemies.

"You sure did. Come on, we have now secured the site as the last of the guards have surrendered. I believe Ayanna, your MI6 mentor, wants to see you," Jane says.

We make our way slowly back to the front of the house, passing groups of guards in handcuffs or plastic hand ties kneeling, subdued. A shout comes from the doorway. It's Ayanna. She runs over to us, a huge smile stretched across her face. Dropping a rifle, she hugs me and draws the other two closer.

"I am so relieved that you are ok. What a team!" she gushes. "I heard that you acted like a superhero, Maisie, destroying the Chinook." I give a weak smile back, and stumble, as the pain in my leg is rapidly increasing. She quickly grabs my arm.

"Come on; we must get that wound seen to. *Medic!*" she shouts. I lay down on the grass where once sat the helicopter, surrounded by army trucks and response vehicles. A man races to me and begins to assess the damage.

I start to feel relaxed, induced by the painkillers and welcome their soothing work. The swirl of people around me seems to merge into a mix of colours and effigies, which are no longer recognisable. The drugs he's given me must have forced me to shut down. Sounds are making no sense to me anymore, as I'm carried to a waiting ambulance. I never knew that such drugs existed. Not surprising that some people get hooked on them. Once inside, the chaos and noises dumb down as the doors are closed. I squint at lights on the roof, which are now turning into snakes, slithering here and there.

I turn to who I think is the ambulance person, although my eyes are heavy with sedation, I can't really tell. I feel a prod on my arm as a drip is delivered. The doors open again, and I think I hear Jaz. She wants to come with me. That's sweet. I hear myself say, *"thanks Jaz,"* in a slurred voice. The door closes again and my body sways from side to side, as the vehicle moves.

A warm hand is placed on mine. It's comforting. Reassuring. I turn to the person who is sitting next to me. I smile and try my best to focus. The chaotic curly hair and the drippy eyes are not what I see, though. The eyes appear harsh and filled with venom. The medic who was with me is sitting in the corner, but red is smeared across his chest. I shake my head as I think the drugs are giving me hallucinations.

The voice that I thought was Jaz's, has changed tone and is issuing words that are hateful and menacing. I attempt to pull back, as the hand that once gave me comfort, is grasping it hard and violently yanking it.

Through my blurred vision and rising anxiety, I am forcing an image of the person who is with me.

It can't be…

62 - AMBULANCE RUN

I have a moment of anguish as my eyes are refocusing on this interloper. Their grip is tightening around my arm, the force draining away any blood. The cannula is pulling sharply across my skin, making me want to yell. The next thing I have to deal with is sharper still; a knife is pushed up to my throat. I attempt to steady my breathing, except, the bloody cannula is causing me so much pain I feel compelled to yank it out. One thing with this extra agony, though, I am waking up and getting more focused, with the effects of drugs wearing off.

"Well darlin', you thought we had all been blown to shit. Sorry to disappoint. Anyone who is anyone in the world, has body doubles, so ours did the trick on the chopper." She leers over me, her dreads dangling like leeches across my chest. "Shame all that effort went to waste; quite impressive all the theatrics with the motorbike." Her hand presses the knife harder against my skin, the sting tells me it's broken; I feel a trickle of blood.

"So, what do we do now? I have a plan, darlin'. Let's see if *'Maisie G'*, as you like to be called, has any limits to the pain she can suffer before she says goodbye to the world." I flinch as she finds the spot on my leg and pushes brutally hard.

I clench my teeth and suppress a yell. Becoming more aware because of my torture, I see that I'm strapped down on this bed, my arms fixed by Velcro restraints. Not good.

I think about shouting out, but the knife at my neck is millimetres away from my jugular, so that would be suicide. I glance around trying to find something that I could use to get free. The equipment in an ambulance is all about saving life, not ending it, so I'm sadly lacking any useful weapon. I do spot something that has potential though. First, I have to get these restraints off.

"It's been a revelation about your fathers' ingenuity. Who would have thought that their daughter's DNA would be the key to unlocking this secretive information." She presses again, making me wince. "Quite inventive, although maybe a little selfish. I think they were willing to sacrifice their little girl for the sake of keeping this information from the rest of us. From what I've heard, they were always looking after themselves and not others; so why would you be any different?" She moves up close and stares, with her dark mascara now scuffed and running, she has that twisted deranged look I saw on the stage.

"I am sure they were more far-sighted than you," I say, with pointless bravado, but I can't help but provoke.

She snarls, pressing harder and the blade sinks a fraction further. I try to swallow, but the knife digs in more. Adding to my pain, are the road bumps along the driveway. We hit one too hard, sending everything in the back jumping like we are in zero gravity. It has the thankful effect of distracting Cafferty, and she leaves me to bang on the bulkhead, shouting her annoyance.

One of the Velcro strips is not so tight, so I twist my wrist to get my fingers on the flap. As everyone knows, it is never quiet, when undoing. At least, it's worth a try and I pull it quickly, freeing my left arm. I pull out the cannula and switch to freeing my right arm. I improvise and use the cannula needle and jam into her face.

"*Take that, darlin',*" I yell. She screams, while I grab my next item for a weapon. It's a metal walking frame.

Yes, I know it sounds lame, but I have to adapt. I swing it as hard as I can at Cafferty, who now has swung round to face me, having pulled the needle out, knife at the ready. It effectively pins her against the van side as she jabs outwards. I wrench it sideways, catching her neck in the bars. I kick as accurately as I can to her sternum, with my head swimming from the sudden exertion. She blocks it and twists my foot. Still holding the frame, I fall against the stretcher. She lurches towards me. I use the stretcher as a barrier and pull it in between us.

Cafferty screeches with annoyance and rams the bed into my leg, sending a mind-numbing spark of pain through me. Now I'm pinned against the rear doors. A good time to exit? I pull the padding from the bed and wrap it around myself. Lifting the handle, I pray that the vehicle is not moving too fast, and we are not on a main road yet, otherwise I'll be mashed up. The momentum spits me out, and I land awkwardly on the tarmac drive.

Thanks to the padding, I unroll like loo paper along the road, into shrubs and trees, coming to an ungainly halt on a raised bank. I quickly check to see if the ambulance has stopped and scan the surroundings. There looks like a path leading through the woods, so I scramble towards it, holding my throbbing leg. I hear a squeal of brakes, so I'm not hanging around as Cafferty will be on me like a rash.

Normally I can run as fast as an Olympian, but today it's just a hobble and limp, making me anxious about how far I can keep ahead of her.

The tangled undergrowth, trees, and branches, feel as if they are in league with Cafferty, tripping me up and whipping my head as I struggle to get some pace. The forest floor is slippery from wet fallen leaves and pine needles, and considering I have no shoes is also bloody painful. I hear her dulcet yelling, trying to hound me down. I have to push on.

There is a sudden crunching and swishing of branches to my right and someone lurches towards me. Instinctively, I twist away from their attack, dropping low and swinging my good leg around, contacting the back of theirs. They shout and fling backwards, followed by a gloopy scrunch. I don't have time to check what happened; I just see blood spurting out of their chest. I think they were impaled on a horizontal branch.

I keep running, eventually coming to the path's end, leading back to the road again. Surely, I must be close to the house and safety. Where's my backup? I glance up the hill where the road leads to the exit and the shouting. My head and leg join forces to slow me down further, the pain making me stumble. Then, I hear a roar. I lift my weary eyes and see two trail bikes racing towards me.

Feeling like a hitchhiker, I lift my arm. I hope these are friends. They screech to halt and spin round, kicking sand and gravel in my face. Sputtering, I wipe my eyes and hope rises as I see Ayanna on one and Alex, with Jaz on the back.

"Come on, we need to get out of here," Ayanna shouts. I smile and drag my butt to get on her seat behind her. "Are you ok? I wondered where you had disappeared to. Then Jane pointed out that an ambulance had taken you - not ours, so I was crapping myself." She turns and smiles.

I hear a crack of gun fire from the path and road. Ayanna and Alex rev their bikes and we speed off down the drive back to the house, my hair flapping around like a hurricane Sunday. A bullet clangs against the metal of our bike and ricochets off. I'm clinging like a baby monkey to Ayanna, thanking God I have her as my protector. We roar along the tarmac now getting a shimmery coating from the fresh rain falling, the spray washing my face.

Pulling in front of the house, Ayanna kicks out the stand and asks me to carefully get off. Swinging my leg isn't easy, and I see fresh blood soaking my black trousers. Alex and Jaz both rush over and help me staggering.

"Quick! We need backup along the road - assailants are still on the loose," she orders, to a group of SAS troops. Jane races over, as serious as I've ever seen her.

"What the hell has happened?" she demands. "I thought you were in safe hands," her eyes staring at Ayanna.

"The ambulance was a decoy. The four and their boss are still on the loose," I say. "The Chinook was a false flag. I don't even know if the toxin was on it." I feel the weight of disappointment pulling me down and I collapse.

Jaz manages to grab me before I hit the deck.

"Got ya," she says.

"Glad you have," I say, giving a weak smile and begin to drift.

63 - SLIPPERY SOAP

Ayanna ensures that my medics are legit, and they set up a comfortable makeshift bed for me to lie on while they attend to my wounds. A gauze is attached to my throat, as the cut was deeper than I thought. The stab wound on my leg needed stitches, so that is all bound up, daubed with iodine. Alex and Jaz have not left my side; I think they feel the need to protect me from any other mistakes, which I think is sweet. Sergeant Jane has sent a group off along the road to track down Cafferty and Co. I hope they get them. I would be quite happy to be included in the execution squad.

I sit up and watch as Shorty appears, hands tied behind her, the dress dishevelled, her long face written with an acceptance of guilt. She gives me the weirdest glance as she's led into a black Mercedes. I can't help but shout at her.

"*Oi, Shorty!* You were always going to get caught. I knew you were scum when I first met you. Enjoy a long prison holiday," I spit. Her eyes narrow with empty defiance. I wave and blow a mock kiss. Jaz surprises me as she gives her the finger of derision; quite out of character.

"I'm glad she's getting burnt," Jaz snarls. "What she threatened us with was cruel and vicious." Alex nods.

"Yeah. If she was a bloke, I would have kicked her arse all the way to London." I laugh.

"You two are a pack of cards; you so belong to each other. I never would have thought of you being an item." They smirk at each other and hug.

"Neither did we. I was far too good for him," Jaz says. Alex gives a puzzled look.

"Yep, I think you are right on that one, Jaz," I say.

Ayanna walks over, a serious look pasted on her face. She fiddles with her comms earpiece. Jane also has something weighing her demeanour down.

"I have some bad news guys," Ayanna says. "We have lost contact with the escapees. Cafferty and the others have disappeared into the ether. They are like slippery soap." A sick feeling rises in my gut. I attempt to ask a question, but I know it's pointless.

"Yes, not a satisfactory outcome. I have alerted HQ to make them a priority," Jane adds. "We have no certainty that you destroyed the toxin, either. They may still have it." I shake my head.

"What a load of bollocks! We had them in our grasp. How could they escape so easily?" I'm not a happy bunny. Especially, because I put my life on the line.

"I have the feeling that darker and higher forces, than us, are at play. I'm hoping once we interrogate Catherine Short and Delaware, we will get a sound handle on it," Ayanna says. Jane pulls a face.

"MI6 has been compromised - do you really think any rogue operatives will be uprooted? I don't think so," Jane says with derision. I one hundred percent agree.

"Well, I'm ready for a drink," I say, waving at someone who looks like kitchen staff. I ask for a coke. I'm gasping. I don't think I've ever been so hungry and thirsty. As I grasp the stone-cold can, the condensation dribbling down, shoots life back to my body. It's like heaven's nectar. I let out a belch.

"So, what do we do now?" I ask.

"We go back to base and debrief," Ayanna replies. Her face is forlorn; I sense the failure is dragging her down.

"Are we sure that the four and 'Loser' have left the scene? This man is a ghost - he can fade into the background and become anybody," I say.

"We are still combing the area, Maisie. If anyone is still here, we will find them," Jane says with certainty. I raise my eyebrows.

"Ok, but I think you are under-estimating them. I've come across this man before - he seems to have contacts with the British Embassy in Paris; has battalions at his beck and call; arrives in a Chinook and can hold hundreds to ransom. Not your average terrorist," I say. Ayanna nods in agreement.

"We have to weed out everyone that is infected by this guy. And don't worry, sergeant, MI6 will be safe and reliable again," she says.

I, along with Jaz and Alex, have that expression which gives the impression we can neither deny nor confirm that will be the case.

64 - BACK TO BUREAUCRACY

MI6 is the most depressing place when you have to go from meeting to meeting; receive counselling for any fallout from the trauma that you could have received and give an account of my mother and father's ingenuity, which I am very protective of.

"This sapphire," a gnarled older man asks, "is it still in your possession?" I nod.

"So, can we assume that it is safe from any enemy of the state?" he continues. I nod again. He turns to Ayanna.

"I am concerned that if it ever ends up circulating again, it will pose an enormous risk to national security," he states. Ayanna glances at me and back again.

"We are aware of that. But as Maisie has described her 'connection' with it, it is safer with her than anyone else. I know she will ensure that it is locked away, permanently." She nods to me, and I return it.

"Yep - it will never see the light of day again," I say as convincingly as I can.

"It *must* be secure, you do understand?" he reiterates, to my annoyance.

"Yes…yes. *I understand.*" Ayanna's eyes close to slits. Here we go again.

"And this 'Anton' - I do have my reservations about this construct that appears to have been hacking into our systems. I am obliged to ask for it to be assessed by our IT staff. We must not have our systems breached. Again, you understand that?" This guy is ready for a smack in the teeth.

"I cannot divulge anything that Anton has in his database, as my mother specifically told me to keep it from any prying eyes - including MI6's." I watch as he bristles with suppressed anger.

"This is not acceptable, Agent Bolt. Any security breach is intolerable. Miss Greene, you *will* comply with our request. You have no option. So, until you capitulate, I am suspending your access to the building, and we will keep you under armed guard." I look up at the ceiling and then at Ayanna.

"How come you are treating me like one of these terrorists? They are free to roam around and I'm the one in prison. You had better think again, mister." I stare, my face feeling flushed. Ayanna shrugs and side glances at this idiot.

"It does have the overtones of bureaucratic nonsense, sir," she says. "Maisie has been instrumental in thwarting an attack on London and uncovering the conspiracy within our own service." His face gives away the turmoil inside. I think he knows that this is true.

"How can anyone be trusted with secrets of this magnitude? Top level priority information that not only threatens our nation, but world stability? You are asking too much, Agent Bolt." He shakes his shoulders and stands. "It is out of your and my hands. The decision is made." He marches off to the door, talking as he goes on comms, which I didn't notice before. Ayanna leans over to me.

"We only have a small window," she whispers. I give her a bemused look. "I have the pass to get you out, but we have to act quickly," she continues. Glancing around the room, she grabs my arm, pulling me towards the door.

"What are we doing?" I ask.

"Saving your ass, girl."

"What about you? You'll get burnt for this won't you?" She smiles and nods.

"Only if you don't make it look convincing enough."

"Eh? What do you mean?"

"I need you to trust me."

"Ok, but this sounds stupid," I say as we wind through the corridors. "I don't want anything to be brought against you."

"Trust me, ok?" she says smiling.

Ayanna and I run through the building and slow every time another officer walks past, trying to look normal and unhurried. We approach an area I've not been into before. She swipes the pass, and she bundles me through the door.

Inside, there is a buzz of electronics and that smell from overworked computers, so acrid it makes me cough. Racks of CPU's line the room, multi coloured lights flashing in unison. We march alongside them until we reach another door. She swipes again, the lock switching to green. This next room is less interesting, with rows of shelving and boxes.

"Where are you taking me?"

"Somewhere safe and then you can make your escape," she says urgently.

"You are going to be in so much trouble, Ayanna. I know you are on my side, but this is dangerous, if not treason." She smiles and drags me to yet another door.

"This is the exit for all the IT staff and operatives who maintain the systems. They have a secure route in and out of the building, so you can leave without too much hassle. I have a pass here which will be adequate for your exit. It will flag up as stolen but I'm sure you can improvise." She grins. "So, I hope you can stay safe and live a life that is outside of this espionage world. You deserve it." A tear forms in the corner of her eye.

"I'm sorry that I couldn't do that here, but I'm sure you have enough experience to survive away from all this crap. Perhaps one day, we will meet again." I wipe away my own tears. We hug and the warmth of her body merges with my own sweaty emotion.

"I can't thank you enough," I spluttered. "This is not the way I wanted it to end. Say a big hi to Alex and Jaz." Another wave of emotion hits me. "I really am pleased with the way they came out of this." Ayanna nods and smiles.

"Yeah; they did great. Now come on you must go…and one last thing," she smirks. "You have to give me the biggest shiner." I shudder.

"You want me to hit you?" I recoil, shaking my head.

"Come on…for old times' sake," she grins. "You have to make it look convincing."

I stare at her for a second, admiring her black face, surrounded by her curly lob hair style, with those piercing dark eyes. Her bright purple lipstick frames her white teeth, now begging me to hit her, before it's too late.

Smack. I throw a punch which knocks her flying into a trash can. My heart immediately shouts shame to me, and I reach out and help her up, instantly hugging her hard.

"Well, don't hold back, girl," she splutters. I hold her and cringe over the damage I've inflicted on that perfect face. Her lip is split and bleeding, her cheek now swelling.

"Sorry…I'm so sorry," I blubber. "You are the most amazing person I know. Thanks for all you have done. I hope we will meet again one day too." She tries to grin but winces.

"Ok, now *go*," she drags me to the door. "Go and live Maisie G," she says. I turn and smile, holding back more tears. She shuts the door firmly, without any chance of return. I look out to a gate and an automatic pass reader.

I swipe the card and the lock obliges, red to green. The gate cranks open and I find myself on an empty side road, a hollow emptiness echoing in my belly. I'm free but bound by my unexpected loyalty to Ayanna and Jaz and Alex. Tears roll down my face, blurring my vision. I so want to hug them all again; I want more time with them, but a siren shrieks above my head, forcing me to move.

I pull my hoodie up and run along this road and find the nearest bus stop and catch a red double decker. Winding to the top deck, I sit subdued as I am taken along Vauxhall bridge for the last time, glancing back at the MI6 building. I blow my nose and sit as far back as I can in the seat for comfort. This emotion is overwhelming, one of losing friends which I have never had before and now the prospect of an uncertain future.

The bus is giving me an unscheduled sightseeing tour of London's famous buildings as I think over what could have happened if that toxin was released and how horrific it could have been. I allow a self-satisfied smile as I think on how we stopped these crazy plans and saved thousands of lives. Gratitude wells up as I am so pleased that I survived this ordeal and yet regret that Loser and the four horsemen are still not toast. I have to trust that the SAS and MI6 and other security services will do their job in catching them.

A group of tourists clamber up the stairs chattering away and taking photos of everything. They crowd around me, as if there are no other seats. It gives me a sense of insecurity, as my personal space is being invaded. But their happy, smiley faces begin to melt away my self-preservation wall and ease my jarred emotions.

"Greata city, London is," one of them says in broken English. I smile and nod. "You live here?" I ponder for a second.

"No…somewhere in the countryside," I reply and smile.

My watch buzzes and I read the text. Anton is wanting me to return as soon as possible. He has seen that I am a fugitive from MI6. He also says the sapphire has been received and is safely within the vault.

I smile.

The tourist nods to me and asks another question.

"You go there soon?"

"Yes…my friend needs me home."

Acknowledgements

As always, I must thank my family for allowing me to dream and write – without their support I would have never got this far.

Thanks to Mish Piri and his amazing artwork and Paul Bell who tirelessly sorts out my formatting problems. For my proofreaders David and Margaret and the amazing support of Dave and Esther, I am forever grateful.

It's always a privilege to write stories about characters who are chiefly made up from your subconscious but have a tinge of realism and reference to real people you come across in life. I don't know of anyone who is an assassin (by the way!) but the joy of blending traits of individuals who coalesce a storyline into a plot and transform over the course of the book, is one I love.

I am so happy when someone feeds back to me that they have enjoyed reading my work and then proceed to ask when the next instalment is coming out. To you also, I say thank you, as I am deeply grateful that you read them at all!

This series is one I hope to continue, whilst I have readers who enjoy the plotlines and characters that excite my creative writing.

Hope you enjoyed this next instalment of Maisie G!